"I'll do whatever you want."

"What!" Sara gaped at Steve. She couldn't believe she had heard him right.

"You'll sign the divorce papers?" she asked, in a low voice. Why had Steve changed his mind? And why was she so shocked now? This is what she'd wanted all along, wasn't it?

"There's only one thing," Steve said, not moving, not flinching, just staring at her.

Sara's ears rang loudly with this new twist.

"Let's make sure there's nothing left between us." His gaze never wavered from hers. "Spend the night with me first."

Dear Reader,

Every one of us knows that there's that special guy out there meant just for us. The kind of guy who's every woman's fantasy—but only one woman's dream come true. That's the kind of men you'll meet in THE ULTIMATE... miniseries.

Whether he's the man that'll follow you to the ends of the earth or the type to stay right in your backyard and promise you a passel of babies or the guy who'll pull out all stops in his seduction, the men you're about to meet are truly special.

Linda Cajio continues the miniseries. Linda is an award-winning author of nearly thirty contemporary and historical romances. Married with two children, she claims to keep her sanity firmly rooted in humor, and that writing amid chaos is a constant source of inspiration. Linda lives with her family in New Jersey.

We hope you enjoy all the wonderful stories and fabulous men coming to you in THE ULTIMATE... series.

Regards,

Debra Matteucci
Senior Editor & Editorial Coordinator
Harlequin Books
300 East 42nd Street
New York, NY 10017

HOUSE HUSBAND
LINDA CAJIO

Harlequin Books

TORONTO • NEW YORK • LONDON
AMSTERDAM • PARIS • SYDNEY • HAMBURG
STOCKHOLM • ATHENS • TOKYO • MILAN
MADRID • WARSAW • BUDAPEST • AUCKLAND

ISBN 0-373-16715-6

HOUSE HUSBAND

Copyright © 1998 by Linda Cajio.

Chapter One

"Cute butt, babe."

Sara Johanson whirled around, trying to find the person connected to the crude words. A parrot, its gray and yellow feathers puffed up, stared back at her from its perch on the broken-down veranda.

"You're a hot one," it said.

Sara let out her breath. "Gee, thanks."

Stop talking to a bird and get a grip, she thought, tightening her hold on her briefcase. If she wanted to completely close her old life and move on to a new one, she needed all the calm and courage she could muster. Facing a husband one had walked out on four years ago didn't qualify as a stroll in the park.

"What the heck *is* Steve Johanson doing here?" she murmured. She had never seen a better place to stop and smell the roses than the little Louisiana town of Saint Sebastian, with its moss-covered trees, backwater bayous and slow-paced lifestyle. Her hopefully soon-to-be ex-husband, intense and focused, had *never* stopped to smell a rose. She wasn't sure he had even known what a rose was, during their marriage.

The flaking paint and beat-up furniture of the veranda

she stood on amazed her even more. Steve hadn't tolerated a magazine out of place on the coffee table, let alone a pile of car parts sitting tumbled against a side railing. A baby carriage with no wheels doubled as a newspaper recycling bin.

He must have children.

Sara's heart squeezed tight at the thought. Children. She wanted them so badly her arms ached sometimes. She and Steve had talked about it—when she could get his attention away from the job he had loved more than her. They had put off having children until later. Only later never came.

She had to get his attention now, she admitted. She was thirty and her time was running out. Brushing a trickle of sweat from her forehead, she turned back to the graying front door. The navy power suit she'd worn to gird herself emotionally was now stiflingly hot in the late afternoon heat and walloping humidity.

"Is that a rabbit in your pocket or are you just happy to see me?" the parrot asked.

"Just happy to see her."

Sara whirled around at the new voice. This one was human and attached to a man. *Steve.* She searched the face she still saw in her dreams, finding it older, with beginnings of true cragginess. The power she remembered still overlaid Steve Johanson's features, but it was softened, muted somehow, as if he had no need of it any longer. His dark hair, which he'd once insisted be trimmed every fourth Thursday, was pulled back in a ponytail and left to hang in shaggy curls against his nape. His deep tan only magnified the blue of his eyes. They held a fire that had once left her breathless—and maybe still did.

His lack of a shirt certainly took her breath. Sara tried

not to gasp like a teenager at the sight of those strong
shoulders. Thirty-six-year-old men on the doorstep of
middle age shouldn't look that good. A pelt of hair ran
across the breadth of his hard chest before arrowing down
past his navel into the low-slung denim cutoffs. She knew
the hairs were like silk. She had run her hands through
them nearly every day for two years. She had run her
hands lower whenever he asked...and sometimes when he
hadn't, to both their delight.

"Keep looking at me like that and I'll be *very* happy
to see you," Steve said, climbing the veranda steps. "I
always was."

The local Cajun women must fall all over themselves
to jump into his bed. Sara mentally shook herself. She
shouldn't care. She *didn't* care!

Sweat trickled down her back. She ignored it. She
wasn't the unsure girl she used to be. She had risen from
cashier at the ribbon counter to regional buyer of a de-
partment-store chain. She dealt with people and problems
all the time now. She could handle this. After all, she was
asking only for the obvious, for what should have been
taken care of long ago.

She cleared her throat, then realized what a dead give-
away it was to her inner state. "Hello, Steve."

He stopped before her, mere inches away. He stood so
close she could see his pulse throbbing in his neck. The
scents of verdant earth and man swirled through her
senses, causing her own pulse to throb in harmony with
his. He gazed at her mouth. He would kiss her any second
now.

She wouldn't back away, she thought. She wouldn't
show that he affected her sexually. He shouldn't. Not after
all this time. Not after the way their marriage had died.

"Where's my friggin' cracker?" the parrot demanded.

"Don't mind Max," Steve said, finally straightening away and allowing vital space between them. Sara refused to breathe a telltale sigh of relief. Steve took something from his pocket and gave it to the bird, saying, "Max grew up in a raunchy New Orleans bar where everyone got a charge out of teaching him to talk."

"He talks a little too well," Sara commented.

"Yeah, he can put the words together." Steve tilted his head at the parrot. "You want to come in or stay out for a while, Max?"

"What the hell do you think?" Max said.

"Does he understand you?" Sara asked, fascinated and repulsed by the parrot. Not that it was the parrot's fault he had a mouth Eddie Murphy would envy.

"Most of the time, I think," Steve said. "Max, be nice now. We have a guest."

"Shove it up your—"

"Thank you, Max. Thank you so much." His response barely overrode the parrot's last word.

Steve turned to Sara and nonchalantly rubbed his chest. She felt the blood rush into her ears. She patted away the film of perspiration breaking out on her upper lip and forehead. Her skin felt oddly clammy and hot, as if she had run a marathon. He looked so damned cool and relaxed, while her suit and stockings were turning quickly into a torture chamber.

"Your hair is shorter and more blond," he said.

She touched her nape in reaction. "Too busy to work with it longer and Miss Clairol covers the gray."

He raised his eyebrows. "If you're gray now, what are you going to be when you're forty?"

"Dead white."

He made no further comment, but she knew he must have noticed she'd shed the last ten stubborn pounds she had carried when they were living together. She half wished she had worn a clinging dress, just to show him, then wondered why she would even think such a thing. Why would she want him to find her more attractive than before?

He said, "You didn't come here to have a parrot talk dirty to you. I doubt you came here because you were burning to see your dear old husband. So why are you in the lovely town of Saint Sebastian? Frankly, I'm surprised as hell you could even find me."

Sara drew in a steadying breath. "My lawyer did, actually. We sent you mailings—"

"Is that what they were?" Steve made a face. "I thought someone back home was suing me."

"Well, ah…yes." She hated tumbling over the words, a sign that she could still be intimated—especially by a husband she didn't want anymore. "That would be me."

His jaw dropped. "What?"

"Oh, screw it!" the parrot sang out. "Drinks all around!"

Steve strode toward her, his gaze blazing with anger. Sara stepped back, practically sitting in the baby carriage in an effort to get away from him.

"What the hell could you sue me for?" Steve demanded. "I don't have a damn thing left!"

"I don't want anything," she said quickly, to reassure him. "Except a divorce."

He slumped, all the air seeming to leave his body in an invisible *whoosh*. "A divorce?"

"That's a dirty word!" Max said.

"Damn right," Steve said, clearly regaining his composure. "Hell, it's been four years. Why haven't you wanted a divorce sooner? Why want one now?"

"Steve, it can't be a surprise," she said, standing up from her precarious position against the baby carriage. She brushed at her backside, positive the pervading dirt had left its mark there. "We need to close that chapter and move on—"

This was it, she thought. Face him down and finish off her old life. She had worked so hard on building her confidence over the years and felt as if all the effort had culminated at this point. "I've been busy just earning a living—"

"Don't hand me that. I paid you all the support you wanted, along with a lump sum for the house. You got plenty."

"I meant," she continued, undeterred, "that my energies were involved in night classes at college and moving up in the company to where I could support myself. You shouldn't have had to pay for me forever. That wasn't fair, with the way things ended between us. And you know I didn't ask for much, just enough to keep me going until I could stand on my own."

He had insisted on giving her more in support and had refused to accept any returned monies. Why did he make it sound as if she were a gold digger? She'd walked away from their marriage, true, but the marriage was already dead. In fact, she often wondered if he'd even realized she was absent the first few days. Usually, he came home only to fall into bed and sleep for a couple of hours before going back to work. He'd probably missed her when no one had picked up his shirts from the dry cleaners. Or when he couldn't find clean socks. After the honeymoon he had quickly gone from treating her like a wife to a maid—which had been half their problem.

"Watch that climb up the ladder," he commented sarcastically. "Or you'll find yourself out on that pretty backside of yours. I should know."

"What happened?" she asked, her curiosity finally getting to her. She had lost touch with him after the first six months.

He shrugged. "RMX pulled the usual downsizing garbage. I need a drink. You want to come in?"

"Ah..." She glanced at the house, not sure why she was wary. "All right. We do have things to discuss."

He opened the door; it wasn't locked. Sara raised her eyebrows, wondering if the small, rural town was truly so idyllic that people left their homes unlocked. She stepped inside and felt the accumulated heat there blast her. Without thinking, she shed her jacket, then looked at it before deciding armor was no good if one baked to death inside. Five minutes more and she'd be in the bathroom stripping off the stockings.

"I don't have air-conditioning," he said, by way of explanation. He opened several floor-to-ceiling French doors, letting in a slight breeze that did little more than stir the hot, humid air. "Want a beer?"

"No thanks. Could I have water instead?"

"Okay, but we don't get the greatest."

He went into a back room, where she could hear him rummaging in a refrigerator. She took advantage of his absence to look around the sitting room, wanting to see what more it would tell her about this stranger. Like the veranda, the furniture here was vintage reject, with a wall of cinder-block-and-board bookcases. Shells occupied every space—beautiful conch and candy-striped cones sitting beside tortoiseshell swirls and king's crowns. The myriad of colors dazzled the eye, and she picked several up to admire them more closely.

Suddenly, eyes glimmered back at her.

Sara screamed and dropped the shell onto the bookcase. She leaped away from the thing emerging out of the shell exactly the way the baby monster had emerged out of John Hurt's chest in *Alien.* Antennae twitched. Eyes on stalks glared. A huge, heavy claw waved in the air. Sara gaped at it, horrified at what it might have done to her.

Pounding feet approached from the kitchen. "What's wrong? Oh. Made it out again, Ruby?"

Steve lifted the crustacean off the bookcase. The brown legs scrambled helplessly in the air as the creature tipped even farther out of the shell. Its body looked like a lobster's, while its legs and one claw matched a fiddler crab's.

"What is that thing?" she asked, her hand instinctively going to her throat to protect it.

"A hermit crab. He's pretty old, I think. At least that's what his size tells me. You don't often see them six inches across like this. Sorry he scared you. He's always getting out of the birdcage I keep him in."

"*He?* Didn't you call it Ruby?" she asked, then immediately realized how inane the question was. Who cared what the thing was named? She certainly didn't.

"Yeah, it's called Ruby. But I can't keep the pronouns straight for some reason. Maisie, my housekeeper, says it's a transvestite crab."

Steve took the crab over to a shaded corner where a birdcage that could house six parrots sat in splendor. He opened the door and put the crab inside.

"Yep, there's the shell he had on this morning." Steve

pointed to a large, green, swirled one in the bottom of the cage. "Ruby likes to dump his shell and crawl between the rungs of the cage to explore the other shells he sees on the shelves. Normally crabs won't leave their shells unless they feel very safe. Ruby must think he's in Fort Knox, although I don't even know how he's escaping, missing two legs like he is. It'll be a while yet until they regenerate."

"What the heck are *you* doing with that thing?" she demanded, her mind reeling with questions about this new Steve Johanson. "I can't believe you live here. I can't believe you keep a parrot with a mouth that ought to be washed out with soap, and a crab that belongs on somebody's plate for dinner. I can't believe you're living in a house that looks like it was furnished by three college kids during a drunken weekend, and I can't believe you're dressed in leftover cutoffs from the sixties. The man I married wore Armani suits and Nicole Miller ties. He got bent out of shape if his favorite business magazine didn't sit perfectly square on the coffee table. And he never drank cheap beer," she finished, when he took a swig of a can that must have sold in a six-pack for a couple of dollars at most.

"I know it's a shock. Hell, honey, have a drink."

He handed her a water bottle. Not one prepackaged with a brand name on it, but an old milk bottle filled with water chilled in the fridge. No glass. No apology. Just his defiant stare daring her to accept it.

She put the bottle to her lips and drank. The water tasted metallic but refreshing. Sara needed something to wet her throat—and give her a moment to compose herself.

"Look at you," he countered. "Four years ago, you

didn't know what a Brooks Brothers suit was, let alone a subtle power color. You never carried a briefcase, and you never went out of your way to hurt anybody.''

"I'm not hurting anybody," she protested.

"Really? I can't wait to see what the divorce settlement says." He rubbed his chest again. "I bet I lose my shirt. If I had one worth losing."

"All I'm asking is that we end our marriage." She opened the briefcase and held out the papers. "Here. Read them. You'll see."

He didn't touch the papers, just stared at them and guzzled beer.

Sara set the divorce agreement down on the bookcase, where she could squeeze it in. "I know you'll be reassured after you read it."

"I don't buy your moving-on story," he said, making a face. "That's crap. Why didn't you get the divorce four years ago when you walked out on me?"

Why hadn't she? The question had plagued her over the years, yet she had never taken any kind of action, legal or otherwise, on it before. The longer she put off getting a divorce, the more distant it became. The whole process of seeing lawyers and going to court seemed messy and emotionally draining, something she hadn't wanted to initiate. Anyway, she wasn't the only one in the marriage, so she asked, "Why didn't you? I always expected you to do the filing, truthfully...." She was being truthful. "I gave you the grounds for it."

"What a great wife you are," he said bitterly.

"I wasn't," she said, gentling her voice, knowing she had done wrong in their marriage. "I wasn't a good wife for you, Steve. I was useless. I was overwhelmed then and clumsy among the other, more sophisticated wives at

RMX Peripherals. That hurt you with your bosses. I was naive about the hours your job would take, and I couldn't handle the constant separations. You needed someone who matched you in enthusiasm and direction. Someone who understood what the climb required. I wasn't it. We both know that.''

He pointed the beer can at her. ''You've really learned to be a diplomat. But it's all garbage. You were what I wanted. You were shy and vulnerable, and I loved coaxing a smile from you. You were everything my job wasn't, and I needed that to renew myself. I know it was hell for you. I know I was hell to live with sometimes. A lot of times. You know I would have made enough to retire before I was forty. That's what we planned—to sacrifice now and have the rest of our lives together. But you didn't give us a chance. Now you stroll in here and you want a divorce. My life went down the toilet, but yours is dandy now, so let's move on. Who is he, Sara?''

She'd known she would have to face anger. She'd known Steve would never understand that the scenario he sketched was what *he'd* wanted, not what she'd wanted. She would have been more than content to have him work forty hours a week until he was eighty, just to give them a life *together.* ''I'm not looking to remarry. Not yet. But I'm thirty, Steve. I want children desperately, and I do want marriage for that. I think kids need a mother and father, and I wouldn't feel right if I didn't make every effort to provide a husband and father for mine.''

He stepped closer again, just as he had on the veranda. She could almost taste the beer clinging to his lips. She wanted to cling to his lips, even as her mind screamed a denial.

''We wanted children,'' he said, lowering his mouth to

her throat. His lips just grazed her skin, not in a kiss but in a caress that sent delicious shivers along her spine. His breath tickled the highly sensitive spot just under her ear. He'd once known what he was doing. He once knew every inch of her body more intimately that she did. "I'll be happy to be your sex slave and give you all the babies you want."

Sara blinked. The swirling in her veins seized up faster than engine oil at sixty below zero. She stepped around him, forcing him back this time. "Let's get serious, Steve. The papers are there for you to read. Please do it and call me at the Meridian in New Orleans. I'm in room 602."

She picked up her jacket and sailed out the door before he could stop her. Outside on the veranda, she let out her breath.

"Do you think I'm sexy? Come on, baby, let me know!" the parrot screeched at the top of its lungs.

"Oh, God," Sara moaned, and raced down the steps to her rental car.

So much for a firm confrontation. The day had been a disaster.

HE HAD WONDERED if this moment would come. He had dreaded it.

Steve stood in his front doorway and watched Sara get into her car. He crushed the empty beer can and tossed it into a cardboard box that doubled as a recycling bin.

"You only live once, so let's get it on," Max advised from his perch in a corner.

"What the hell…" Steve muttered. "You've got more sense than I do, Max."

Seeing Sara again stirred up feelings he'd thought long dead. Instead, the wounds felt fresher than ever. He still couldn't believe she had walked out on him. Granted, he had been so wrapped up in his new vice presidency at RMX that he hadn't been a good husband. He had barely been there, and had been snappy and critical when he was. He hadn't meant to be; the condition had only been temporary from the stress. He hadn't realized she didn't understand that. After she'd left him, he had been so angry that she hadn't tried harder on her end. He had fully expected her to come crawling back. Only she hadn't. He had refused to waste his time getting the divorce, deciding to hell with her then. If she wanted a divorce, she could make the effort.

She finally had.

Steve grimaced. He hadn't been prepared for the rest of the slide in his life, however. First the rapid cutbacks and downsizing that eliminated his vice president's job, returning him to middle management, where he stewed in humiliation. Another set of cutbacks put him right out of RMX's door, without a regret on the company's part. Nationally, the corporate climate was such that he couldn't get another job in upper management, and he wasn't willing to compromise for less. He had lived on savings and stocks and generally slipped further and further down until an interview-vacation found him stuck here in Saint Sebastian.

He had gone from a two-hundred-thousand-dollar-plus-perks career to running a cleaning service for some outlying tourist hotels. He didn't even own the company he now worked for, and he was forced to supplement his piddly income with shell polishing for tourist shops as well as turning in recycled cans. Even those weren't hustle jobs; he worked when lack of money moved him. Like a leaky roof that needed fixing. His did.

Steve looked at the can bin and wondered just how much he contributed to his recycling. Way too much. At this rate, he'd be rich when the recycling company paid him for the load. God knew he needed the money, but not at the expense of his liver.

"Don't worry. Be happy," Max sang.

"Get a life, Maxie," Steve replied.

"I felt the vibrations.... I felt the gris-gris simmer on my chest...."

Steve whirled around at the human voice behind him, then groaned when he saw his housekeeper, Maisie, coming along the path.

"I'm not having any damned gris-gris, okay?"

When she stopped on the porch, Maisie pushed the hair off her face and stared at him with eyes that literally glowed. Most of the time she looked benign, grandmotherly, Steve thought. Then she had moments like this.

"I told you before," Maisie said. "You don't want to be fooling around with no gris-gris."

She waved the amulet in question to emphasize her point.

"I'm not fooling around with it, trust me." Why the hell had he ever hired a housekeeper who practiced voodoo on the side? Just because her brother owned this house was no excuse.

"Because no one else would work for what you pay, my friend. What other excuse do you need?"

Steve's jaw dropped, although Maisie had answered his thoughts before. Still, the whole mind-reading business baffled him.

"She's the one, isn't she?" Maisie asked.

"One what?" he asked innocently. Maisie looked

through him again—or at least she looked like she did. He made a face. "Yes, she's my wife."

"Change is coming. Big change. Mark my words."

"No kidding. She wants a divorce."

Maisie laughed. "I could make you a love potion and fix that all up again. Or a good-luck gris-gris. I keep telling you that you need one to get out of this hole you're in."

"I'll crawl out on my own, thank you."

He had considered Sara his good-luck charm, his rapid rise at RMX coinciding with meeting and marrying her. His rapid descent coincided with her leaving. Coincided. Coincidence. He wasn't buying it.

He shuddered at the thought of even looking at the divorce papers. Where would he be once he signed them? In hell, probably. Giving Sara her freedom terrified him beyond all logic. Yet how fair was that to her over a marriage he knew was long dead?

"Bye-bye, Miss American Pie," Max told him.

"No kidding, Max."

Maisie just snorted.

Still, Steve thought, Sara *had* looked like Miss American Pie. Although her creamy skin and snub nose enticed, her eyes were still her best feature. Wide and deep brown, they always reminded him of a fawn's, questioning and wanting approval. Combined with her generous curves, they made her irresistible to him. He'd noticed she was slimmer now, her jawline more defined and her full breasts more enticing for the narrower waist. Even with her new haircut, she still had that same gentleness he remembered so well. Yet she exuded a feminine strength she hadn't possessed before. He wanted to explore that. He also wanted to hurt her as she had hurt him.

"I'm losing it," he said out loud.

"You never had it," Max replied, then whistled. "Here, chickie, chickie."

"You want the woman, just take the woman," Maisie advised.

"I need a beer," Steve muttered. Between housekeeper and bird, he was being driven to drink.

He fetched a second can, popped the top and took a big swallow, the beer flowing down his throat. The "must" teased his senses, the slight bitterness of the brew settling his stomach.

He might still want Sara in a sexual way. But Sara wanted a husband and children. Children they should have already had together. Clearly, she had to get rid of husband number one before she opened the door to husband number two. She might deny there was no candidate for a new life mate, but Steve didn't buy it. Otherwise, why would she bother with the divorce? No, she wanted children now because she had a father for them. And it wasn't him.

He hated the idea of her with someone else. She was unfinished business, no matter how illogical it sounded. His emotions didn't want logic. They wanted closure.

"I'll make you a love potion to end all love potions," Maisie said, coming into the kitchen. Max sat on her shoulder, a perch he liked above most others.

If only it was that easy, Steve thought to himself. He shook his head. "Don't be daft. Besides, it would never work. The love is dead all around."

"You are lying through your teeth, boy. Now that ain't nice. Is it, Max?"

"When the moon is over Miami, I'll be a fool for you," Max sang, bobbing his head up and down.

"I hope you're not a prophet, Max," Steve said.

Maybe he should finish this business with Sara. One way or the other.

Chapter Two

The waiter bringing room service wasn't the waiter bringing room service. It was Steve.

"Too bad Max isn't here," he said, eyeing her terry-
cloth robe. "He'd have a lot to say."

As Sara held her hotel room door open, she clutched
the shawl collar closed, hoping Steve had no clue she
wore nothing under the garment. Why the hell had she
taken a shower when she returned to the hotel? Why had
she blithely opened the door without asking who it was,
even though she'd been expecting dinner from room service? And where was the damn corporate power suit when
she needed it?

In the dirty-clothes bag, that's where.

"Did you sign the papers?" she asked, not unblocking
the entrance to the room.

"Not hardly." He smiled. "I thought we should talk."

"Let's talk later," she began, only to be interrupted by
a waiter pushing a meal cart toward them.

Perfect timing, she thought.

"Room service," the waiter announced, his lilting ac-
cent overly cheerful to her already frayed nerves.

Sara opened the door wider to let in the waiter. Steve
followed right behind before she could stop him. At least

he wore a shirt, she thought, gazing at the Dirtbusters logo on his back. Unfortunately, she needed to be wearing one, too.

She signed off on the bill, adding a good tip for the waiter, who practically bowed his way out. The door shut behind the man, leaving her alone with Steve. Sara swallowed back a sudden lump of fear. And anticipation. She grimaced, refusing to wonder at what she might be anticipating. It had better be nothing, or she was dead meat.

She finally turned back to her husband, only to find him popping the lids off the room service dishes.

"Josephine's Orange Roughy in Mango Salsa," he said, sniffing. "A great choice, but her Jerked Chicken is even better."

"You know the chef here?"

"I know everybody in the hotel business around here. Do you always answer your door in a robe and nothing else, or did you anticipate the waiter would appeal for dessert?"

"I'm not naked!" she lied, annoyed with his insult.

"Of course you are. Your hair is wet and you never wear underwear when you're in your robe right after a shower. I should know. I stripped you out of one more times than I can remember."

Sara refused to blush. "I could do things differently now."

"But you don't."

"Why would you care?"

"Who said I did?"

"You did, when you asked about the waiter."

He flopped on the bed, right in the middle of it, lying in splendor on the bird-of-paradise spread. Crossing his legs at the ankles, he reached out and lifted a roll from the bread basket. "Just curious if you were getting your next husband lined up already. Don't read anything more into it than that.''

She wouldn't, she thought. Only why did she feel so damned deflated?

''Steve, what do you want?'' Sara demanded, realizing she could spend hours sparring with him—and feeling deflated. She only wanted him out of her room...so she could get dressed...so he wouldn't be in her bed...so she wouldn't be half-naked. Her blood thickened at the reality.

He finished the roll in a few bites, then said, ''It depends on what you want.''

''I don't have time for this,'' she muttered, moving the cart over to the room's only chair. She sat down and placed her napkin on her lap.

''What's the rush?'' Steve asked. ''This is Louisiana. Life is leisurely.''

''No kidding,'' she said under her breath, eyeing him. Did he have to wear shorts that tightened in the most strategic of places? Did he have to lie on her bed like he owned it? ''Did you read through the divorce papers?''

''Nope. I've been thinking. What do you need a divorce for? A lot of women are having children without marriage now. It's accepted, so why are you so hot for a new husband?''

''I told you earlier, I'm not comfortable without a husband and marriage. I know it's fine for others, but it's just not for me.''

''You really do want the vine-covered cottage, don't you? I bet you want the requisite dog and cat, too. You always did.''

''My parents had that, and I want the same for my children. I have the time to begin the process now. And if vine-covered cottages sound pedestrian, I'm not apologizing. I'm as bourgeois as they come.'' She sliced off a portion of the fish and ate it, savoring the burst of fresh fruit and delicate spices that enhanced the blander meat. "This is marvelous."

Steve grinned. "I told you Josephine was good."

"She is. And this is the low-fat platter." Sara wished the words back. They revealed too much about herself.

"It's looking good on you." He rolled over on his side and propped his head up with his hand. "I should have told you earlier how sexy you look."

"I don't look sexy," she replied in a withering tone. At least she hoped it was withering.

His gazed dropped to her breasts. "They look very sexy to me."

Sara glanced down to find her robe had gaped open, revealing nearly all of one breast and half of the other. She yanked it shut, even as her face heated. To occupy herself, she shoved another bite of the fish into her mouth. This time it tasted like ashes.

"I always loved it when you blushed, Sara. I always loved to make you blush. Do you remember the time you were out weeding the garden, on your hands and knees, and I came up behind you—"

"No! I don't remember!" she lied, trying to stop the flood of memories. She ate another hunk of the roughy, to shut herself up. Only her mouthful of food went down the wrong pipe, and she began to cough. The coughing fit got worse when she couldn't clear the problem. Her eyes watered with the spasm.

Just as she finally swallowed the lodged food, Steve shot off the bed. She tried to signal that she was fine, that things were just about back on track, when he yanked her out of the chair. Her knee banged hard against the cart, sending it spinning away from her. Steve pulled her back against his chest, pressed his fist just under her breastbone.

He jerked her rib cage upward and proceeded to bounce her up and down in a Heimlich maneuver gone mad. What she'd eaten thus far, now settled nicely in her stomach, threatened to revisit in a most violent way.

"I'm all right!" she gasped, horrified that she might toss her cookies right on the spot.

Steve gave her one last jerk that pushed all the air from her lungs before he relaxed slightly. "Are you sure? Nothing came out."

"That's because it went down *before* you started shaking me like a rag doll." She drooped in his embrace, her legs too weak to take her weight.

"Oh." He held her against him, his hands spreading along her stomach, just under the lower curves of her breasts. His thumb rested naturally on the bare skin of her cleavage.

Sara knew she ought to break his hold, but she was too rattled from his lifesaving technique to do it smoothly. Above all, she wanted to do it smoothly, so he wouldn't know he had any effect on her.

His hand rubbed against her stomach, the tips of his fingers slipping in between the lapels of her robe to touch her skin. She froze. He bent his head along the side of her neck, his breath wreaking havoc on her flesh when he inhaled her scent. "What's the shampoo?"

"Coconut milk extract," she said hoarsely, and cursed herself for responding to him. Yet she couldn't stop her blood from throbbing in her veins, throbbing in places that brought heat to her face and chest.

"It's... Hell, I wish I had the words for what it does to me." His hand slipped fully inside her robe, finding her breast. He rolled his thumb across her nipple. It hardened, aching for more of his touch.

His tongue circled the sensitive outside edge of her ear.

His breath on her flesh sent delicious rushes down her spine.

Sara tried to breathe herself, tried to say something, but she could only sag in his arms, already helpless against the storm rising inside her. His arousal pressed against her derriere. How many times had some of the best lovemaking between them started like this?

Not lovemaking, but plain animalistic sex, she thought. The two of them tearing their clothes away. She had always been so bold with him in private—once he had taught her how.

She wanted him again, and she shouldn't. She wouldn't.

Somehow, she pulled herself out of his embrace. She yanked the robe closed and turned to face him. He grinned at her, unrepentant.

"You sure you want a divorce?" he asked.

"Yes," she practically hissed at him.

"The mouth might say yes, but the body says no way."

"It's just a natural response," she told him. "We did have feelings for each other once, and they surfaced for a moment. Big deal. It happens to lots of divorced couples. One time. Only it doesn't change anything. Our marriage is long dead and it needs to be finalized."

There, she thought. She had faced the worst and confronted it with nonchalance. She was doing fine. She only wished she felt that way.

"Well, you are ready to make babies."

"Steve, if you're only here to drive me crazy, go home. If you're here to discuss the terms of the agreement, then stay."

He flopped back down on the bed again. He was only doing it to put her at a disadvantage, she chanted over and over in her brain. Unfortunately, her body insisted on resurrecting the feel of his hand on her breast, followed by the urge to strip away her robe and climb into the bed with him. She swore she would get an overdose of novocaine next time she was anywhere near this man. How the hell could he create this inside her?

"I wasn't sure why I came here, but a notion did pop up." He chuckled. "Ironic, isn't it?"

She refused to take the bait. "What's your idea?"

"You have no guarantee any new husband you pick will be better than me. You could do a lot worse." He smiled ruefully. "Well, maybe not. But I have the advantage of being the devil you know rather than the devil you don't. And I'm out of sight and out of mind. Why waste time and money getting a divorce when I might be willing to step in and do the job myself? After you're pregnant, you don't have to see me again."

She stared at him, stunned. "You're nuts."

"Oh. I would like to have some visitation rights, though. Several times a year I get to see the kid, and when he or she is old enough to travel, the little one could spend part of the summer here."

"Are you crazy?" she demanded. "I want a husband who is *there* all the time—"

"I could be that. Hell, why didn't you say you were looking for a house husband? Anyone could do the job—"

"I mean I want a husband who loves me and whom I can love! Not a marriage of convenience for kids."

He stared at her for the longest time. "We did once love each other. Don't discount it."

She drew in a deep breath, not wanting to hurt him and not wanting to think about the implications of loving him again. "I meant I want a stable man who's calm and steady and on whom I can rely."

"He sounds like a Milquetoast geek with no personality and five thousand pens in his pocket protector."

"He sounds like a very nice man."

"You know what you'll get from a guy like that? Kids who are just like him. Bland, with no passion. No surprises. No love to last a lifetime. It's like you've gone through a computer dating service and checked off all the likes and dislikes until you've created a perfect dummy. But he won't be a real man, and your marriage won't have a soul, Sara. Neither will your children."

"You're being ridiculous," she said, to shake the feeling he knew more about this than she did. Yet she couldn't shake the feeling that he was right.

"I don't think so."

"What about child support?" she asked, trying to show him how impractical his suggestion was. "I know I'll need help with expenses, and no offense, but you don't have the salary you used to. How would you pay?"

"I'd manage." He sounded sure of himself. That worried her.

"Are you telling me you have some grand love for me?" she countered, trying to put him on the spot.

"Hardly." His gaze raked her, leaving her feeling oddly stupid and embarrassed. "I'm saying why go to all the trouble of getting a husband who won't make you happy in the end? Why discover you've got to go through another divorce, this time with kids who will suffer, when you already have a husband whose foibles you know? On the plus side, I'm intelligent, halfway decent looking, have good health and all my teeth. I'm also occasionally fun to be with, and I don't make rude bodily noises in public."

"What more could a girl ask for?" Sara muttered, her

head spinning. She had fallen into a vat of insanity. She must have.

"I can't think of another thing myself." He stretched out on the bed. "Here I am. Let's make a baby."

STEVE GRINNED at his wife's astonished expression. He had had no idea what to say when he came to the hotel, but the moment his proposition left his mouth all his instincts clicked together in surety. He had felt the same way when he'd gone after the Electronic Data Systems account. He'd gotten the account, and Ross Perot's former company, EDS, had poured tens of millions of dollars annually into RMX's coffers. That never would have happened if Steve hadn't instinctively kept pursuing his hunch.

Sara suddenly whirled around and grabbed the water glass from her room service tray. She dumped the contents right in the middle of his crotch.

"Yow!" he yelped, leaping off the bed, his nether regions soaked and already chilled to the bone.

"You needed cooling off, Steve," Sara said, "and a return to reality."

"You can take your reality and shove—"

"You've been hanging around with your parrot too long," she interjected. She strolled over to her closet and picked out a dress. "When I come out of the bathroom, be ready to discuss the divorce agreement or be ready to leave. The choice is yours."

She sailed into the bathroom like Cleopatra having triumphed over Rome, and shut the door behind her.

Steve plucked at his wet shorts, trying to keep the ice water from penetrating his skin even more. "The least you could do is hand me a towel."

The door clicked open and one flew out of the bathroom, smacking him in the face.

"Thanks," he muttered, snatching it before it landed on the floor. He rubbed at himself, although the thick terry cloth was useless. He wouldn't get dry unless he changed, and he wouldn't get changed unless he left. That gave Sara the victory. He had had total control of this meeting, yet she had turned the tables within a second. All his instincts now said, "Idiot!" His instincts were right.

"This isn't like you at all, Sara," he complained loudly, so she could hear him. "You never would have tossed ice water at me before."

"I told you I was different. I learned to stand up for myself over the last few years. I've had to."

"No, you didn't. You could have stayed married to me."

She didn't answer.

"Okay, so I was a lousy husband," he admitted. "But I've changed, too. Or haven't you noticed?"

She emerged from the bathroom. The little sundress she wore, sleeveless and skimming her curves, sent his blood pounding faster through his veins. The strappy sandals only added to the internal mayhem. He loved New Orleans in the springtime—the humidity made everyone wear fewer clothes early in the season. Look at how it made Sara dress. A couple more minutes and he would boil himself dry.

"Why are you wearing that?" he asked. "The heat notwithstanding."

She paused, looking down. "What? What's wrong with it?"

"It's like you'll be hitting the bar at any moment—"

"You're sounding jealous again."

"I'm not," he assured her. He only wished he was sure.

Damn, he did sound possessive. And sounding possessive gave power to her. "Never mind. Look, I can't go through the lobby like this. Unless you want me to tell everyone I pass that it's a kinky sex thing you have, you'd better figure out how I'm supposed to get dry."

"Me?"

"Yes, you. And don't think I'll sneak out of here, because I won't. I'll go right through the lobby, and that's a promise."

"You would tell everyone, wouldn't you?" She made a face, then straightened. "What makes you think I would care what strangers think of me?"

"Because you haven't changed all that much," he said, banking on that being the truth. "You may be more bold, but you always were Miss Proper Behavior. You could have given Emily Post lessons...except when we were alone."

She waved her hands. "Just dry off."

He held out the towel. "I'm not doing very well. Why don't you help me?"

"I think I'd rather eat porcupine needles for breakfast." She gestured toward the bathroom. "I have a hair dryer, if you want to use it."

"I don't know," he mused, stroking his chin. "I'm kind of getting used to a frozen pen—"

"Steve!" she yelped, her face turning red when he finished the anatomically correct word.

"Maybe you threw the water at me to preserve your favorite part of my anatomy forever. A nostalgia thing."

"Just get in the bathroom or I really will throw you out, and damn what you say or what anybody thinks!"

She sounded as if she meant it. Steve retired to the bathroom, deciding he had taken back some of the control.

He paused inside the door, looking at the sink countertop. Hair spray and perfume bottles stood side by side, and a makeup bag sat unzipped. Brushes and eye shadows stuck halfway out. He remembered vividly how their master bathroom had used to look like this and how lonely the house had felt without the little touches of femininity that were so much a part of his marriage. The good part.

How many times had he come in late, her already asleep, and smiled in pleasure at finding a pair of earrings on the dresser? Or her shoes slipped off and sitting drunkenly next to the closet door? Or her facial-cream jar next to the sink? He had loved those little things that said a woman was in his life, and he had missed them after she'd left him.

"How are you doing in there?" she called out.

"Fine," he replied, reaching for the hair dryer and plugging it in. He turned it on the High setting, then turned the nozzle to his affected area. He caught sight of himself in the mirror.

"There's nothing like blow-drying one's crotch and getting a cheap thrill in the process," he called out.

"Geez, Steve. Get a life!"

"Max tells me that all the time."

"Max is right. You ought to listen to your bird more often."

He wouldn't touch that with a ten-foot pole, Steve thought in amusement. When he was dry finally, he walked back out into the bedroom area.

Sara had her hotel room door open, her purse slung over her shoulder. "I'm buying you a drink."

"Trust me, you don't need to get me drunk to have your way with me. Now that I've been iced and blown dry, I'm more than ready."

She smiled sweetly. "I'm sure you are. Now get down to the bar before I kick you there."

"You like the rough stuff now, eh?"

But he walked out of the room meekly, knowing he had baited her enough. What was it about the verbal sparring that he couldn't resist? This new Sara didn't back down. At least she hadn't yet.

Tommy, the bartender, arched his eyebrows and gave a knowing smile when they entered the bar. Steve wanted to stuff the man into one of the potted palms that littered the place. Steve had spent far too much time in this bar—in many bars in and around New Orleans.

When they sat down on the high stools, Tommy said, "Well, well. Who is this now, Steve my man?"

"My wife," Steve replied, glaring at Tommy.

Tommy's knowing grin died a fast death. "Oh."

"A beer and a white-wine spritzer," Steve said.

"A daiquiri," Sara corrected. "Light on the rum, please."

Steve raised his eyebrows. "You've changed your drink."

"I've changed a lot of things," she replied. "That's my whole point in this. What are we doing married when neither of us are even the same people we were before?"

"I see a lot of the old you, Sara. And I like what I see of the new."

"Thank you."

She didn't quibble, apologize or downplay her accomplishments, showing her new confidence. Neither did she return the compliment. That didn't surprise him. He had a hard time believing where he was, too, sometimes. Someone once said, "Pride goeth before a fall." His pride was still down for the count.

After their drinks came, Tommy wisely disappeared. Steve took a long gulp of beer. Sara took a more dignified sip of her strawberry-colored concoction. Part of her hair fell across her cheek. Giving in to a sudden urge, he reached out and pushed the short strands back off her face, reveling in the way they seemed to wrap around his fingers. He allowed his palm to trail across the soft skin of her jawline.

Sara took his hand and set it firmly on the bar's hard mahogany surface. "Let's stop playing games, Steve."

"You used to like games. I remember when we played strip poker and you kept losing and getting more clothes. I think you emptied your closet—"

"I don't play games anymore."

"That's bad, Sara. You've got to relax. I'll tell you what. We'll play strip poker again—"

"No, thank you."

"Party pooper."

She smiled. Amusement didn't reach her eyes. "All right then, let's play a game."

"Oh, goody." He began to unbutton his shirt.

"What are you doing?" she demanded, tensing.

"Getting rid of as many pieces of clothing as I can before we play strip poker. I want to make sure I lose."

"Keep it up, and I'll make sure you never walk again."

"Keeping it up isn't the problem."

"Walking will be, if you don't get serious."

He downed more beer. "If I have to. All right. What's your game?"

"What will it take for Steve to sign the divorce agreement? Obviously, you want something."

"You."

"I doubt that. Do you want money? Is that it? Do you want me to pay back those support checks?"

"No, I don't want you to pay them back," he said, angry that she would think it. Hell, he might always be short of cash now, but he wasn't a damn leech to sponge off his now-successful wife. "I don't want your damn money, okay?"

"Then what do you want?"

"I made my proposition."

"I doubt you were really serious."

"Try me."

"No thanks. Why not be honest for once and really tell me what you want?"

"Nothing."

"Then why not sign the divorce agreement?"

"Hell, I don't know!" he admitted, irritated with her pressing. "Why are you in such a hurry for me to sign it?"

"I told you, because I want to move on, to start really building a new life for myself."

"You had a life, a good life with me. But you chose to leave it."

"You were never home for our quote, good life, end quote," she said, tightening her jaw. "You were more married to that job than to me."

"I encouraged you to get out more, to take up a hobby or some classes at the college. *You* preferred to be home."

"Enough." Sara waved her hand. "That was four years ago. Anyway, it just proves the point that we would never work out. We need closure, Steve. Both of us."

He didn't understand himself. Even with internal, EDS-type clickings, good-luck charms and Maisie's voodoo feeding his superstitions, plain common sense still told him he ought to sign and end the old life. Maybe that was his whole problem—he hadn't been willing to let go before. Maybe he ought to listen to Sara and do it now. Yet that meant he wouldn't see her again.

No series of clicks occurred in rightness.

"Let me think about it," he said finally, stalling. If nothing else, he *ought* to think about it.

She relaxed. "Good. Well, I think I'll go up to my room. I'm really tired from the flight and all."

"Sara..."

She turned to him, her wide brown eyes looking expectant.

He couldn't think of a thing to say that would persuade her to stay at the bar with him. Certainly, he couldn't think of a thing to say that would persuade her to allow him to go upstairs with her. Here he was again, he thought, trying to breathe life into something maybe better left dead. "Come to dinner tomorrow night. I'll give you a decision then."

She pursed her lips. He wanted desperately to kiss them.

"All right."

He grinned. "Eight o'clock."

"Eight o'clock."

He wondered what he would say at eight o'clock tomorrow evening. He wondered if the dinner would last past eight-fifteen.

Chapter Three

Just as Sara raised her hand to knock, Steve's front door opened.

An older woman with chocolate skin and fire in her gaze motioned for her to enter. "I knew you would be here, right at this moment."

Sara stepped over the threshold. "You did?"

"I read the bones this morning. They tell me everything. Big change is coming, yet no change at all."

Sara resisted the urge to back out over the threshold. "Is Steve Johanson here?"

The woman laughed. "Now where else would he be when I'm cooking?"

"Jamaica!" Max's squawk was faint. Since he wasn't on the porch or in the living room, Sara assumed the bird was in one of the back rooms.

The woman said, "He's in the kitchen with me. He likes to help me cook." Then she called out, "It's not too late for baked parrot, Max, so you watch your mouth!"

"I'm a dirty bird!"

"He's got that right," the woman commented. "Come in, child. Don't stand there by the door like I'll bite you."

Sara decided discretion was the better part of staying alive. She had no clue who this woman was, but she wouldn't argue with her. Besides, the smells from the kitchen were pretty good. She only hoped Max was in a cage and not standing on the stove, stirring with a claw.

She stepped inside. The house was cooler than yesterday, but still warm.

The woman laughed again. "I'm Maisie, Steve's housekeeper. And you're Sara, his wife."

"Not exactly," Sara said, holding out her hand to shake Maisie's. "We're getting a divorce."

Maisie laughed again and gripped Sara's hand in her strong one. "You just be thinking that, girl, and you'll get what you want. Don't worry."

"Okay." Relief shot through Sara when Maisie finally let go. The woman's touch had an odd, tingling feel to it, like electricity. Now that was ludicrous.

Maisie laughed again.

Sara glanced around the clutter in the living room. It hadn't changed since she had been here yesterday. She doubted it had even been dusted. Sara wondered what kind of house Maisie kept, then decided she didn't want to know.

One of the displayed shells moved. Maisie caught sight of it and clucked in disapproval. She went over and lifted it up. Sure enough, Ruby emerged. Hung out of the bottom, actually. Sara shivered at the sight of the hermit crab's large, threatening claw.

"Ruby escape again?" Steve asked, coming into the living room. He wore a cotton, plaid shirt and shorts.

Sara was glad she'd opted for a light blouse and pleated slacks, rather than the power suit. She wanted this night to go smoothly, in amicability, not in anger. Besides, sweating to death in a trussed-up outfit couldn't help her cause.

"We should have called him Houdini." Maisie opened

the birdcage and set the creature inside. "I told you this was no good. These crabs, they see the pretty shells, they want the pretty shells. He'll be slipping through the cage wires every chance he gets."

"Aren't I paying you to cook dinner and not give advice?" Steve asked, glaring at her.

Maisie raised her eyebrows. "The advice I give for free, boy. You want to keep messin' with me, you'll find yourself with worse *wanga* than you already got on you."

"My *wanga*'s fine the way it is," Steve said, knowing a *wanga* was a bad-luck spell cast on someone's soul. Maisie was always going on about that.

"So you think!" Maisie stalked out of the room.

"Your life is certainly different," Sara commented.

Steve shrugged. "Not everyone's got a voodoo priestess for a housekeeper."

Sara gaped. "You're kidding!"

"No. She talks a good game, but she's harmless, really."

"I don't even want to know about that *wanga* thing."

"Don't get excited." Steve grinned at her. "A *wanga*'s a spell, but I'll live."

"Oh." Sara eyed the birdcage. Ruby crawled up the skinny wires, clinging effortlessly. "Can you lock him up or something? I don't even want to think about him getting out while I'm here. How can you stand it?"

"Ruby doesn't hurt anything, Sara. He just wants a pretty new shell, like Maisie says." Steve stared at the cage. "I'd put him in the tank with the babies, but sometimes bigger crabs bully younger ones. I don't know if Ruby actually would, but I try to be cautious."

"Babies!" Sara panicked. "You've got more of those things?"

Steve laughed. "Yes. Relax, honey, they don't bite. They only pinch, and that's when they feel insecure."

"Then give them to a psychiatrist!" Sara glanced around wildly. Baby crabs! She sat down in the nearest chair, feeling that if she didn't, she would pass out. "What the heck are you running here? A home for unwed hermit crabs?"

"Feels that way sometimes." He took her hand and pulled her upright. "But you'll like the babies. Come and see them."

Sara resisted. "No way."

"I told you, they don't bite."

"They pinch, remember?"

"Only if they need a psychiatrist."

"I think you do."

"Probably." Steve yanked her along, into the dining area, where a fish tank rested on top of a linen chest. Although the tank had the requisite sand and coral, it was devoid of water. Instead it held a small, hollowed-out rock that served as a pond, several sponges, some plastic palm trees and a live tree branch with withering leaves. Shells of all kinds, smaller than the ones in the living room, littered the bottom of the tank.

"Okay, guys, here comes the hand of God." Steve reached in and picked up a tiny, lavender-colored, speckled shell.

Sara had to chuckle. The whole scene did look like the hand of a god lifting a believer up to the heavens. Steve turned the shell over to check inside the opening. Sara wondered what his eye looked like to whatever creature was inside.

"Hold out your hand," Steve said.

"You're kidding. There can't be one in there," Sara

answered, staring at the shell. It would fit on top of her thumbnail with room to spare.

Steve took her wrist and flipped her hand over. "Palm out flat."

Her curiosity getting the better of her, she did as he asked. He set the shell in the middle of her palm. After a few moments, Sara felt the slightest of tickles against her skin. Slowly, almost undiscernibly, the edge of the shell raised. She could barely make out the legs and claws when they emerged, they were so small. Ruby had been a dark color, a reddish-brown, but this one was pale pink. She caught sight of the sweetest little face. Antennae waved at her.

"Oh, my goodness, it looks like a miniature ET," she whispered, awed by the creature so different from the monster in the living room. "Does it have a name?"

"Pansy," Steve said. "There's also Murgatroyd and Ogglethorpe." He reached in and took two more shells from the tank, then set them on the chest itself. Two crabs eventually emerged, slightly bigger than little Pansy, but still with the sweet, heart-shaped faces and unfrightening countenances. "See? They're not so bad."

"No, they're not. I understand now why you don't keep Ruby in here with them. He's way too big. Oh!" Pansy began exploring the human hand she sat on. Sara stared in fascination as the crab moved slowly along her palm. Suddenly, Pansy made a sprint toward her arm. Sara grabbed the crab before it fell off.

Steve took Pansy from her, and put all three babies back in the tank.

"What are you doing with them?" Sara asked.

Steve shrugged. "I've become a kind of crab-rescue center, I guess. I found Ruby on a beach in Florida, fending off about ten seagulls. I thought a guy that tough ought to get a break in life. He came up with two legs missing not too long ago. I have no idea how, but he'll have new ones when he molts again. It's an amazing process. He'll shed his outer layer and be very soft and pink, but bigger...."

Sara stared at her soon-to-be ex-husband in astonishment. She felt as though she was listening to a science show for hermit crabs.

He added, "This trio I came upon one by one. Murgatroyd was from a pet store. He was the only one left and I felt bad for him. Ogglethorpe was clinging to a dead hibiscus in my front garden, right after a hurricane. God knows where he blew in from or how he survived. I found Pansy in a load of shells I was sent because I polish them for tourist shops. I noticed her peeking out of a shell in one of the bags I had just opened."

"How awful." One part of his explanation caught her attention. "You sell shells, too?"

"Say it three times fast." He grinned, then sobered. "It supplements my income. Life here doesn't require good old corporate hustle."

"I can't imagine you without it."

"I discovered it wasn't all it was cracked up to be. Shells aren't in great demand in the New Orleans area."

Sara gazed at him, confused. "This isn't like you. Or at least it's not like the Steve I remember. You would have seen the crabs' plight as survival of the fittest and walked away. In all four cases."

He shrugged again, the self-effacing gesture another foreign emotion, one the old Steve never would have used. "Maybe I like thumbing my nose at the animal behaviorists who preach noninterference. Maybe I'm raising dinner for thirty years from now."

"Now that's more like you," she commented. Only she

knew, just from the way he handled the little guys so gently, that he wasn't the old Steve and the crabs would never be dinner.

Bad thinking, she admitted, realizing that softened feelings opened old doors better left closed.

"Dinner!" Maisie called out, bringing a loaded platter into the room. "It's Love Chicken."

Sara wanted to ask what Love Chicken was, but didn't know if she could handle the answer. Don't Ask, Don't Tell had its place—especially when the cook was a voodoo practitioner.

The chicken dish turned out to be one of the best Sara had ever eaten, to her relief. She and Steve didn't really talk about anything during dinner—or rather, they didn't talk about anything important. The conversation stayed light, mostly catch-up on Sara's parents and sister and on his family, although Steve clearly didn't keep in regular touch. Sara didn't want to bring up the divorce until she sensed the timing was right, and so far it hadn't been. Why Steve stayed silent on the subject, though, worried her. After all, he had offered to give her an answer tonight.

Maisie left after serving coffee. She vanished with a broad smile, which only added to Sara's foreboding. Silly, she told herself. So what if the woman was a voodoo priestess? Maisie hadn't cast any spells. At least Sara didn't think so. She hadn't heard any chanting in the kitchen.

"How about a stroll by the bayou?" Steve suggested.

Sara hesitated. A stroll by the bayou seemed innocuous from a romance standpoint. But she had heard of alligators. "That sounds dangerous. What about alligators?"

"We've got a few, but not where I'll take you."

That sounded ominous, with danger waiting in the wings.

Once she got out on the bayou, however, things weren't so bad. In fact, they were spectacular. Moonlight bathed the ripples in the water crystal white on a midnight black lake. The Spanish moss gleamed silver on the tree trunks, and it seemed as if she and Steve were the last living creatures on earth. The warm breezes heated her skin. The verdant scents of fertile soil and life-giving water filled her nostrils. Even the birds cooed right on cue.

The damned scene was right out of *No Mercy*. All it needed to make it complete was Richard Gere and Kim Basinger handcuffed together and wading through the water. Sex was in the air.

"How long are you staying?" Steve asked, as they strolled along a dirt path that followed the lake.

"I have some vacation time accumulated," she replied, making sure she kept a good arm's length from him. "A couple of weeks, but I don't expect to be that long."

"How long do you expect to be?"

"That's up to you."

He laughed. "You better have a long time coming to you, then."

She refused to be baited into a confrontation. She cleared her throat and asked, "Have you thought about the divorce agreement? You said you would give me an answer tonight."

He shrugged and rubbed his stomach. "I thought about it, and I don't know."

"Why would you want to stay married to me?" she asked, trying to remain logical, rather than defensive.

"I don't know the answer to that one, either." He looked up at the moon, its light illuminating his profile. He had a square jaw and a snub nose that always turned her on. She used to love sitting in the car with him, just to have a reason to stare at his profile.

Sara grasped her waning control and yanked it firmly back into place. "You're not making sense, Steve."

"Maybe not, but then again, I don't have to." He reached down and picked a flower. He handed it to her. "It's a wild orchid. The locals call it a swamp orchid."

She admired the whitish bloom, the yellow-brown speckling on its tongue.

"It's beautiful," she breathed.

"Just like you."

"Not hardly." But his words were too intimate, disturbing her senses. She spotted another flower and distracted herself with collecting it. "Here's another pretty one. And one over there, too."

"That's jasmine and an azalea."

She began picking more flowers until her hands were full.

"You've picked enough," Steve advised. "Why take more?"

She paused, straightening with another orchid in her hand. "Why not? They'll make a beautiful bouquet."

"They give more for years if left for the birds and bees to pollinate."

She smiled at him. "You *are* different."

"Just respectful of nature. I make some of my living from it now."

Steve sat down on a log that had fallen a long time ago, from the looks of it. "Relax for a while, Sara, and enjoy the view."

"It's getting late," she began.

"So? What does that matter?"

"I suppose it won't hurt." She sat down gingerly, again keeping her distance. A good distance, maybe not the size of the Grand Canyon, but far enough that she was safe from him.

She stared out over the bayou, watching the current endlessly stream by, almost sensual in its slowness.

"This water has been flowing by here since time began," Steve said in a soft voice. "I often wonder what it would think about the world. Probably not much."

Sara gazed at him, openmouthed. When had he become a philosopher? Albeit a pragmatic one, but a philosopher all the same. She wouldn't ask, she thought. The answer was bound to get her into trouble.

He seemed to be all the things she had always wanted him to be. Relaxed. Gentle. Patient. She had glimpsed this in him during their time together, but only enough to have her wishing for more—and hoping to change him. That had been her fatal mistake in marrying him. She had thought love would bring out all the things she wanted in a husband.

She knew he had wanted her to be more outgoing, and wondered if he, too, had expected marriage to change her.

"You look like you're pondering the weight of the world, Sara."

He smiled at her, his face all shadow and light from the moon. The warm breeze lifted the shaggy ends of his hair. She felt the breeze ruffle her own hair, pulling sensuously at the strands. The scents of water and earth wafted through her senses in nature's most erotic aromatherapy. She had the overwhelming urge to trace his jawline…to wrap her arms around his neck.

"I'm pondering a lot of things," she whispered. "You, mostly."

His smile grew more intimate. "I've been pondering you ever since you arrived on my doorstep."

He reached across the space separating them and took

her hand in his own. The flowers fell to the ground. Maybe if he had dragged her down in passion, she could have resisted. Maybe. Instead, he pressed his lips to her palm in the lightest of kisses. Sara just stared at him, frozen. Her brain warned her to pull her hand away, to walk away, but she couldn't move. All the old sensations shot through her.

He kissed her palm again, then leisurely kissed his way past her wrist and up her arm. Sara leaned toward him, shivering at the heat rising in her veins. His head lifted and this time his lips touched her own. Sara felt pulled into a gentle maelstrom, the velvet darkness swirling all around her. Emotions long buried rose up strong and true again. His lower lip rubbed along her own, teasing her mouth open. She needed no encouragement, eagerly mating her tongue to his. The darkness swirled faster and deeper, her head spinning dizzily. She hadn't forgotten how he could make her feel, no matter how much she had tried to suppress the memories. One kiss and she craved him all over again, just as she always had.

Somehow she felt Steve's hands at her back, and her body was pressed as deliciously to his as she remembered. She wrapped her arms around his shoulders, her fingers stroking the unfamiliar hair at his nape. She found it erotic and somehow totally masculine. Swashbucklers had hair like this, she thought. Ancient chieftains and heroic warriors of old had worn their hair this way—all of them men's men, the definition of virility. No wonder men loved women's hair long, she thought dimly. It felt so good.

Steve eased his lips from hers, but she reached up and renewed the kiss. She couldn't stand the thought of him not kissing her like this, and yet she didn't understand the thought at all. He kissed her again...and again and again, endless kisses that captured her and turned her into a creature of feeling. All logic, all warnings, deserted her.

When his fingers went to her shirt, she desired it. When his hands freed her breasts for his mouth, she willed it above all things. When his tongue laved her nipples into aching points, she cried out gladly at the throbbing in her veins. The breeze did nothing to cool her heated skin.

She got his shirt off and reveled in the feel of his bared chest against her breasts. It was like coming home, she admitted. The hard wall of his chest, the silky hairs arrowing down past his waist, had always made her feel feminine and sexy, playful and dangerous, loving and comforted. Whenever she had had erotic dreams about him after their breakup, she had always remembered the way his chest felt against her skin. She couldn't fight this, she thought, pulling him closer in her embrace.

He moaned, his mouth turning to fire, planting stinging kisses along her chest and throat...across her breasts and torso. Their lovemaking felt as wonderful as it always had—and yet better. More poignant. More knowing. Sara moaned and rained kisses along his shoulders, nearly biting him in her desperation.

She wanted more. Everything just one more time.

SHE WAS SEDUCING HIM.

Steve tried to pull air into this lungs, but they weren't having any. He tried to control his response to her, but he was already out of control. The moonlight bathed her skin a stunning alabaster. It only enhanced all the primitive urges clamoring inside his body.

And Sara. She was like a bird in flight. Soaring. Dipping. Challenging him to take her to even greater heights. Since she had left him, he had never been able to rid himself of the way she had responded to his touch. Lying in his bed alone, he had been haunted by the passion she had had. She still had. Only now it was overlaid by a stronger femininity. She had a true inner confidence that met him more fully now, enhancing his desire for her. He wanted her so much more than he ever had before....

A deep bellow split the air.

Sara jumped back. "What the hell was that?"

"Just an alligator," Steve replied, reaching for her again.

"Alligator!" She slapped his hands away. "I thought you said there were no alligators around here."

Steve took a deep breath, marshaling his desire. He didn't want to, but all sorts of emotions spun through him. He knew he had to reassure Sara—on several fronts. "He's pretty far away. Just a bull calling for a mate. You can hear them for up to a mile."

"That's all?" She shivered and pulled her shirt back up, covering her beautiful breasts. "That's hardly enough. We should go."

His entire body cried out with unsatisfied need, but he admitted the truth at last. "We can't make love tonight."

"Who said we would?" she demanded indignantly.

He swatted at a mosquito buzzing around him. "Your body and mine. Five minutes more and we would have been happily making the baby you want. And don't try lying about it. I might be washed up on the corporate ladder, but I'm not a total idiot."

"Oh, God," she muttered, covering her face with her hands for a moment.

Steve knew she felt regrets. He ought to feel some himself, but he just couldn't. "Sara, this proves we still have feelings for each other. I know I came on strong at the hotel, but maybe I was right. I've been thinking a lot since you came here. We only need to get to know each other again—''

She grabbed up the rest of her clothes and began pulling them on. "It was just sex, Steve. Nothing more."

"Oh, no, it wasn't."

"Okay. It was just almost sex."

"It was more, and you know it."

"What about the moonlight and breezes? We could have been any two unattached people in a setting right out of *The Big Easy*. Who the heck *wouldn't* want sex?"

"You can go ahead and think it was just physical, but you know different. Deep down, feelings still exist for both of us. We need to explore them before we make love."

"Steve, this was a mistake. And could we talk about this later? When we're decent?"

"We're decent now. In fact, we were just feeling pretty damn good about each other—"

"Forget it." She shoved him hard enough to put him off balance. Before he could recover, Sara scrambled to her feet.

He pounded the log. "Dammit, Sara. Stop ignoring the obvious!"

"I'm not ignoring the obvious." She buttoned her blouse up to the neck. "I'm keeping the obvious in perspective."

He stood. "If you think I'm giving you a divorce now, you're crazy! We just need to talk about our feelings for each other."

She didn't answer. Instead, she stalked away. Steve went after her. That damn alligator, he thought in disgust. If it hadn't bellowed, they never would have stopped their lovemaking. Now she was ticked off with him. When was the last time doing the right thing had gotten him what he wanted?

"Running away again won't solve anything, Sara."

"I didn't run away before, and I'm not running away now. I'm walking away from a situation that has no future." She glanced at him. "Button your shirt, Steve."

"I like the wind on my chest hairs."

"Men have no dignity when half-naked."

"That's right. Just shred our egos." He tried buttoning his shirt while still trotting next to her. His foot caught on a rock, and he went tumbling headfirst on the path. "Dammit!"

Sara kept on walking. "I'll find my way back on my own, thank you, Steve."

He got to his feet and ran after her again. Unfortunately, she was just about at the house. And her car. When he finally caught up to her, he grabbed her arm and spun her around to face him.

"Listen to me," he said, glaring at her in the dim light. "This changes everything, Sara. You can't deny that. We're back in each other's lives again. We may be for a long time."

"Thank you for a lovely dinner, Steve, and tell Maisie I enjoyed her wonderful meal." Sara disengaged herself from his grip and went to her car. She opened the door, got in, then said, "Do us both a favor, Steve, and sign the divorce agreement."

She slammed the door with a finality that would have satisfied a movie director.

Steve watched the car drive away. "In a pig's eye, honey. In a big, fat pig's eye."

Chapter Four

"I know I forgot to call, Mom. That's why I'm calling now."

Sara glanced heavenward for supplication. She was thirty years old and still had to call her mother.

Her mother's voice was smug. "Moms worry, child, which you will learn soon enough."

"What do you mean by that?" Sara asked, her gut churning as she remembered last night with Steve. Did her mother know about the near lovemaking between her and Steve? Had he called and told her?

"I mean," her mother said, chuckling, "you'll learn after you have this baby you're so all-fired ready to have. Much as I am looking forward to you giving me a grandchild, I am *not* looking forward to being called Grandmother. And you're still young. So how is Steve?"

Sara could hear the interest in her mother's perky voice. She had always liked Steve, an amazing thing when one considered Marjorie Carter's cool reaction to brash salesmen who called at the house. When Sara left Steve, her mother had given her a no-nonsense lecture on the foolishness of young brides, then had followed up with a sympathetic shoulder to cry on. Her father had been about the same. He liked Steve, too.

Sara took a secret delight in informing her mother of Steve's current circumstances. "He's living in a ramshackle old house with a voodoo priestess for a housekeeper, four hermit crabs, a mouthy parrot and alligators practically outside his door."

Marge burst into laughter. "Oh, God, Sara. I would have loved to have seen your face. Your man-god is definitely off the pedestal."

"He's my husband, not my 'man-god,'" Sara corrected caustically. Her mom had always liked Steve best, sometimes better than her own daughter. It was enough to cause a mother-daughter complex.

"It's nice to hear you acknowledge the relationship. What the heck is he doing with a voodoo priestess as a housekeeper?"

"I don't know." Sara was thoroughly exasperated with her mother. "This is *not* helping me, Mom."

"I know." She chuckled again. "I'm sorry, honey. I totally support you, you know that. I just find the situation ironic. I take it Steve did not sign on the dotted line."

"Not hardly."

"It's pride on his part, probably. He's a very proud man, you know. And he never liked failure. Anyone could see that."

"It's nice to have a psychologist's secretary in the family. I guess you're telling me I have to convince him divorce is not failure."

"Sure you want to?"

"Yes." Sara forced the word out, knowing what hesitation might say about her—especially to her mom.

"Okay." Her mother sounded very dubious.

"I wish you could be a little more supportive, Mom," Sara blurted out, frustrated with her mother's lack of enthusiasm.

"Honey, I am supportive of you. I hope you know that."

Her mother sounded entirely too soothing for Sara's jangled nerves. Sara felt like she was a kid again. How did mothers manage to make their adult children feel that way? She'd better start taking lessons for her own parenting time, which she hoped happened sooner than later and not through Steve's help.

"I know you're supportive, Mom." Her mother truly was. "I guess I'm upset with Steve and I'm taking it out on you."

"I can understand that. But maybe you ought to consider why he upsets you. Maybe your feelings aren't as dead as you think."

"Mom, I think you've gone nuts if *you* think that. You know what my life with Steve was like."

"Oh, he needed a wake-up call, that was obvious. But you did need to give him a second chance."

"I gave him a hundred!" Sara snapped.

"Maybe you should take a look at this new Steve with the falling-down house and mouthy parrot. Maybe he's a different man than he was. He certainly sounds like it, although he's managed to be just as interesting."

"Goodbye, Mom," Sara said firmly, and hung up the telephone.

"Moms!" she snorted. If playing devil's advocate was a mother's prerequisite, then Sara intended to break the rules. No way would she make her child crazy with presenting the other side when the other side was dead and buried and no longer existed.

Her mother's words only reminded her of how foolish she'd been with Steve. Maybe Maisie's Love Chicken was aptly named. Something had definitely got out of hand.

Sara pressed her fingers to her suddenly warm cheeks,

trying to dispel the heat of embarrassment. Nothing out of hand about it, Steve's hands had been all over her…and hers all over him. She must have been nuts. Thank goodness for screaming alligators. Right now, she deserved to be one's dinner.

What she needed was to regroup. Her mother had made a good point about Steven looking upon divorce as failure. Sara needed to show him the marriage had been a mistake in the first place and the divorce would wipe the slate clean. It meant dredging up a lot of memories—ones neither of them wanted to face—but she would have to do it. Once the trip down memory lane had been accomplished, Steve would be more than ready to sign the papers.

Sara lowered her hands and took a deep breath. "Okay, now let's find the clothes that make the woman. The calm, sensible, unaffected woman."

She opened the hotel closet and viewed the few clothes she'd brought. One suit, power color. One pair of decent slacks. One blouse. All too damn warm for New Orleans in April. She also had that one sleeveless dress he had already seen, plus some jeans and T-shirts that seemed like a parka and heavy leggings in the current spring heat here. The *sultry* heat.

"Great," she muttered, thinking that she was even turning the weather on. This was not a good thing.

She did a little shopping, settling on some more light sundresses and sandals, none overtly revealing. The thought of meeting with Steve in the evening chilled her faster than a blast from the Arctic Circle.

Making a decision, she went out to his house. She figured Maisie would be there cleaning and she could track down Steve through the voodoo woman. Heck, if nothing else, Maisie could throw some prophetic chicken bones and track him that way.

Instead, Sara found Steve himself. He sat back in a rickety wicker chair on the veranda, his feet up on the railing and his eyes closed. He did open them and gaze at her as she got out of the rented car. Immediately, Sara was all too conscious of the way the new dress skimmed her body. She stopped at the bottom of the veranda steps, unwilling to go farther.

Max gave a wolf whistle, cocked his head and said, "I want me some of that, man!"

"Thank you, Max," Sara said with all the aplomb she could muster. "You're too kind."

"Max is never kind. He's usually right, however." Steve eyed her speculatively, his blue gaze sensual. Very sensual. Sara's awareness rose to extreme levels until she felt like a prime pork chop in a butcher's case. Max was far less intimidating. Steve rubbed his bare chest, drawing her attention and her body's physical response. His simple gesture had her blood pumping hotly in her veins.

"I'm just curious," she said, "but do you own more than one shirt?"

He grinned. "Not if I can help it."

"I can tell. Well, it's your skin cancer."

Steve's grin faded. "What?"

"You know, the UV rays and all that bad stuff from the sun. Scientists recommend we stay covered and out of the direct light for our health." Sara smiled, feeling as though she'd quenched any sensuality in his near nakedness. "But, of course, it's your choice."

"Does this mean you care?" Steve asked, his confidence coming back.

"As I would for anybody risking his health," she replied, liking her general answer.

"If you think I'm sexy, come on, baby, let me know," Max sang happily from the Rod Stewart tune, then gave another wolf whistle.

"Speaking of sexy," Steve said, "I was thinking about last night, and the way you kissed me, all hot and aching—"

"I was…caught up in a moment," Sara interrupted.

"Come onto the veranda and we'll talk about it."

She felt as if she was about to walk into the lion's den. Unlike Daniel, she was bound to get chewed up and spit out. Going down memory lane seemed less palatable than when she'd been alone in the room and desperate for a game plan.

Sara looked at the free chair—on the other side of Steve. She'd have to pass far too close to him to get to it. Going up the steps, she perched on the porch railing next to Max's stand.

"Hubba, hubba," Max said, eyeing her with his head cocked again. His beady little eye looked positively gleeful.

A good ten feet separated her from Steve. A very safe ten feet. Sara took a deep breath to brace herself. "Have you reconsidered your stance from last night?"

"About signing the papers?" Steve pursed his lips. "What do you think?"

"Yeah, what do you think?" Max repeated.

"I think you should think logically and sign them," she replied to both man and parrot. "There's nothing between us anymore—"

"There was very little between us last night. Maybe you could have fit a nail file, but I doubt it."

"Yes, well." She paused, knowing she was losing control of the conversation. "Why aren't you working today? It's a weekday. I thought you cleaned rooms."

"I do. I did work this morning and I will again later."
He shrugged. "It comes and goes."

"But your business won't grow or even remain stable
unless you hustle a little, nurture the client list—"

"I hustled and nurtured seventy-hours-plus a week and
where did it get me? Down and out in the corporate and
marriage world. Now I do things at my pace. When I need
to push, I do. When I need to enjoy, I do, too."

Sara wanted to shake him. His attitude was uncharacteristic of him, totally uncharacteristic. It hid a lot of bitterness. She felt to blame and had a nearly overwhelming
urge to wrap him in her arms and do some major nurturing
of her own.

Lord help her, Sara thought, shocked by her urges. She
couldn't afford such notions. She couldn't even *think* of
them. She had to kill notions and quickly. Feeling panicky
and urgently needing something to help her break away
from her collapsing emotions, she said, "I'm in love with
someone."

The words hovered in the air like frozen stalagtites.
Sara gasped. Where the hell had they come from?

Steve's feet hit the plank flooring with a bang. He sat
upright and stared at her. "What did you just say?"

Sara stared back at him. If she denied the words, she'd
look like the complete idiot she was. Yet how could she
explain her carelessness? Stalling for time until she came
up with something halfway reasonable, she said, "You
heard me."

"Hot dog!" Max squawked. "Here we go!"

"You said before that there was no one else in your
life and now you're saying there is." Steve's voice reminded her of a runaway locomotive gathering horrible
speed before it crashed.

"Yes, well...I suppose I shouldn't have." Sara began,

trying to salvage a little dignity. She was doing a damn lousy job of it. "I wasn't fair to you."

"Damn straight. You should have told me right from the beginning."

The confused apology she'd been scrambling for went right out of Sara's head. She asked, "Would it have made a difference if I had?"

"What the hell kind of question is that?" he snapped, clearly furious. "You know it would have."

Dredging up every bad moment in their marriage looked more hurtful than sensible now. To tell him she'd found someone else was hurtful, too. Unfortunately, she'd already done it. Maybe her pea brain had a reason for popping out about another man. Maybe it had done it as a protective measure. Steve was so angry, he wouldn't come near her again. That was a plus. He might kill her, but he wouldn't kiss her. That was a big plus, too.

"I'm sorry," she said. "I didn't want to hurt you. Now I have."

He opened his mouth, then shut it. Clearly, he'd been about to say he was hurt, before changing his mind. Her mother was right about him being a proud man. Maybe the idea of Sara loving another man would make divorce seem like less of a failure to him. After all, while he might have some control over job and opportunity, he had no control over love. No one did. Maybe he would find another man a more acceptable reason for the divorce. Maybe he'd just want to wash his hands of her now.

Sara's heart skipped painfully at the thought.

"I'm not hurt," he said. "Just confused over why you told me the opposite."

"I—I thought it was better that way," she said lamely, then added, "I didn't think you'd refuse to sign. We haven't even see each other in years and the marriage is long dead."

"You sure didn't act that way last night," he told her. "You were all over me like gumbo over rice. For someone in love with another person, that's a strange way to act."

"I told you I just got caught up in the moment."

"One helluva moment."

"Crapola," Max announced in general, but summing up the conversation succinctly for Sara.

She shrugged at Steve, hoping for nonchalance. "It was a mistake, a lot of old emotions up for a last gasp. Maybe I wanted to be sure about my feelings—"

"Are you telling me last night I was just a guinea pig for your feelings?" Steve interrupted angrily.

"No. Oh, no. I wasn't thinking that at all. I just got caught up in a moment," she repeated. Boy, but her arguments were getting lamer and lamer. Not a good sign.

"Sure?"

"Yes."

"So who's the guy?" Steve asked.

"Nobody you know."

"I want to meet him."

"What?" Sara gaped at him. She could feel her eyes bulging. Her stomach churned in distress. His suggestion was ludicrous, far more ludicrous than he'd ever know.

"I want to meet him," Steve repeated. "I want to see this guy you have all picked out to father your children. I want to see whether he's a Milquetoast or not. I want to see you're happy with him—"

"I'm happy, I'm happy," Sara exclaimed. *Meet him?* Now Steve had gone nuts.

"Good. I'll be glad to see you happy."

His gaze pierced her. She felt trapped—and terribly

guilty. Now was the moment to say she'd lied, that she was only kidding.

And that sounded horrible.

"I don't see any purpose in your meeting him," Sara said, stalling.

"I do," Steve began.

The front door opened, and Maisie came through with a tea tray. The tray held mismatched mugs and a chipped clay pitcher of what looked like iced tea.

"Whatcha got there, babe?" Max asked, then whistled.

My salvation, Sara thought gratefully. Even if only for a moment.

STEVE WANTED TO THROW the pitcher and mugs across the veranda. That act would hardly calm his mood. He didn't want his mood calmed. He wanted to kill.

The other man.

"You're making a bad mojo," Maisie warned in a low voice as she set the tray on the little, wrought-iron table. Mojo was the charm of one's well-being. "You want good mojo, you have to have happy thoughts."

"Mojo yourself right out of here," Steve muttered.

"*Tsk, tsk.* It's bad to smart-mouth someone like me," Maisie said, straightening.

"Here, chickie, chickie!" Max crooned.

Sara smiled at the parrot.

"Max is gonna have more luck than you with that girl," Maisie whispered.

Max leaned toward Sara and squawked, *"Voulez-vous coucher avec moi, ce soir?"*

Sara blushed and laughed.

"See?" Maisie said triumphantly, and went back into the house.

Steve clenched his teeth against making a sarcastic

comment. He was in enough trouble already. Glaring at Sara, he wondered what the hell she was playing at. She looked very cool and sensual in the sleeveless dress that hugged her curves. Did she have any clue what she did to him? She had to. She must have dressed deliberately to entice him. Even feeling that way, he only knew he didn't want her enticing anyone else. The thought of another man tormented him.

Another man. She'd been here two days, shoved divorce papers under his nose, then kissed him silly. She'd even denied having another man at their first meeting. Now, all of a sudden, his worst nightmare arrived. How could she have kissed him last night the way she had, if she loved someone else? What was this?

Get some answers, he decided. He always functioned better when he had all the answers.

"What's his name?" Steve asked.

"That's not important," Sara said, her voice sounding weak and shaky. "About the papers, you see—"

"When I know about this guy, then we'll talk papers." He wanted to get up and pace, but was afraid he'd go right over and shake her.

"Papers, papers, papers," Max shouted, rocking from side to side on his perch.

"What's his name?" Steve demanded once again.

Sara hesitated, then looked away. "Mike."

"Mike," Steve repeated.

"Mike!" Max echoed, in a learning mood.

"What does it matter?" Sara said. "You don't know him."

"He's what brought you down here," Steve said. "So indulge me."

"It seems silly," Sara protested.

"Mike's a silly bird," Max said.

"You know it, Max." Steve stood and walked over to Sara. She shrank back a little on the railing, as if just realizing what her news bomb had released. A big stink. And Steve intended to make one. "Where did you meet him? What does he do? Have you slept with him yet?"

"Okay, that's enough," Sara said, straightening.

"Now you've done it," Max intoned.

"Answer the questions, dammit!" Steve demanded, practically in her face.

Sara pushed him back, taking him by surprise. She stepped around him before he could recover. "Look, just forget all this stuff. It's not important."

"Not important!" Steve gaped at her. She was turning his life upside down yet again, and she said it wasn't important.

"Hot damn, baby!" Max shrieked.

"Oh, shut up," Steve told the bird.

"Oh, shut up," Max repeated. He then went on a rampage, chanting "Oh, shut up."

"I don't think I'm asking too much, to know about this clown you have to replace me."

"Oh, shut up," Max sang, very operatically.

"I think it's my right to ask, especially if you want the papers signed."

"Oh, shut up," Max bellowed in a deep voice.

"I don't see why you're making a big fuss, Sara. Just tell me who he is…or did you not bother to tell him you already had a husband?"

"Oh, shut up!" Max squeaked out in a high, piping voice.

His tolerance level lower than zero, Steve rounded on his pet and shouted, *"Shut the hell up, Max!"*

Startled, Max skittered back, flapping his clipped wings and losing his balance. The parrot accidently flipped off the perch, yet managed to land upright on the veranda floor.

"Help! I've fallen and I can't get up!" Max squawked, his feathers all puffed up in fright.

"Hell," Steve said, disgusted with himself for losing his temper with a bird.

"Poor little guy," Sara said, immediately bending down and extending her hand before Steve could rescue his parrot.

"Watch out," Steve said, while Max climbed up onto Sara's wrist. "He bites sometimes."

Steve extended his own hand for Max.

"Bite this, pal," Max said, and snapped at Steve.

"Dammit!" Steve exclaimed, snatching his hand back before Maxie got a chunk of it. Everybody wanted a piece of him today.

Max climbed up Sara's bare arm, his claws clearly gentle on her flesh. He perched on her shoulder and began to play with her hair. The damn thing seemed content, its feathers unpuffing back to normal.

"I don't like this," Steve said, eyeing his cantankerous pet.

"He's fine," Sara assured him. "Believe me, I'll yell if he does anything."

"Don't leave any presents on her dress, Max," Steve told the parrot.

"Blow it out your—"

"Just don't you do it," Steve said, overriding the parrot's comment.

"The bird, the bird, the bird is the word," Max sang, then went back to playing with Sara's hair.

Max's antics at least had distraction value. Steve knew his anger had diminished to controllable levels, meaning he controlled it and it no longer controlled him.

He realized badgering Sara wasn't the best way to accomplish what he wanted from her. He would have to put his curiosity about *Mike* on the back burner.

"You better sit down," he said, pointing to the chair he had vacated. "Max will be settled in for a while, if I know him, so you're stuck for the duration. If you sit, he might get interested in the seat back and move to it."

"Thanks." She sat gingerly on the wicker seat.

"You can sit back," Steve said in amusement. He was pleased he could be amused at the moment. "You won't hurt him."

"Okay." Sara sat in a more comfortable position. Max continued his hairdressing chores.

Steve wondered what he was supposed to talk about, now that he wasn't talking about "the man." *A guy of Sara's.* He hated the whole idea of Sara having a guy other than him.

"Could we start over?" Sara asked.

Hope rose in his heart. "Sure. I'd like us to try."

She nodded. "I came out today to talk about your signing the papers. I'd like to keep it strictly to that."

"Oh." So much for his high hopes.

"So, will you?"

"No." The word came out without hesitation.

"Steve." Sara sighed in frustration.

He grinned wryly. "I've heard you sigh my name in more intimate circumstances. It sounds a whole lot better then."

"Please."

"That, too." He held up a hand. "I'll be good. Max'll probably peck my eyes out if I'm not."

"What will it take for you to sign?" she asked, more businesslike than he had ever been.

He had a lot of answers on his lips, but all sounded

less than impressive. Clearly, she had someone new in her life, and who the hell was he to hold her back?

But why wouldn't she talk about the guy? And why the hell would she be all over him when she loved someone else? If she'd just been caught up in the moment, then he was still an executive vice president of RMX.

That gave him an idea.

"A million dollars and I sign," Steve said, pulling a number out of a hat. An outrageous number, but he liked it. His marriage was worth a million to him. More. It was priceless. At least he wasn't going out without a down-and-dirty fight.

Sara gasped and half rose from the chair.

Max squawked, "Look out now!"

Sara sat back down. To Steve, she said, "You're nuts."

Steve shrugged. "You asked. I told you."

"But it's ludicrous. Where would I get a million dollars from?"

"Choice investments. You must have made some. Take a second mortgage out. I know. Have the new boyfriend cough it up. You're worth it, honey."

"I don't—" Sara broke off and made a face. "Steve, can't you be halfway reasonable about this?"

He didn't want to be reasonable about anything again where she was concerned.

"My mother said this morning that you were a proud man." Sara leaned forward. "She would be so disappointed to know you're selling yourself for money."

"And to think I like your mother." He did, too. He wondered if he should try and enlist Marj Carter's help. Marj would ultimately side with Sara, no doubt. Any mother would side with her child. His own mother had sided with him. His father hadn't. Dad had always liked

Sara better. His father had also never forgiven him for losing the prestigious job.

Steve had never involved either set of parents in his problems with Sara, not wanting to put them in the middle. Tempting as it might be, he wouldn't do it now.

"Look, divorce is not a failure. It's a resolution to dissolve something already dead." Max chose that moment to walk onto the back of the wicker chair. Sara stood up. "I've got to go. You need to think about what *you* want, Steve."

She hurried off the veranda and into her car.

"Oh, hell!" Max shouted, flapping his clipped wings.

"The situation calls for stronger words than that, my friend," Steve commented while Sara's car roared to life.

"Don't you be teaching that parrot any more bad language," Maisie said, emerging from the house. "Oh. You didn't have any tea. You should have. I put a special spell on it."

"Just what we needed," Steve grumbled.

"You probably did."

"She's got another man."

"She tell you that?"

"Yes, she told me that," Steve retorted. What the hell. Let Maisie turn him into a zombie for smart-mouthing her. He couldn't feel more miserable than he did right now.

Maisie burst into laughter. "That girl's got another man like I've got *a* man. And you know I don't have a man. Don't want or need one. Ya'll are too messy and stiff-necked."

Steve paused in his misery. "You don't think she does?"

"Anyone can see your Sara ain't blossomed except around you. 'Course she's gonna tell you she has a man.

Nothing spooks another man away faster. Then she gets what she wants."

"A divorce," Steve finished.

Maisie snorted. "She only thinks she wants one."

"You don't think she does?"

"You sound like a broken record, boy," Maisie said, with a sniff of disdain. "But I think she will if you keep acting the way you do...with the brains of a pea pod."

"Yeah, man!" Max squawked, bobbing his head up and down. "Yeah, man, yeah, man, yeah, man."

"Hush up, Max," Maisie said, putting her wrist out for the bird. "Better get on before he wants parrot for dinner."

"Who needs ya, baby?" Max commented, then climbed up on Maisie's arm. He went all the way to her shoulder, cuddling his head under her ear.

Maisie chuckled. "By the way. Ruby's missing again from the birdcage, and Pansy's buried herself in the gravel like she did last month. I think she's going to shed that body of hers. The little girl is growin'!"

"Mmm," Steve said absently. He wondered if Maisie was right. If so, that easily explained why Sara had been like a woman too long on a desert island last night, why there'd been no mention of another man and why one had popped up out of nowhere.

"I got things to do," Steve said, jumping off the veranda.

"But what about Ruby and Pansy?"

"Pansy will show up in a week or so, bigger and better. Look under the fanciest shell for Ruby. He's bound to be there." Steve headed for his truck.

"Don't you think you ought to put on your fanciest shell?" Maisie called out. "You ain't hardly dressed proper for grappling with a wife."

Steve stopped and looked down at himself. He looked up and grinned at his bossy housekeeper. "I thought I was."

"Ding-dong!" Max squawked.

Steve let him have the last word.

Chapter Five

Sara stepped into the hallway and shut her hotel room door, intent on going to dinner. Not that she felt like eating...

"Good. I caught you."

Sara groaned, knowing the male voice anywhere. She had heard it enough over the years of her marriage. Hotel security stank, that was for sure, otherwise they never would have allowed Steve up in the halls.

The last thing she wanted was to tell more lies about another man, like she had that afternoon. She'd never felt more high-school immature than when driving away from his house. She calculated her chances of success in getting back into her room and locking the door before Steve reached her. She doubted she would make it. Besides, he'd probably camp out until she was forced to emerge. The retreat had more high-school immature written all over it, anyway.

She glanced up and swallowed back a sudden lump of anxious femininity. Steve looked great in black linen slacks and a cool white shirt. He wore the sleeves rolled to the elbows, showcasing his tanned, corded forearms. Her senses surged to awareness of him as pure male—as her chosen mate.

"Mate my ass," she muttered, to give herself some backbone. Louder, she said, "Hello, Steve. What do you want now? Two million? I'm afraid I'm on my way out. *Alone.*"

"Actually, I came to apologize," he said, when he reached her. "I've been pushy and aggressive...bull-headed." He grinned. "So what else is new? But I should have been more of a gentleman about it."

"So you don't want a million to sign the papers?"

He laughed, positively jovial. "No."

Sara didn't know what to say, surprised by Steve's attitude. And his appearance. And his new look. She was really liking the hair. She just didn't trust him. Not one inch. "Okay. Now what's this about?"

He shrugged. "Nothing more than what I just said. You're going out to dinner. I haven't eaten. Why don't I take you somewhere nice to eat?"

"Thanks, but I'm only going downstairs to the hotel restaurant."

"Have you seen New Orleans at night?" he asked. "Knowing you, the answer's no."

"Hey, I get out," Sara protested.

"So you mentioned earlier," Steve replied, clearly referring to her "man."

Sara's cheeks heated until she felt like the top of her head would come off from the boiling temperature inside.

"But you haven't gotten out to the French Quarter yet, have you?"

"Not really," she admitted.

He took her arm, sending delicious shivers of awareness along her nerve endings. "Good. I'll show you a New Orleans you won't see otherwise."

"That's what I'm afraid of."

But she allowed herself to be led down the hall. This

new approach by Steve intrigued her. She couldn't help it; she had to see what he was up to now. Maybe if they found some common ground, he'd come around to her way of thinking.

She ignored the little voice inside her that said, "Fat chance."

She tried to put distance between them in the elevator, but the hotel had a convention and people began squeezing in on each floor. She was pressed up to Steve's side, her body tingling scandalously, as conventioneers used the elevator to go to dinner. Most were women. Some were in deep discussion.

"They can't just have sex. They *have* to be in love first," one said.

"And then they have sex," another added. "But only if it works for the story. People tend to forget that."

Sara glanced at a woman's name tag, then swallowed. She and Steve were in an elevator filled with romance writers. They were clearly at some sort of writing conference.

Lord help her, she thought. Where were the divorce attorney conventions when one needed them? In Minneapolis, no doubt.

Steve caught her eye and grinned. Sara looked away. Fortunately, the women's discussion turned to plots and characters and publishing in general. Sara sighed in relief when the elevator doors opened on the lobby.

Steve put his hand to her back to guide her out, his fingers strong and warm at her waist. Sara wondered if the romance writers knew the sensations that were shooting through her at Steve's touch. They went way beyond pure sex.

"You stay in interesting places," he said.

"Yeah...well. Luck of the reservation," Sara replied. "Maybe we shouldn't go to dinner together."

"Why? Did those women get you thinking?" he asked.

"Who, me? No." Okay, so she'd brave it out.

To her surprise, Steve talked about everything but their relationship during dinner. He had her laughing over some of his cleaning stories. He sounded as if he genuinely enjoyed the job in some ways. The old Steve would have starved in the gutter before he'd have taken such employment.

But the old Steve obviously hadn't, when faced with reality.

"Steve, what did your parents say when you came down here?" she asked. His father had been very proud of his younger son's position in a big company.

"Not much." Steve grew quiet and poked at his Shrimp Remoulade with his fork. Finally, he added, "Let's just say my dad doesn't see the point. I think the downsizing left him more bewildered than it did me."

"I'm sorry. What about your sister? And your brother?" His older siblings had been as ambitious as Steve had been. Joan was an attorney for a Philadelphia law firm and Rich a surgeon.

Steve laughed dryly. "They think I've had a nervous breakdown."

"None of us were there for you, were we?"

"Doesn't matter now."

But it had mattered then, she thought, feeling guilty. If she had known...

What would she have done if she'd known what was coming for him? Would the marriage have been better or worse? It had been threadbare enough without the loss of his career to stress it further. She knew it wouldn't have survived.

"This seems an odd place for you to wind up," she said. "You're a Northerner, and you have no family or friends here. At least, I wasn't aware of any when we were married."

"We're still married."

"When we were *living* together," she corrected.

He grinned at her. "No, I didn't and don't have family or friends here. I came down for a job interview with a company here, decided to take an impromptu vacation and got stranded, frankly. It seemed as good a place as any to get a do-over."

She chuckled. "I'm not sure what you're doing over with a cleaning company."

"A helluva lot of rooms, believe me. Does your new guy know he's committing adultery?"

Sara gaped at the sudden turn of conversation.

"I assume you're sleeping with him," Steve said. He paused and raised his eyebrows. "Or aren't you?"

"I don't think that's your business," Sara snapped.

Steve burst into laughter. "I'm your husband. I don't know who else's business it would be when a wife's committing adultery. So does he know?"

"Oh, like you've been Mr. Faithful," she scoffed. She couldn't imagine that ever happening to randy Steve Johanson.

"Actually, I have been Mr. Faithful," he said, gazing at her. "I have no clue why…except I made a commitment I was intent on keeping."

Sara sucked in her breath. She had never thought…never *once* thought Steve would have been faithful to her. In fact, she'd tortured herself thousands of times with visions of him and another woman together. Knowing any reaction other than a light one would give away her confused state of emotions, she said, "Lordy, Steve, you went right over the line on commitment."

"Interesting that one of us did."

"I have nothing to apologize for." That was the truth. "So I won't. We make choices based on desires and need. You made yours. I made mine."

"Based on desire *and* need, no doubt."

He sounded so jealous under the sarcasm she had to hide a smile. It wouldn't hurt for him to think she hadn't pined.

"So does your guy know he's committing adultery? That must be an eye-opener for him."

"He knows the circumstances."

"Does he also know you're looking for a baby machine?"

"For someone who's not pushy, you sure are pushy."

"Some habits die hard," he told her. "You're one of them."

She wished he wouldn't stare at her that intently. His blue gaze always seemed to strip her to bare skin. She wished things had been different. But they hadn't. She had to keep that in mind.

"How's Max?" she asked, changing the subject altogether.

"He's fine."

"No aftereffects from his tumble?"

"He hates me, but I'll live with it."

Sara had run out of conversation.

"Finish your dinner, and if you're a good girl, I'll take you to a strip club," Steve promised.

"Oh, that's enough to make me eat my cauliflower." Sara made a face. "You can't be serious."

He shrugged. The man had become positively Gallic. "This is New Orleans. Let the good times roll and all that. Okay, so we'll just walk the streets like the rest of the masses.''

Sara grinned. "I definitely prefer streetwalking to stripping."

"You'd make a fine New Orleans *femme*." Steve laughed.

They did walk, neither saying much, just taking in the gaudy sights of the French Quarter. A cool breeze had come in off the river, and Sara was glad she wore a jacket for the evening. Steve didn't seem bothered by the change in the air. He had always been a furnace. On cold nights back in Philadelphia, Sara would gratefully snuggle against him. That had almost always led to lovemaking.

Sara pushed the thought away, then stepped away from Steve. She needed to put physical distance between them. A thousand miles would be best, she thought. His solution to her desire to have a baby was absurd. So why had she thought about it more than once?

A crowd of women surged around them, separated them even more. Sara saw Steve's head and shoulders above them. Once the people passed, a large expanse of sidewalk lay between them. Sara felt as if it epitomized their marriage. No matter what was good in it, the gulf would never be filled.

Steve casually walked back to her, making a mockery of her gulf. "Did you see that crowd? I think they were those romance writers from your hotel."

"Really? I didn't notice." She truly hadn't. Her thoughts had been occupied with him.

"Come on. I'll buy you a tacky T-shirt and a cheap mask from one of the souvenir shops. Every tourist needs one."

"But I'm not a tourist."

"Tonight you are."

He bought her the tackiest T-shirt with pushing-the-envelope risqué comments about crawfish on its front. But the feathered mask more than made up for it, cheap or not.

"It's gorgeous," Sara said, admiring the silkiness of the peacock feathers.

"Too bad Mardi Gras has passed," Steve said. "You could have worn it for the parades."

"This place must be a madhouse then," Sara said.

"No sane local comes into town during the celebrations."

"Which means you were here every night."

"Thank you for your vote of confidence. Not me. I'm dumb, but not foolish."

Sara just laughed.

Eventually, they made their way back to her hotel. The lobby was filling with the returning romance conventioneers. A number of women eyed Steve. Sara's jealousy did a slow burn. She knew the women's interest had nothing to do with their occupation. Steve had always attracted women. Little old ladies fell all over themselves to get his attention. He was just one of those people that everyone noticed.

"Thanks for the lovely evening," Sara said. She meant it. Other than a few bumps, the evening had gone well enough.

"You're welcome."

He kept walking with her to the elevators. Sara paused when they reached the doors. "I can find my way up."

"I know you can, but I'll feel better escorting you to your door."

"No, thanks," Sara said quickly.

"I insist. I am still your husband."

His tone was calm, soft, as if he'd suggested a bike

ride. She knew he wouldn't back down without a big fight. Even if he lost, he probably wouldn't. The growing group of women around them were quiet enough to hear any conversation. Sara couldn't make a fuss without causing embarrassment. Everyone would be embarrassed—except Steve.

"Fine," she said.

"Sullenness does not become Electra," Steve said, chiding her.

"You can't have your cake and eat it, too, Marie Antoinette." She smiled wryly. "I would be happy to smoosh it in your face, however."

The women around them chuckled.

Steve leaned over and whispered, "I think you inspire them."

"I hope so."

"You deserve a book," a woman said to her, and handed over a romance novel she took from her oversize purse. "If you like this, buy more. More of mine."

Everyone laughed.

"I'm better than the guy in the book," Steve said.

Sara grinned. "Don't bet on it."

The women laughed again, and the author signed her book for Sara, who clutched it like a lifeline.

The elevator they boarded rose slower than Mount Everest from the Indian Ocean. Even the other occupants couldn't distract Sara from the growing fear of losing the battle that was bound to take place when she and Steve reached her door. She didn't doubt Steve's interest in seeing her to her room had less to do with safety and more to do with getting her alone in her hotel bed. Now that was dangerous—extremely dangerous.

When they emerged from the elevator, Sara said, "You

can see my room from here and nobody's in the hall, so thanks—''

"I won't bite," Steve said, snorting in disgust. He took her elbow. "I only want to be a concerned husband, something I neglected before. What are you worried about? You've got this other guy. Other than one caught-up moment, you ought to have no interest in me sexually. Or do you?"

Sara stopped dragging her heels and kept pace. "Don't be ludicrous."

"You keep saying that." He grinned. "Why are you obsessed with that word?"

Everyone was a psychologist, Sara thought. She knew she ought to be flattered by his concern, but she just didn't trust him. "I'm not obsessed with *anything,* okay? I simply find this situation less than reasonable." They arrived at her door. "Thank you for the dinner, the souvenirs and the walk. I am now safe at my door, all you could ask for."

"I'll check inside, to be sure the room is secure."

"No, you won't," Sara said sternly.

"I'm not leaving until I do."

"The hotel is first class and very secure. The room is fine."

Steve folded his arms across his chest. "Sorry. I look or I stay."

"This is…" Oh, no. She wasn't going down the ludicrous road. "Fine. But I will check my room myself. You stand over there." She pointed to the other side of the hallway. "I'll leave the door open, and you can watch. I promise to scream for you if some guy grabs me, all right? And it better be all right or I'm screaming now for the hotel security. Don't test me on this."

He was silent for a full minute. "Agreed."

She smiled in relief. "Good."

Sara unlocked her door and marched into her room. She checked the bathroom and opened both sliding, mirrored doors of her closet. She looked in every corner. Steve watched her through the open door. Sara went to the bed. She swallowed back a sudden vision of her and Steve on it, writhing in passion…naked and writhing in passion….

"Get a grip," she muttered, steeling herself. She knelt down on her hands and knees and looked under the bed. Kate Moss couldn't have fit between the floor and the low, low, box spring mattress.

"All clear," she said in satisfaction, then heard a suspicious click behind her.

She realized the flaw in their arrangement as soon as she straightened. Steve stood on her side of the door. Her closed door.

"Steve, don't even think what you're thinking," she began. "I'll scream right now—"

"Tempting as that is, I'll sign the papers."

"What?" Sara gaped at him.

"That's what I came up here to tell you," he said. "I didn't think you'd want our business broadcast around the hotel, especially one filled with writers looking for inspiration."

Sara sat heavily on the edge of the bed. Her heart beat painfully, her stomach knotted sickeningly and her head throbbed. A lump of tears formed in her throat. She couldn't believe she had heard him right and, oddly, it hurt like hell to think she had.

"You'll sign?" she asked in a low voice.

"No million dollars," he said. "No material attachments of any kind. I'll sign the papers."

A knife stabbed her heart. Why had he changed his

mind? But what hope was there for a marriage that had been no marriage? That still had dead ends?

"Spend the night with me first," he said, not moving from the door.

"What?" Sara's ears rang loudly at this new twist.

"That's all I ask. Spend the night with me. Not to make babies. Let's make sure there's nothing left between us. Then I'll sign." His gaze never wavered from hers. "Think about it."

He opened the door and was gone.

SCARED TO DEATH, Steve rushed back to the hotel before eight the next morning. He was positive that at any moment Sara would check out and run. If she hadn't already.

Where the hell had his brain been when he'd made his condition for signing the divorce papers? In his pants, that's where. He had only thought that making love would rekindle his marriage, that as soon as they had been intimate, Sara would realize they could try their marriage again. She would know he would be capable of giving her everything she wanted. Home, hearth, kids. Well, kids and all the attention she needed or wanted. He would never neglect her in the future.

But all the reactions she might have to his demand had raced through his mind the entire night. Bolting like a scared rabbit had been his worst nightmare. He couldn't blame her if she had. He blamed himself—for being a total idiot.

"Is she still here?" he gasped out to the desk clerk.

"I beg your pardon?"

"Sara Johanson. She's a guest here. At least she was when I called an hour ago."

The clerk frowned.

"I'm her husband," he added. "We had a fight. Please, just check."

The clerk still frowned but checked the computer. "She's still registered. I can't give you her room number."

"Not a problem. I know it."

He raced through the lobby toward the bank of elevators. A woman sitting at the lobby garden restaurant caught his eye. He skidded to a halt.

Sara sat at a small table, sipping coffee and reading a newspaper. She wore jeans and a T-shirt, and she looked no more perturbed than a cat sunning itself on a windowsill. Certainly, she didn't look like she was going anywhere fast.

He walked over to her table. She flushed slightly when she saw him, then smiled. It didn't reach her eyes. Steve reevaluated "perturbed."

"Good morning," she said, her voice cheerful.

He sat down in the chair opposite her.

"Would you like some coffee?' she asked. "Call the waitress if you do."

He stared at her, not believing what he was seeing.

"I was just reading that there's been a big snowfall back home. Seven inches in April." She shook her head while flipping a page. "When was the last time that happened? I can't remember ever seeing a big storm this late in the season. The weather's crazy all over, isn't it?"

"Sara," he said, finally finding his voice and interrupting her report.

She looked up. "Yes?"

He said the only thing he could think to say. "You're still here."

"Yes." She went back to her newspaper. "There's a story, too, about that big, illegal, tire-dump fire near Route

95 in Philadelphia. Did you hear about that here? It weakened a half mile of the highway right above the Center City exit. What a mess—"

"Did you think about what I said?" he asked, and immediately wished he could retract the burning question. The answer would devastate more than a half mile of him.

"Yes," she replied, and sipped her coffee. She went back to her newspaper.

He waited. He couldn't stand it. "Well?"

The waitress stopped with Sara's breakfast—eggs, bacon, grits and toast. The woman set the plate down in front of Sara, who thanked her and actually smiled in clear appreciation of her morning meal.

"Would you like anything, sir?" the waitress asked.

"Coffee," he said, watching Sara set her napkin on her lap and pick up her fork. "And a beignet."

The waitress wrote it down and disappeared.

"I'm starved," Sara said, and tucked into her breakfast with relish. Steve stared at her, stunned by how unconcerned she was. She'd looked astonished last night. Shocked. Flummoxed. Vulnerable. He had wanted her vulnerable to him. God knows, he was *very* vulnerable to her.

"Oh. The white crocodiles here in New Orleans had babies," she exclaimed after swallowing a bite of food. "I read it earlier. They were up at the Philadelphia Zoo several years back. I should have gone to see them. Maybe I'll go while I'm here—"

"Sara!"

His voice carried over several tables. Heads turned their way.

"I'm only three feet from you," Sara said. "You don't have to bellow."

"I apologize." He should let it go. He shouldn't ask. "What are you playing at?"

Okay, so he'd asked the *second* most burning question in his head.

"I'm having breakfast," she said.

"You were upset when I left last night."

"I don't think so. Surprised, yet not surprised. You always bargained. I feel like I've been in negotiations ever since I arrived. Why should last night be different?"

"I think we should talk about it," he began.

"No need."

"No need?"

She shook her head.

He sucked in his breath. "Then you've made a decision."

"No."

"You're still thinking about it."

"No."

"You haven't made a decision and you're not thinking it over," Steve repeated, confused.

"Right."

"What the hell *are* you doing?" he demanded in a loud whisper, conscious of his last faux pas.

"Eating breakfast. And here's yours."

The waitress set his coffee and beignet down in front of him. Steve stared at the cup and plate, not seeing them at all.

When the woman left, Sara said, "Beignet, huh? I think I'll try one over at Brennan's this afternoon. They're supposed to be famous."

Steve wanted to shake her, to make her stop toying with him. She was doing a damn good job toying with him, and she had to know it.

"I was serious last night," he said. He had been and he wasn't going to deny it.

"So I figured." She started eating again.

He decided to push things, just to see what she would do. "You have to spend the night with me, if you want me to sign the divorce papers."

"So you told me."

"You don't believe I meant it, do you?"

Sara propped her elbows on the table and crossed her hands one over the other. The fork hung from her fingers. "Oh, I'm sure you meant it. Why would you say it if you didn't?"

Why would he? She'd asked one damn good question, because he didn't know what *he* meant at this point. He had rushed to the hotel to stop her from leaving because of his "condition" for a divorce. Now, facing her calmness, her lack of concern, every inch of him demanded that he stick to his guns for pride's sake. Certain parts of him had a baser reason for doing so, but they shouldn't count.

"So if you're not still thinking it over, what are you thinking?" he asked. He wouldn't get caught in a breakfast wrangle again.

"Nothing."

"You're not going to do anything?"

"Nope."

He glared at her. "You're not making a lick of sense."

She smiled. "Neither are you."

Stalemate, he thought.

She motioned for the waitress. "I've got to go—"

"Where?"

"I have a tour this morning."

"A tour?"

She nodded. "I'm going on a paddleboat cruise to some of the river plantations."

"Oh." He stared at her as she paid the waitress. "You're not thinking, you're not leaving and you're going on some sightseeing thing like a regular tourist?"

"I am on vacation." She patted him on the cheek as she walked by. "Have fun at work."

Work was not fun, however. When Steve was forced to fill in for one of his sick cleaners, he knew the day had capped itself for confusion and misery.

He was in complete limbo. Sara had done it on purpose, he decided, yanking the plug on the vacuum cord out of the wall socket in the last room he had to clean. His final client, Highway 10 Motel, was done.

So was he.

Sara had managed to tie him up in knots—by doing nothing! She had hooked him and reeled him in like a hungry catfish. She must be hell in negotiations, he admitted. As good as he had ever been.

Maybe he had suffered a little temporary insanity when Sara had walked back into his life. Maybe he thought everything would magically change back if she loved him again. Maybe that was why he'd made those ridiculous propositions about signing the divorce papers. Maybe he wanted her to admit she had no other man. Maybe he only wanted to see just how much she wanted a divorce.

Lots of maybes, he thought, but no answers.

Life was *not* magic, Maisie's practices notwithstanding. He needed to rethink his strategy. Big-time. Only how? What a mess he'd made of things.

Maisie was waiting for him when he pulled his battered truck up behind the house. She waved at him as he opened the door, calling out, "Good! You're home. Come inside quick."

Steve took the kitchen porch steps in one stride. "What? What's wrong?"

"I need a big favor from you," Maisie said, as they went into the kitchen. "My daughter has to have emergency surgery tonight. I need to be there, and I can't take my grandson."

Steve spied a portable sleeping basket on the table at the same moment he realized where his housekeeper was headed with her "favor." He didn't even wait for her to say it. "I can't take care of a baby!"

"But you want to make them fast enough," Maisie countered, then waved a hand. "I *have* to get to the hospital now. Michel," she continued, pronouncing it the French way, "is an angel. It's easy, Steve. You feed him when he's hungry. You change his diaper when it's wet or messy."

"Diaper!"

Maisie grinned. "You wore them, my friend. I put his bottles in the fridge and his diapers are in the bag there." She pointed to a quilted bag next to the basket. "You'll have no problems. I wouldn't ask if I didn't have to. You'll be fine. It's just for a few hours. Oh, Ruby's out again. Find that crab and keep him away from my grandson."

Steve gaped at her in horror. "Maisie, are you nuts?"

"Just don't drop Michel."

"Sweet Jesus!"

"The Lord will watch over you both, don't worry. I'll be back as soon as I can."

His housekeeper hurried out the back door before Steve could stop her.

He was alone with a baby.

Steve heard a rustle from the basket. It sounded like a gunshot to his panicked ears. All became quiet again. He inched closer to the table until he could see inside the basket. A baby slept. Black, curling hair framed its dark features. Steven's heart beat wildly in his chest, then calmed. If Michel slept the whole time, baby-sitting wouldn't be too bad, he thought. It wouldn't be too good, either.

A baby!

Steve cursed under his breath. What the hell was he supposed to do with a baby? Michel twitched in his sleep. Steve felt as if he'd been hit again by a shotgun blast when the little arms flung up in the air. Once more Michel settled into stillness. Steve watched for long, long minutes, waiting for disaster to strike.

Help, he pleaded silently to the universe.

He heard a car engine draw closer along his driveway.

"Thank you, thank you," he whispered, grateful that the universe had made Maisie come to her senses and return for the baby.

He rushed to the back door to let her in, but heard the car instead stop at the front of the house. Steve frowned. Maisie usually came around to the back.

He tiptoed past the baby before running for the front door. Max, on his living room perch, squawked, startled by Steve's energy as he flung open the door.

Sara stood on the other side, poised to knock. She looked gorgeous in a russet-colored tank top and wrap-around skirt.

"I'll spend the night with you," she said.

A wail of outrage shattered the house.

So much for help.

Chapter Six

Sara staggered back at what sounded exactly like a baby crying in Steve's house. Of all the things she'd expected to encounter, a baby wasn't one of them.

Steve gazed at her, cursed, then ran toward the back rooms.

"A horny man rises to the occasion," Max intoned from his perch.

"Sara!" Steve shouted as the crying began in earnest.

Sara hurried inside, pushing the door shut behind her.

"Don't go there," Max shouted.

Sara did anyway. In the kitchen, she found Steve. The panic in his eyes was obvious.

"Michel's crying," he said, giving the name a French pronunciation. "I thought Ruby bit him, but he didn't."

"You put a hermit crab in with a baby?" Sara exclaimed, horrified.

"No! What are you, nuts? Ruby's loose in the house again, and I thought he got in the basket somehow." Michel's cries hit a crescendo Pavarotti would have admired. Steve pointed to the basket. "Do something!"

"But I don't know what to do!" Sara's own blood pressure rose from the infant's stress. "Where's his mother?"

"In surgery. It's Maisie's daughter. Maisie left Michel with me."

Sara's jaw dropped. "What is she, nuts?"

"My words exactly. Dammit, he was supposed to sleep the entire time."

"Somebody should have told him that."

"No kidding. You're the one who wants babies. Do something."

Fear shot through Sara. Wanting one and being faced with an unhappy, screaming infant were two entirely different things. Clearly, Steve was useless. Steeling herself, she gingerly reached into the basket and lifted the baby. Something told her to hold it to her body. She cradled little Michel to her. He immediately rooted at her breast and clamped onto her nipple through her clothes. Sara yelped. Michel spit out material and cried, too.

"Those don't work, son," Steve said, chuckling.

"Thank you very much," Sara replied in withering tones while she shifted the baby to her shoulder. The little boy squirmed and cried. To think she had come here in a cold, calculating move to get the divorce papers signed. After her success at breakfast with Steve, she had told herself it was all in the attitude. She could withstand one night of unspontaneous sex that would prove she had no more feelings for Steve. He had had a point—an ugly point, but an apt one.

But never had she thought she'd have to deal with this!

"I bet he's hungry," Steve said. He went to the refrigerator and got out a bottle. "Here."

"It's cold." Sara made a face. "You have to warm it first."

"But the kid'll scream down the house in the meantime."

"So I'll be deaf in one ear. Get a pan of water going on the stove and put the bottle in it."

As he did, Sara awkwardly crooned to Michel and patted his little bottom. "He's wet, too."

"I guess we should change him." Steve eyed the baby. "You do that and I'll look for Ruby."

"Wait a minute," Sara said. "Why should I change him? You're the baby-sitter."

"Hey, I'm cooking his dinner and looking for a loose hermit crab. Or would you rather find Ruby?"

"I think I have the better end of the deal," Sara muttered. "But not by much."

Steve left the room faster than Superman beat a speeding bullet.

"Lucky for you I'm not three men," Sara told the baby.

With one hand, she laid a bunch of newspaper sections on the kitchen table. She laid Michel on them. Michel screamed sorrowfully while Sara held him with one hand and tried to open the quilted diaper bag with her other. The little lambs and kitties on the bag didn't fool her. The thing was a menace to open. She grappled with the zipper, then got a diaper out.

"You can do this," she told herself.

Michel yelled in disagreement. Max squawked in the background, responding to the baby crying.

She discovered the baby was more than wet when she got his soiled diaper open. Her stomach flipped at the stench.

"Found him," Steve announced, coming into the kitchen at that moment. His triumphant expression changed. "Puh! What is that smell?"

"*Eau de Michel,*" Sara replied. This was no worse than a litter box on cleaning day, she thought. Only it was.

"He's on my kitchen table," Steve protested.

"I put papers down," she said, ineptly cleaning Michel's tiny bottom with wipes she found in the diaper bag.

"That's a baby, not a dog."

"Fine, I'll take the papers out."

"Oh no, you won't. How can a little baby do all that?" Steve asked, looking at the old diaper.

"Amazing, isn't it?" Sara said.

Michel, in his gratitude, squirted her.

Sara gasped in dismay as the front of her top displayed a lovely trail of wet spots. Belatedly, she stepped out of the line of fire.

"Kid's got good aim," Steve commented, chuckling.

Sara stopped her ministrations, holding the baby's legs in the air before sliding the fresh diaper under him. "One more word out of you and I walk out that door."

"I'm Silent Cal," Steve promised.

"You better be."

Something hissed on the stove.

Steve cursed and lifted the pot off. "The milk boiled out of the top of the bottle,"

"Then get another bottle out and start again," Sara told him, taping up the diaper at the baby's waist. When he was properly covered, she raised her hands like a cowboy after roping a calf. "Victory!"

Michel still cried.

Sara picked up the baby and rocked him on her shoulder.

She looked at the dirty diaper. With one hand, she wrapped the newspapers around it. When she let go, the sections slowly reopened like a rotten rose in bloom.

Steve looked at the wad. "I'm not touching it."

"What a baby you are," she said. Taking a deep breath,

she picked up the rolled newspapers and their inner secret and dropped everything in his trash bin.

"I'm not touching that, either."

"Just watch the pot this time, Steve."

"Okay. But when will I know when it's done?"

"I don't know. We only want the bottle warm."

"But what's warm enough for a baby?"

Sara paused. She truly didn't know. "I guess when it feels warm to us. People test it on their wrist. Surely, you've seen it on TV."

"Yeah, but is warm to us warm to him? Or is it too hot?" he asked.

"This is amateur night, isn't it?" Sara admitted, pushing away her rising uneasiness. "We can't panic. The baby needs us."

Steve watched his new pot. "I bet babies sense panic like animals do and attack."

"Don't say that."

"Okay, I won't."

Michel seemed calm at the moment, surprising her. Maybe he was happier with a dry, clean bottom. Lord knows she would be, Sara thought.

Curious, she asked, "Where was Ruby this time?"

"In one of the new shells," Steve replied.

"I thought it was Pansy who liked to change shells," Sara said, remembering her introduction to the hermit crabs.

"She does. Ruby does it strictly for the escape value."

"Don't you think you ought to put him in a more secure cage?"

"I'm planning to get around to it eventually."

Sara looked heavenward. "Today would be a good time. We've got a baby in the house."

Steve grinned. "I like the sound of that...especially from you."

Sara pressed her lips together. She hadn't had a Freudian slip and she wasn't about to have another. "Just get that crab in a cage that works."

"But the formula—"

"I'll take care of it."

Steve frowned, but went on his new assignment.

"Men," Sara sniffed, looking at the water simmering in the pot and trying to gauge if the warming bottle was ready. She took it out and awkwardly splashed a little formula on her wrist. It felt lukewarm. It stood to reason that mother's milk had to be at room temperature. Well, close enough. Michel screamed in her ear, as if sensing food at the ready. "That's good enough for me."

Sara repositioned Michel without dropping him, although she dipped him dangerously at one point. Michel latched eagerly onto the bottle's nipple when she got it close to his mouth. His eyes closed as he sucked down his meal.

"I guess it's warm enough," Steve said, when he came into the kitchen and saw her feeding the baby. He held Ruby in one hand. The crab hung half out of its pretty pink, spiral shell, its antennae moving continuously.

"Steve, what if Ruby falls out?" Sara said, stepping away from the crab.

"Nah. These guys only come out if they want to. They have two legs that secure the back half of themselves in. Ruby's just trying to figure out where he is."

As if to make a liar out of Steve, Ruby leaned even farther out of the shell, but didn't fall out. Steve tipped the shell back slightly, to keep disaster from happening.

"Where are you going to put him?" Sara asked.

"I'm not sure," Steve admitted. "I have a metal pail on the back porch. I think I'll put him in that."

"Can he climb out?"

"I doubt it. The sides are steep and I'll put a lid on top, just in case."

Steve took care of his escape artist. Sara, her arms aching, sat down at the table. She did it slowly, so as to not startle the baby. Michel watched her over the top of the baby bottle, his little mouth still working hard for his dinner.

"Even though I'm not Mom, this isn't so bad," Sara said to Michel.

Michel just stared, his eyes a beautiful brandy color.

"The women are going to fall all over you," Sara cooed, smiling at the baby.

Michel let go of the bottle and wailed indignantly.

Sara silently cursed and shoved the bottle back in Michel's mouth. The baby fussed for a moment, then accepted it again.

"I stand corrected. It won't be the girls falling all over you," Sara said, and braced herself for another mind-numbing scream.

Michel ate.

"I'm not going down that road," Sara told him, relaxing. "Don't worry, Grandma will be back soon."

"Boy, I hope so," Steve said, carrying a pail that made frantic scrabbling noises. "Ruby is one unhappy camper."

"A couple hours won't kill him. Maybe he'll learn to stay put."

Steve only laughed.

Michel let go of the bottle's nipple. He didn't cry or fuss, however.

Sara frowned. "He can't be done. He just started."

"The bottle's hardly touched," Steve said, as she held it up. "He only drank a quarter of it."

"I better give him some more." Sara tried to guide the nipple back into Michel's mouth. The baby turned away once or twice before finally accepting it.

"I guess he just needed a little break," Steve said. He set the pail down.

"Not here," Sara told him.

"Ruby can't stay outside tonight. The weather's supposed to change and the temperature will drop. Crabs need heat, not cold."

"He can't be where the baby is, either, in case he gets loose again. Put him in the dining room for now."

"You're getting downright bossy in your old age," he commented, then moved Ruby to the other room.

"Old age," Sara muttered darkly. "Look who's talking. Mr. Sixteen. Michel, I'd tell you not to be a man when you grow up, but there's no hope. Just don't be a dumb one, okay?"

The baby grinned around the bottle. Sara's heart warmed, happy to see the baby responding to her.

Steve came in and watched her feed Michel. A deeper warmth settled inside her, one that pleasured and disturbed. She found it far too easy to imagine more scenes like this with Steven. She forced away the notion. The poor baby would suffer if she weren't here to help. That was all this was, not real life.

She managed to get more than half the bottle's contents into Michel, even though he rejected the nipple more and more frequently. At last she held the bottle up. "Shouldn't he be finishing it?"

"I would think so," Steve said. "But he obviously doesn't want it."

"I don't think I could force any more in," Sara said. She looked at Steve, stricken. "Do you think he's sick?"

Steve looked at Michel. "I don't think so. He's not crying or anything. Maybe he's got to burp. Then he might have more room."

"Maybe." The idea seemed sound to Sara. A baby had to be burped after a meal. Steve made a good point, too, about the baby not being upset anymore. She shifted Michel to her shoulder and patted his back. "How about this, Steve. We got a baby diapered and fed. Semifed."

"And rescued from a hermit crab," he added. "Don't forget my contribution."

She laughed, noting the parrot was quiet. "And even Max has calmed down."

"Not bad for a couple of amateurs."

"We could be pros before we know it."

The innocent words hung in the air. Sara admitted she liked the sound of them. She liked the quiet and the feel of the baby's body against hers. Michel smelled so sweet with that wonderful baby smell, and he was so helpless as he snuggled on her shoulder. Her breast pressed into his little tummy in a satisfying maternal manner. She liked looking at Steve while holding a baby. She liked the idea that they were "pros" together.

"This is nice," Steve said.

Sara smiled. "Yes, it is."

Michel burped.

She and Steve laughed together.

Sara stopped laughing when she felt something hot and wet on her shoulder. She lifted the baby away at the same second he brought up his dinner. It landed all over her silk top.

"Oh, no!" Sara wailed.

"Yuck!" Steve gasped, while holding his nose from the sour-milk odor suddenly pervading the kitchen.

Michel gave his opinion in another blast of half-digested formula. He had the nerve to smile right afterward.

"Steve! Help me!" Sara cried out, not knowing what to do. She tried not to breathe, but couldn't help herself.

"I think amateur night is back," Steve said.

"Steve!"

"Okay, okay. I hate to say this, but you probably ought to hold him until he's done being sick."

"Thanks a lot!"

"It's only logical," he said in his defense. Unfortunately, his defense had common sense to it, much as she hated to admit it.

"Once he's done, I'll take him and you can go clean up," Steve continued. "Use the shower if you want. Take any of my clothes you need. Maisie'll clean yours. She had the nerve to tell me he was an angel."

"The guardian angel of puke is more like it," Sara said.

Michel obliged on cue.

Wonderful, she thought as a new wave of baby horror hit her square in the chest.

Calculated seduction and babies just didn't mix.

This was *not* the future as she'd imagined it.

STEVE WAITED until Michel had actually fallen asleep before he set the baby back in his portable basket. They'd had to change Michel's clothes, too. The diaper bag now had only one fresh shirt and pair of socks left.

The continual beating of water against a wall in the bathroom told Steve that Sara was hell-bent on taking the longest shower in the history of affronted womanhood. Boy, had Michel affronted her.

"And to think she wants one of you guys," Steve whispered to the baby.

Probably not now, he admitted in amusement. Hell, he didn't even want to *make* a Michel. That was saying a lot, too.

Michel slept peacefully. Innocently. His Cupid's-bow mouth made sucking motions and the miniature fingers curved toward the small palm. Steve gently reached out and touched them, amazed at their perfection. The fingers wrapped around his own forefinger, the grip trusting.

Steve's heart shredded into a thousand pieces and rebuilt itself again. But everything was different. More tender. More vulnerable. More needing.

"Damn," he muttered, silently vowing to do everything to protect Michel for however long his guardianship lasted. He would not fail this baby.

His arm began to cramp, but Steve left his finger in Michel's grasp, not wanting to disturb the infant.

Steve heard the shower go off and eventually Sara padded back into the kitchen. She wore an old Eagles T-shirt of his and a pair of his jeans rolled up at the ankles. Her hair was combed back from her face and forehead and still damp from the shower. She looked as innocent as Michel and as sexy as he had ever seen her. Nothing was more arousing than a woman in a man's T-shirt—especially Sara in his.

Steve wanted nothing more than to make love to her until she had ten Michels. A hundred.

"Stinker," she said in a low voice, making a face at the baby. "You throw up all over me and go to sleep for him."

"Some of us have the touch," Steve said.

"I hope your arm falls off." But she smiled ruefully at him. "I guess since he's sleeping he must be okay."

"He's sure acting like it," Steve agreed.

"Is he hot? Does he seem sick to you?"

"No."

"I wonder what made him ill before."

Steve shrugged. "He's a baby. He probably doesn't need a reason."

Sara shook her head. "I'm sure he's got a reason, but that seems gone now, for which I'm grateful. By the way, I washed my clothes and Michel's out in the sink and hung them over the shower rod. Is that okay?"

"Sure. My dryer's on the fritz but you can hang them out back on the line if you want."

She nodded, then asked, "Have we heard from Maisie yet?"

"No."

"I hope her daughter's okay."

"Me, too." Steve nodded toward the sleeping baby. "Especially for this little guy."

They stood silently together and looked at the baby. The only sounds in the house were the scrabbling of Ruby's claws against the metal pail and the occasional flutter of Max preening his feathers.

The baby's grip finally eased, and Steve retrieved his finger. He rolled his shoulder to get some blood back into it. "Now I know what Maisie's talking about when she said he was an angel. He's one now that he's sleeping."

"Kissed by God," Sara said, smiling at Michel. "We've done it. We've calmed a baby, fed and diapered him and put him to sleep."

Steve's pride swelled at the accomplishment. The achievement outranked closing a million-dollar deal. Those had become all too commonplace in his former life, while this was unexpected and unlikely. To do it with Sara made baby-sitting all the sweeter.

A noise erupted from the basket—a rude sound like someone squeezing air out of a balloon. Or someone sitting on a whoopee cushion. Worse, the sound was a little too ripe for just gas.

"Your turn to change," Sara announced.

"Oh, no. Not me!" Steve protested.

"Oh, yes. Definitely you. I had my turn on diaper duty already. Now it's yours."

"I can't," he said, being honest with her. "*I'll* be sick if I do."

"Your turn to clean that up, too."

"When did we designate turns for diaper duty? I don't remember voting for that."

"I took a count while I was in the shower. One to nothing, so I made an executive decision." She reached out and touched his shoulder. "Tag. You're it. That should cover all the bases."

"Remind me never to let you shower alone again." Steve grinned when she flushed. More noise rose from the basket. Steve stared at Michel with the growing realization that he had to do the dirty work this time. "How can a baby sleep through all that?"

"I don't know." Sara shuddered.

Steve frowned at her. "Do you think we should wake him up and change him?"

"I think *you* should let him sleep and *you* should change him after he wakes up," Sara replied.

"It...the stuff won't hurt him?"

"Oh." Sara's eyebrows shot up in surprise. "I didn't think of that. I don't know. I guess you better wake him and change him, Steve. Just to be safe. I'll get newspapers."

"I feel like I've got a puppy instead of a baby," Steve

muttered, after directing Sara to where he kept his own dailies for recycling.

He put his hand under Michel's arm to lift him, but the baby's head bent slowly back. Michel opened his eyes wide. Steven got one hand under the baby's head, but he wailed anyway.

"Hurry up!" Steve shouted to Sara.

"Stop shouting!" she shouted back. "You'll scare the baby."

"Like you won't. Honey, we scared the you-know-what out of him the moment Maisie walked out my door."

Sara got the sections down on the table again. Steve laid the baby on it. Michel only cried louder.

Max squawked loudly from the other room, adding to the noise level.

"Don't ever use this table again," Sara said, giving Steve a fresh diaper. "No amount of disinfectant will cure it."

"My thoughts exactly."

The telephone rang. Sara deserted him, saying, "I'll get it."

She answered the telephone while Steve wrestled open the baby's clothes.

"It's Maisie," Sara said.

"Thank God." He opened the old diaper and closed his eyes. "Oh, God."

Steve felt a buzzing in his ears until he could barely hear the baby crying and Sara talking on the telephone. The room went dark for an awful second. He realized he was about to pass out.

Get a grip, he told himself, getting a grip. The world righted itself. He opened his eyes. He was still faced with Michel's "gift." The kid hardly looked kissed by God at the moment. Steve took a deep breath to steel himself for the job ahead.

It was a mistake.

"How could something so little be so smelly?" he gasped, holding his nose.

"Maisie says she has to stay overnight," Sara said, holding her hand over the receiver's mouthpiece. "Her daughter has complications and she'll be in surgery longer than they expected."

Michel screamed. Steve knew how the child felt.

"Tell her that's fine—whatever she needs," he muttered, while dealing with an outraged baby in desperate need of a diaper change.

"We woke him up to change his diaper," Sara said into the phone, after telling Maisie not to worry. "Oh. Okay, but won't it make him sick or something?"

"What are you doing to me, kid?" Steve asked, realizing Michel needed a clothing change as well as a diaper one. How the hell *did* a little thing like him do so much? Maybe he was ill.

"Ask her if he's ill," Steve said to Sara. "He got sick and he's filled a diaper. Twice."

Sara asked, but Steve was too engrossed in changing Michel's diapers to discern the answer from her response. He finally got a fresh diaper on the kid. Feeling the way Sara had, he proclaimed, "Victory!" and lifted Michel up on his shoulder the way he'd seen Sara hold him. Michel fussed for another minute, then settled down.

"Not bad," he crooned to the baby. He patted Michel gently on his backside. Nothing like a fresh, clean bottom to make a person feel better, Steve thought.

Sara got off the phone. As she cleaned up the table—at arm's length—she said, "Maisie doubts Michel's sick.

He's still on fluids so he's suppose to be…loose. He's a good little pooper. Her words. Literally.''

"I can attest to that. So he's okay on that end."

"Evidently." Sara grinned wryly. "I asked about him not drinking the entire bottle. Maisie says that's okay, too. She says babies tell you what they want. She says we probably fed him too much the first time, which is why he was sick. His stomach was getting rid of the extra. She says that's also why he went again. It's got to come out somehow. Her words."

"The woman has pearls of wisdom. Okay, so we haven't done him irreparable harm." Steve smiled at Michel, then at Sara.

"Nope. We're okay. Oh, Maisie says we shouldn't wake him to change his diaper. He'll wake up fast enough if it's irritating him. She says it normally doesn't."

"Another pearl of wisdom too late. Sorry about that, Michel." To Sara, Steve said, "What about her daughter? Is she going to be okay?"

"Maisie thinks so, but she needs to stay. I don't blame her."

"Me, neither. Well, we'll cope. The kid ought to just sleep now."

"Let's hope. Maisie says you're making good mojo tonight. Whatever the heck that means."

That he was getting a good rating of any kind from Maisie pleased him. "She owes me for this."

"I doubt you'll collect." Sara cocked her head. In a low voice, she said, "I think he's asleep."

"Really?" Steve tried to look at the baby's eyes, but couldn't see his face. The infant wasn't fussing, his body quiet against Steve's.

"I think he likes you," Sara said. "More than me. At least he hasn't been sick on you."

"Give him time." Steve put his hand to the baby's neck and began to shift him to the basket.

Michel opened his eyes and cried.

"Okay, okay," Steve soothed, returning Michel to his shoulder.

Michel stopped fussing and laid his head down again.

"I'll wait until he's really asleep," Steve said.

"It works for me," Sara agreed.

"Will you stay with me until Maisie gets here?" he asked.

She smiled. "Sure. I said I would."

"Thanks. But this doesn't count for spending the night," he said.

She chuckled.

Steve relaxed. "We'll talk about that later."

They waited until Michel was sound asleep. Steve waited ten minutes more. He tried once again to put Michel down in the basket. Michel woke up and fussed. Steve replaced the baby on his shoulder.

"I'll wait a little more." Steve wondered how long "a little more" would be. His back was starting to hurt from standing in place. The baby wasn't heavy, but Steve's arms protested maintaining the same position. Yet he liked holding little Michel. He liked the way the baby felt in his embrace, but this was becoming too much of a good thing.

"I think we have another problem," Sara said. "Michel's not liking the basket."

"But I can't hold a baby all night," Steve protested.

"I think you're going to have to, or we'll have one angry baby on our hands. He likes you."

"A little too much." Dismayed, Steve stared at Sara.

Sara laughed. "Remember what Maisie said about him letting us know when he's unhappy."

"Want to bet that will never happen?"

"Not on your life. I think he's attached until he's seventeen."

"You're enjoying this, aren't you?"

She nodded, her expression amused. "I can't lie. I am. But you look kind of cute with a baby."

"I do?" Maybe it would be worth holding Michel all night if it gave Sara tender feelings about her husband.

"Why don't you try sitting in the living room while holding him?" Sara suggested, picking up Michel's portable basket. "If he lets you sit down, then you might as well be comfortable. Maybe he'll sleep more soundly if you're comfortable, and then we can move him to the basket."

"Good thinking."

Steve took a couple of tiptoe steps to see if movement disturbed Michel. When it didn't, Steve followed Sara into the living room. Ruby scraped around his makeshift prison when they passed, no doubt hopeful of an early release.

Steve sat on the edge of his beat-up easy chair. Michel started, woke, then settled back into sleep again. Sara giggled. Steve made a face at her. Feeling braver, he sat back. Michel woke again, fussed a little, then went back to sleep. The chair cradled Steve and he sighed in relief. Michel sighed, too.

"Oh, brother," Sara said in disgust, taking the couch.

"The babes are back!" Max called out.

Michel whimpered, but didn't move otherwise.

"Maybe this isn't such a good idea," Steve said, eyeing the bird.

Sara shrugged. "The baby didn't wake up—"

"He almost did."

"But he didn't. Let's see what happens. If Max acts up, we can always move."

To Steve's consternation, Max began eyeing him back. The bird tilted his head one way, then the other.

"I think he's going to attack the baby," Steve said, worried about the meaning of the bird's antics.

"Max will be a good boy," Sara said. "Won't you, Max?"

"Parrot for dinner...*brack!*" Max squawked.

"See? He understands the dynamics involved."

"I just hope you understand my parrot better than I do."

"Me, too."

Max stayed put on his perch, parrot dinner obviously not on his menu. The room quieted. The baby slept soundly on Steve's shoulder. Steve felt more relaxed in the chair, his arms now supported as he held Michel.

"I can feel his heart beating," he whispered to Sara.

Her eyes widened. "Wow."

"No wonder you want this. It makes you forgive the mess. Almost."

She smiled at him, her gaze shining with emotion.

"Did you really come to spend the night?" he asked. "To sleep with me one last time?"

Her expression went blank, and she looked away. Finally, she looked back at him. "Yes. I thought about it while I was on that plantation tour. Your reasoning had merit, although you're pretty mercenary about it."

"Me? Who's here to sell her body for a signature?"

"Who wants to buy a body for a signature?"

Steve acknowledged her own reasoning had merit this time. "Stalemate. You must want this guy of yours pretty bad to be with me for a night."

Sara stared at him for the longest time, then sighed.

"There is no man in my life. It was only something stupid I said in a stupid moment, stupidly thinking you would sign the papers then."

Steve's heart leaped and beat as fast as the baby's. "Maisie was right. She said you didn't have a man."

"Maisie?" Sara exclaimed.

Steve shushed her to keep her from waking the baby.

"How could you do that?" she said, her voice only slightly lower in volume.

"Me?" Steve's shock woke Michel, who whimpered. Steve patted his back, while saying in a lower voice, "Me? What did I do?"

"How could you tell Maisie?"

The big trick was how could he tell her how he'd told Maisie without looking defeated and vulnerable? He'd hated those two emotions. "Never mind that. We need to talk about why you came tonight."

"That doesn't matter," Sara said. "It's a moot point anyway with Michel here."

"Once he settles and is in his basket, we can begin 'spending the night.'" Steve intended to spend it with all the skill he was capable—and then some. To hell with signing. By the time he was done, she'd be begging to stay. So much for feeling defeated and vulnerable.

Michel suddenly burped—and christened Steve down the front of his shirt.

"Hey! Hey!" Steve yelped, holding Michel away from the mess.

"Oh, no! Not again!" Sara exclaimed, running over to take the baby.

Before she did, Michel threw up one last time. And grinned.

Chapter Seven

Sara woke with a crick in her neck, an ache in her back and a charley horse toying with her thigh. Even as she realized she was in pain, she realized it was morning.

She had spent the night with Steve.

"The baby!" she gasped, leaping off the couch. She hollered in pain when her leg gave under her weight.

Max squawked, startled out of parrot slumber.

"What? What?" Steve said, shooting upright in the easy chair. Michel, on his shoulder, shot upright with him.

The baby jerked, then cried.

"Thank God, he's okay," Sara said, relieved to see he had snoozed safe and sound on his favorite spot, Steve, all night.

"Dammit, Sara." Steve glared at her, his eyes red rimmed after the long night. "He's only been asleep for three hours."

"I'm sorry." She rubbed her leg and rolled her shoulders to ease her body's complaints. "Here, let me take him for a while."

She lifted the baby and settled him on her shoulder. After a disoriented cry, Michel calmed down and looked around.

"Waa! Waa!" Max wailed in a perfect imitation of Michel.

"That was quick," Sara commented.

"Not really," Steve countered, rubbing his face. "He's had hours of lessons from the master there. Many *long* hours of lessons."

Sara smiled in amusement. What a night! Steve now wore a new set of clothes, thanks to Michel's efforts. The old ones hung on the outside line with hers and Michel's. She'd made the transfer when it became obvious the shower rod would collapse under the weight of wet clothes. Michel was in a cut-down Harley-Davidson shirt of Steve's.

Steve looked exhausted and very human. Her mother was right, Sara thought. Steve had toppled off his pedestal. Yet she found him more appealing, more warm and caring than she did during their marriage. Now he was just a man. A man who needed the other half of himself. The old Steve had needed nothing and no one. This Steve had needed her desperately last night—to help with a baby, of all things.

Sara knew deep down in her bones what women had known for centuries. The mutual give and take of family life was an emotional as well as a physical necessity between the sexes. Never had she felt more equal to Steve than she did now.

Michel rooted around at her shoulder. "I think he's hungry, and he needs changing, too. I'll do it."

"It's your turn anyway. I changed him at three this morning." Steve leaned back in the chair. Then sat up again. "Maybe we shouldn't feed him. He turns into the puking machine when we do."

"He's not hot, and his color's good," Sara said. "I

don't think he's sick. We really overfed him last night, and that was the problem. I'll be careful this time.''

"How did you become such an expert?"

"I haven't. I'm just using logic."

She left Steve to think about that and took the baby into the kitchen. She got him changed while she warmed a bottle. Both tasks were accomplished without a hitch.

"Look at the time," she said to Michel. "It's eight-thirty. The dummy adults really-wore you out, didn't we?"

Michel tried to put his fist in his mouth.

"Breakfast is coming right up," she agreed, then added, "I hope that's not prophetic."

"Me, too," Steve said from the kitchen doorway. "I need coffee."

"Why don't you sleep for a while? I feel fresh," she lied.

He rubbed his unshaven jaw. "I'm too tired to sleep. You do his breakfast and I'll do ours."

"Deal." She checked the warmed bottle for temperature. Satisfied it was okay for drinking, she cradled Michel and held the nipple toward him. Before she gave it to the baby, she said, "Now remember, you have to tell *me* when you've had enough."

Michel clamped eagerly onto the nipple.

"Polly wants a friggin' cracker!" Max shouted from the living room.

"You better feed him, too," Sara told Steve.

"Lord knows what he'll do if I don't." Steve got a box of sunflower seeds from the pantry. As he passed Michel, he touched the baby's cheek and said, "I'm almost out of clothes, pal, so if you nail Auntie Sara... Aw, go for it, kid."

Sara firmed her lips, annoyed with the innuendo. Steve

kissed her on the mouth before she realized what he intended. He walked out of the room, whistling.

"He always was too damn cheery in the morning," she said out loud.

A short time later, she heard a car on the driveway just as Steve strode into the kitchen. "It's Maisie! She's coming around the back."

"Thank God! We're rescued." To Michel, she said, "Grandma's here. Life is back to normal."

Michel grinned around the bottle.

"He's cute when he does that," Steve admitted.

"He knows it, too." Michel's "Uncle Steve" was the same way, Sara thought.

Steve held open the back door for Maisie, who looked as tired as they did. But the older woman smiled.

"When I saw all the clothes on the line back there, I thought I had me a bunch of naked people in here," she said, taking off her sweater.

"Michel didn't like his dinner. Again," Steve said.

"When you give him too much of it, he won't." Maisie came over to the baby and smoothed back his hair as he fed. "He's not feverish. You're making up for lost time now, aren't you, *mon petit?*"

"Do you think it's too much?" Sara asked worriedly at the disappearing contents of the bottle.

"He'll let you know." Maisie laughed. "Ya'll are afraid of that."

"You bet," Steve replied. "You sure he's not sick?"

Maisie shook her head. "You'll know when babies are sick, too. They're fussy and yet listless. They have no interest in anything, least of all food. This boy's eating up a storm. You two fed him at the wrong time and fed him too much, besides. He let you know that."

"All over our clothes," Steve said ruefully. "How's your daughter?"

"Better, but still not out of trouble," Maisie answered, looking somber. "They think she might have a tear in her liver now, so she may have more surgery today. We'll know after some tests. Being a mama never stops, not even after your kids grow up and have their own children. I don't think I worried this much when she was three and had a bout of pneumonia."

Sara stared down at Michel. He was a lifetime commitment. She'd known that, of course, about children, but Maisie's words opened up a realm she hadn't considered. It didn't scare her off having her own, however. But it made her think of all that would be involved.

"What's this on him?" Maisie asked. She started laughing. "Did you initiate my grandson in a motorcycle gang last night?"

"We ran out of clothes for him, too." Steve said.

"And nearly for us," Sara added.

"Well, it's a good thing I figured you'd need more," Maisie said. "Steve, go get the packages out of my car."

Steve glanced at Sara. "Okay."

After Steve went outside, Maisie surveyed Sara critically. "How are you holding up here?"

"All right, I think." Sara grinned. "We called it amateur night. I doubt the Three Stooges could have done worse."

"You look good with that baby."

"You think so?"

Michel picked that moment to let go of the bottle. Sara set it down on the table and lifted the baby to her shoulder.

"Here's the trick," she said to Maisie, while gently

patting Michel on the back. "He usually leaves me a present at this point."

Michel burped a simple, little, very dry burp.

Sara laughed.

"You need to put a cloth down on your shoulder," Maisie said, rummaging in the diaper bag. "Keeps your clothes clean 'cause babies spit up all the time."

"Now you tell us," Steve said, coming in the back door. His arms were filled with packages. The screen door closed behind him with a bang.

Sara had an ominous feeling their baby-sitting chores were not at an end.

"You learn by doing," Maisie told Steve. She sat down in a chair and sighed heavily. "I hate to ask you to keep Michel for a while but I must. Chloe is touch and go. I need to be with her. I should be with her right now, but someone has to take care of settling Michel, too, while she can't. Chloe's all I got since her brother, Big Michel, passed away. I have no spell for this. Just love and worry."

Sara heard the heartbreak in Maisie's voice. Another darker, tragic aspect of parenting surfaced in her mind.

"Don't worry about the baby," Steve said.

"We'll care for him as long as you need us to," Sara added.

"Thank you." Maisie reached across the table and took Sara's hand, her grip tight and shaky but filled with gratitude. She then grasped Steve's.

"I know I ask too much, but I don't know where to turn," the woman said, her voice breaking.

"You turn to friends," Steve replied, hugging his housekeeper.

Sara gazed at the husband she was desperate to be rid of. He'd never given a thought to work or to himself in this crisis, but was going all-out to help Maisie. She couldn't see the Steve she'd known even considering such a thing. At best, he would have hired someone to take care of a baby entrusted to him. And then he would have put it from his mind.

Help me, Sara thought, *but maybe this is a man not to lose.*

Maisie cried a little, then took control of her emotions. She issued orders like a general as she laid out baby clothes, blankets, diapers and other sundries. She set two large cans of formula powder on the counter.

"There's enough here for a week!" Sara blurted out without thinking. "That's okay. Not to worry. We can handle it."

Maisie glanced at her in amusement. "Scared ya, didn't I? The good Lord willing, I don't expect to be a week. But I wanted to be sure you two had enough to last in case Chloe has more problems and I can't get away. I don't expect that to happen, now. Steve, there's a playpen in my trunk. I figure you need that, too. The basket's only good for a little while as a crib."

Steve nodded and took the car keys from the older woman.

While he retrieved the playpen, Maisie said to Sara, "You'll be just fine, girl. How long you suppose to be in New Orleans?"

"Several more days," Sara replied.

Not nearly long enough, she thought, looking longingly after Steve.

"HE'S STILL SLEEPING."

Steve stared at the baby lying flat out in the middle of the playpen. Michel's little chest moved up and down rhythmically, but other than that, he lay perfectly still. Unmoving. Steve's stomach churned with anxiety.

"I think something's wrong," he said. "Michel's been asleep for four hours."

He and Sara had had a late breakfast and an early lunch while the baby napped.

Sara stared into the crib and frowned. "He didn't sleep well last night. Maybe he's just making up for lost time. You ought to, too."

"I can't sleep," he said. "Not with the baby like this."

"Steve." Sara turned him to face her. "The last time we woke him up, we paid for it. Dearly. Let the child sleep, Steve. Babies sleep a lot."

"You sure?"

"What did Maisie tell us?"

"That Michel would tell us what he needs when he needs it."

"And what is he telling us now?"

"He needs to sleep. I hope."

Sara grimaced. "Go do something with Ruby. He can't live in that pail forever."

"I know, but it's on your head if anything's wrong with the baby."

"Thanks a lot. Load me with impossible guilt."

Steve let out his breath. "I'm sorry. That was completely unfair of me."

"And stupid," Sara added.

"And very stupid."

He pulled her into his embrace, giving her a hug of contrition.

Sara sighed and patted him on the back, then extricated herself. "We're both tired and cranky."

"I'll go do something about Ruby."

Much as he wanted to bring Sara close to him again,

Steve knew now was not the time. She was probably right. Michel was only catching up on lost sleep from last night.

Steve went out to the back shed and found some old chicken wire some former occupant had left. It wasn't too badly rusted, so it would do for a makeshift fence around Ruby's birdcage.

He checked on the little crabs after he went back into the house. Murgatroyd, Ogglethorpe and Pansy were all fine. Like Michel, the three were snoozing in their shells. One less worry.

He set Ruby, the master escape artist, back in the birdcage and wound the chicken wire around the cage, closing the crab in.

Sara chuckled as she watched him. "It's ironic that you use a birdcage for the hermit crab and not for the bird."

"Max hates it in there. He prefers a perch, so I just keep his wings clipped."

"Gonna meet at the YMCA." Max sang the short verse of the Village People's song over and over again.

"We ought to muzzle him before he wakes the baby," Steve said.

"I thought you wanted Michel awake."

"I'm on your side now. Remember?"

"That's scary." Sara plucked at the shirt she wore. "The baby has his clothes but I'm still in yours. I suppose I should go to my hotel and get some."

"And leave me here alone with the baby?" Panic shot through Steve at the thought.

"What could happen? Don't answer that. Oh, well. I wonder how long Maisie will be."

"I don't know," Steve said. "It could be a couple of days. Maybe more. I don't think Maisie's telling us everything about Chloe's condition."

"I have the same feeling." Sara straightened. "Whatever she needs for the baby I'll do. I'm just a little worried, though, that someone might be trying to reach me. Besides clothes, I could have some messages."

Steve had an idea. "If we're brave enough, after Michel wakes up we could drive to the hotel—all three of us—and get your clothes and any messages. Maisie did leave his car seat."

"Would it be safe?" she asked.

"I would think so. I'll drive carefully," he promised.

"I mean, should we move the baby?"

"Now who's being overprotective?"

Sara smiled sheepishly. "Me. Okay, when he wakes up we change him."

"Your turn."

She made a raspberry at him. "My turn, thank you for reminding me. And we'll feed him, too, assuming he wants it."

"If he doesn't, we'll take a bottle with us. He's bound to want it halfway to New Orleans."

"Or halfway home."

"Wherever the bottle isn't, if we don't take it," Steve finished with a grin. He and Sara had a master plan for traveling with Michel. "This is kind of fun."

Sara looked down at Michel. "It's good."

Steve stood next to her. "You really want one, even after what we went through last night?"

"I do," she said in a low voice.

"My offer still stands."

Sara didn't say anything. Steve grimaced. He never should have said anything, yet the words had left his mouth before he thought. That she didn't refuse could mean she was thinking over his offer. Or it could mean she was infuriated with him and was afraid to yell at him for fear she'd wake the baby.

Michel shifted and stretched, then blinked sleepily. He lifted his head and looked at his surroundings. He tried to move but was still too young to make his arms and legs obey his brain.

Sara bent down and lifted the baby. "Hello, big boy. You waking up? And, yes, your two idiots are still here."

Michel gurgled at her, his angel status in place.

"I resent that," Steve said. "We're bunglers, not idiots."

Michel, to his delight and Sara's, behaved himself during the necessities of changing and feeding. Steve got the baby seat strapped into the middle of his truck's bench seat. He rationalized that this way both he and Sara could see the baby while they drove into the city, rather than have the baby in the back of Sara's rental car, where neither could watch over him.

Sara came outside with Michel. She had the diaper bag slung over one shoulder and her purse over the other.

"Are you kidding me?" she exclaimed when she saw the driving arrangements. "We can't take a baby in the truck!"

"Why not?" he asked, surprised by her reaction. "What's wrong with the truck?"

She opened her mouth, then closed it, temporarily stymied by the question. She opened her mouth again. "Is there a seat belt in there for the middle? You've got to belt the car seat into the main seat. I know that much."

"Already done."

"Is there a seat belt for me? I'm not going in that thing without one."

"It's on the passenger seat, waiting for you. The car's a bench seat, with room for three. Feel better now?"

"Not really."

When Michel was safely secured in his little seat, Sara admitted, "Okay, so it works."

"See? I'm not a total loss."

She smiled at him. "I guess."

They drove to her hotel, Steve being careful as he promised. Michel fell asleep before they were even out of the driveway. He stayed asleep for the entire trip into New Orleans.

"The kid can sleep when he wants to, can't he?" Steve commented, in awe of Michel's reversal from yesterday's wide-awake baby.

"Should we wake him just to go in and get my things?" Sara asked, when they pulled up in front of her hotel.

"Good question. How about if I stay here with him while you go in? That way he can still sleep. Maybe he'll sleep all the way home, too."

"You really are on this sleep bandwagon now, aren't you?" Sara chuckled in amusement.

Steve lowered his chin and looked at her over the top of his sunglasses. "Hey, I'm very adaptable. Besides, he was awake before, so I know he's okay."

"All right, then I'll get some things and I'll be back in a few minutes."

An idea burst full-blown into Steve's head. The practicality of it made sense from several angles. He had a feeling Sara would hate it, but he decided to throw it out there anyway. Taking her arm, he said, "Wait a minute. Sara, I want you to look on what I'm about to suggest from a wholly objective point of view. Just take the personal right out of it."

"Last time you began something like this, you were taking that vice president's job with the eighty-hour work week,'' Sara told him, her eyebrows raised in a cynical arch that matched her voice.

"And that had merit," Steve said. "If you had been objective about it."

"Instead, I was normal about it. We had this argument years ago—"

"No, we never had this argument," he interrupted. "That was half our problem."

"Then let's not have it now, years after the fact. What do you want me to be objective about?"

Steve took a deep breath. He had to make his presentation perfect in order to make this sale. He wondered how far he had fallen down the ladder of persuasive abilities, then pushed the notion from his mind. He needed confidence to pull this off.

"Maisie doesn't know how long she'll be, right?" he reminded her.

"Right," Sara agreed cautiously. "Several days, she thought."

"Maybe even more."

Sara didn't contradict him.

"You're planning to go home in a few days, right?"

"That's right." Her voice sounded very sure, yet puzzled. She still hadn't figured out where he was headed. That was good, because she had to listen.

Sara added, "Of course, if anything got worse here for Maisie, I'd try to stay longer for Michel's sake, if I could. He would need me then."

Steve wanted to object that he needed her more and that he was competent enough to handle the baby alone. But those responses were bound to defeat his purpose.

Careful now, he thought, as he said, "Maintaining a hotel room while you're at my place is a sad waste of your money—"

"Oh, no," Sara said, opening the truck door.

Steve gripped her arm tighter to stop her from getting out.

"Look, I'm only suggesting this from a practical standpoint, so hear me out. Please." He rushed on. "You said you'd stay the entire time Maisie needed to be at the hospital. That could easily be the rest of the days you have scheduled here. And you'd only have to run back and forth to get more of your things. This hotel is expensive, too. You've got to be paying the rack rate, or have just a small discount at best. Unless you came down on some travel-agency plan?"

He let the question hang. Eventually she shook her head.

"Three days at my house with the baby and you'll have wasted what?...more than six hundred dollars?"

Sara's gaze flickered, and he knew he had made a hit.

"Unless you're Trump, that's a waste of good money."

"It wouldn't work," Sara said. "Me staying with you."

"It worked already for a night," he replied, letting go of her arm. He sensed she was still listening even as she protested. "It worked very well. You have to admit that. This is simply a practical move because of particular circumstances. I promise to be a gentleman."

Sara laughed. "That's a laugh. You've been trying to get me in bed ever since I arrived."

"I've been trying to get you to give our marriage a second chance. There's a huge difference." Of course, if sex got him there, he wouldn't object. "This is a different situation, Sara. It's a—a time-out for us. You know you'll be at the house all day and night with Michel anyway. This would save you time and money. And give you more sleep. God knows, you don't want to be spending the few

minutes we get while he's sleeping driving back and forth
between my house and here.''

"And what happens if I check out today, and Maisie
comes for Michel tonight?"

"Then you can always check back in here. No problem.'' Steve finally let go of Sara's arm. She got out of
the truck and shut the door fairly quietly, considering he'd
poleaxed her with his suggestion that she move in with
him for the duration.

Steve sighed as he watched her disappear into the hotel.
"Good effort, but a no-go from the get-go.''

What did he expect? That she would magically fall
back in love and say okay because he wanted to be with
her?

When the truck clock showed nearly a half hour had
passed since Sara left, Steve began to worry. She was
taking far longer to get her things than seemed normal.
He debated whether to wake Michel in order to go get her
or whether to stay put.

He no sooner began unbuckling Michel when she
emerged with luggage. Steve rebuckled Michel, who began to fuss. Steve got out of the truck and helped her
place her garment bag and small carry-on in the stowage
area behind the cab seat.

"I guess you're bringing everything to be safe,'' he
said, when she settled on the passenger seat.

He was about to close her door when she said, "I'm
bringing everything because I checked out.''

She stared out the front windshield while she said it.

"You checked out?'' he echoed, positive he hadn't
heard right.

"I checked out.'' She faced him. Her expression was
anything but soft. "Forget saving money and time, Steve.

That's a bunch of bull concocted by you to make your point. You were always good at that.''

"But I meant it," he said. She made him sound as if he was a manipulator extraordinaire.

"On some level, no doubt, you did." She gazed at him with a firmness that Donald Trump would have envied. "However, I do save a bundle by staying with you. While that's not your ultimate reason for your offer of hospitality, I'm not a wealthy woman and it's cost me plenty already while you're trying to resurrect a failed marriage. With that failed marriage in mind, I also see a practical side to this. Whatever residue is between us needs to be wiped away. The most efficient way to have this out is to take you up on your offer until it's obvious we have nothing to resurrect." She took a deep breath and went on. "Here's the deal. I'll stay to help with the baby *and* to prove to you that you're clutching at straws. We have a dead and buried marriage. Once I show you that, you sign the divorce papers, and as soon as Michel's back with his family, I'm out of here. All right?"

Steve grinned, undaunted. "All right!"

Chapter Eight

It must be heatstroke.

Not yet willing to go back into the house, Sara stood on Steve's back porch and shivered at the cool evening air wafting down from the north. Yep, she was definitely suffering from heatstroke. She had to be, to have taken Steve up on his "objective" offer.

She would never have considered it if he hadn't mentioned cost. That had concerned her, because she didn't have an endless credit-card limit. She'd checked her account with the front desk and discovered she already had nearly a thousand dollars on her bill thus far. The thought of several more days of paying for a room she wasn't even sleeping in persuaded her to consider his offer. She even came up with several other reasons why staying with him while Michel was there would be advantageous to her.

She would be on hand for the baby.

She wouldn't have long drives into New Orleans for things she needed.

She wouldn't have to wear Steve's clothes.

Oh, boy, did she have reasons.

The porch door opened.

"He's crying and your mom's on the phone," Steve

said, leaning out. He looked far too pleased with himself. No doubt he and her mother had had an interesting conversation.

"Okay." Sara sighed. Reality was about to sink in real fast.

Inside, Sara took the phone. Steve took the baby.

"Hi, Mom," Sara said, while watching Steve walk the kitchen floor with Michel on his shoulder.

"I come home from the movies and pie at the Honeybee Café with your father. Imagine my surprise to hear your message on my answering machine that you're now staying with Steve. Imagine my further surprise when there's a baby crying in the background. My angel, you work fast."

"Faster than the speed of light, Mom." Sara made a face. "I suppose Steve told you what happened."

"No. He and I barely said hello."

Her aunt Fanny, they barely said hello. Sara bet the phone had rung five minutes ago, while she'd been outside. Her mother probably had more poop on the story than Michel could deliver.

"Steve's housekeeper's daughter is in the hospital. She couldn't leave her grandson with anyone else but Steve. I walked in and saw the baby needed help." Steve grinned at Sara as she added, "Don't read any more into this than there is."

"So you haven't been to bed with him yet."

"Mom!"

"Sex cures a lot. Just look at your father and me. When I'm infuriated with him, a good night in bed will have me extremely content with him. He's very good, especially with his—"

"I don't need to hear this, Mom. I don't want to."

"Sara, honey, I'm old. I'm not dead."

"I just wanted to let you know where I was. Now, goodbye."

"Wait, wait! All right, I won't be an open mom. I suppose some lines in the mother-daughter relationship should never be crossed."

"I'll say," Sara murmured.

"How are you doing with the baby? You must be thrilled to be taking care of a little one."

"We're okay." Sara sighed.

"Not as much fun as you thought, eh?"

"We had some miscues...." Steve laughed over Michel's unhappiness, catching on to what the women were discussing. Sara added, "We accidentally overfed him and woke him to change his diapers."

Her mother laughed. "I don't miss that at all."

"I can understand why." Michel's crying increased in volume. Obviously *he* didn't understand why.

"He sounds very fussy," her mother said. "It's probably colic."

"Colic?" Sara had heard of the condition. The word had an ominous ring to it, and she knew from general women's talk that colic was a dreaded thing. "Are you sure? He was fine all day. In fact, he slept most of it away."

"Oh, well then, he may have his days and nights mixed up, especially after doing all that sleeping." Her mother laughed again. "You're in for some fun."

"You make the Marquis de Sade look like a pussycat," Sara grumbled, plugging a finger in her free ear as Michel fussed louder. Steve gave her a desperate look and took the baby into the dining room. To her mother, she said, "Michel's grandmother said he'll tell us when he wants to eat and to sleep. And when to change the diapers."

"Oh, good Lord, no. Never let a baby take control or

PLAY...

"ROLL A DOUBLE!"

GET 4 BOOKS

AND A

FABULOUS MYSTERY BONUS GIFT

ABSOLUTELY FREE!

SEE INSIDE...

NO RISK, NO OBLIGATION TO BUY...NOW OR EVER!

GUARANTEED

PLAY "ROLL A DOUBLE" AND YOU GET FREE GIFTS! HERE'S HOW TO PLAY:

1. Peel off label from front cover. Place it in space provided at right. With a coin, carefully scratch off the silver dice. Then check the claim chart to see what we have for you – FOUR FREE BOOKS and a mystery gift – ALL YOURS! ALL FREE!

2. Send back this card and you'll receive brand-new Harlequin American Romance® novels. These books have a cover price of $3.99 each, but they are yours to keep absolutely free.

3. There's no catch. You're under no obligation to buy anything. We charge nothing – ZERO – for your first shipment. And you don't have to make any minimum number of purchases – not even one!

4. The fact is, thousands of readers enjoy receiving books by mail from the Harlequin Reader Service®. They like the convenience of home delivery...they like getting the best new novels BEFORE they're available in stores...and they love our discount prices!

5. We hope that after receiving your free books you'll want to remain a subscriber. But the choice is yours – to continue or cancel any time at all! So why not take us up on our invitation, with no risk of any kind. You'll be glad you did!

YOURS FREE!

FABULOUS MYSTERY GIFT COULD BE YOURS *FREE* WHEN YOU PLAY "ROLL A DOUBLE"

"ROLL A DOUBLE!"

Place label here

SCRATCH HERE

SEE CLAIM CHART BELOW

154 CIH CDVR
(U-H-AR-02/98)

YES! I have placed my label from the front cover into the space provided above and scratched off the silver dice. Please send me all the gifts for which I qualify. I understand that I am under no obligation to purchase any books, as explained on the opposite page.

NAME _____

ADDRESS _____ APT. _____

CITY _____ STATE _____ ZIP _____

CLAIM CHART

4 FREE BOOKS PLUS MYSTERY BONUS GIFT

3 FREE BOOKS PLUS BONUS GIFT

2 FREE BOOKS

CLAIM NO. 37-829

he'll run you ragged. He'll tell you, but he's got to have some direction, too, especially with sleeping.''

Sara had never felt more confused from the conflicting advice. Maisie certainly sounded sensible and it had worked during the day. But she trusted her mother, too. "What do we do, Mom?"

"Don't let him sleep more than three or four hours in a morning or afternoon nap, for a start. Try and keep him awake for a little while in between. Let him sleep as long as he wants at night. It'll take several days to turn him around again. Oh, and don't be so fast to pick him up when he fusses. Sometimes babies fuss for five or ten minutes, then settle back down.''

"He'll be cured just in time to go back to his grandmother," Sara said, looking heavenward. "What about the colic? What if he's got that?"

"If he calms down when his sleep times are corrected, then he was just unhappy, not full of bellyaches. If he doesn't, then you just have to ride the colic out.''

"Wonderful.''

"If you weren't told, he probably doesn't have it, although maybe Steve's housekeeper doesn't know. Children keep their parents in the dark about things. We *love* being mushrooms. I understand there is medicine to help colic nowadays. I'm sure you would have been given medicine if he had colic. So it's the day and night thing…unless he's going through a growth spurt. That could explain his fussiness.''

"A growth spurt?" Lord help them, Sara thought. It sounded like Michel would be taller than Steve in a few hours.

"Kids kind of grow overnight. Or so it seems. It's a fussy time for a week or two.''

"Great, just great," Sara mumbled, thinking of these new baby calamities looming on the horizon.

"This will give you a nice preview. What did you think? Babies were all sweetness and light? You weren't. You insisted on waking up every night for nine full months. How old is this baby?"

"I don't know."

"He sounds young. Is he sitting up? Does he crawl?"

"No." God, new horrors. "When do they do that?"

"Between six and ten months or so, depending on the child."

"He's not that old." She didn't think he was.

"Then it's probably something."

"Thanks a lot, Mom," Sara said dryly.

"Oh, anytime...except between the hours of midnight and eight in the morning. You're on your own then. It's called Mother's Revenge. But do call the baby's pediatrician right away if he's feverish or violently vomiting or anything else that seems unusual. Vigorous crying is just unhappiness most of the time."

Sara's head spun with instructions. "Okay."

"Good luck with Steve and the baby, honey. This has been an interesting trip for you."

After Sara hung up, Steve came back into the kitchen. Michel still fussed, although he was less angry about it.

"What did she say?" Steve asked.

Sara pushed her hair back from her face. "She told me things I didn't need to hear, from her sex life to growth spurts."

"Sex life?" Steve grinned. "At least she's got one."

"But I *don't* need to hear about it." Sara shuddered. Dammit, she hated being surrounded by people with happy sex lives.

"What's this growth-spurt stuff anyway?"

Sara told him all the baby lore her mother had relayed.

"Colic?" Steve looked shaken. "You mean he'll cry like this *all night?*"

"That's what she said. But she says we let him sleep too much today and he might be fussy now from it."

"But Maisie said he'll tell us what he wants. And he told us he wanted to sleep."

"And my mom says you have to give babies direction. She says we were lousy sleep cops." Sara looked at the baby, whose unhappiness manifested it in a fierce wail of displeasure. Max began squawking in the living room.

"I'll kill that bird," Steve vowed.

"We fed Michel about an hour ago and he ate well but not too much, so it's not food." She shuddered again. "I learned my lesson on that one."

Steve rubbed the baby's back and crooned to Michel. "Poor little guy. He probably just wants his mother."

"I'll give him mine," Sara commented, putting on some coffee. If Michel intended to fuss all night, she might as well be awake for it. The only advantage she could see about a days-and-nights-mixed-up, colicky, growth-spurting baby was that he kept Steve at bay sexually. The last thing she needed was a happy sex life, like her mother. Confusion, not contentment, would result.

"Now what else did Marj say that bothered you?" Steve asked. "I know she did. I could always tell."

Sara shrugged. "It's a mother-daughter thing."

"We can never please our own parents, can we? Do you know my father's still ticked at me for our split up?"

"Really?" Sara's eyebrows rose in surprise. Steve's father never had that much to say to her.

"He always liked you best, better than me. He liked my job better than me, too. Needless to say, he wasn't happy that I lost both."

"But losing your job wasn't your fault."

"But losing you was."

Sara shook her head. "I was too young then. We both know it. I was certainly too insecure. There was fault on both sides."

"So what's wrong with now?"

His question stabbed at her. But this was one of her reasons for being here.

"I can't go through it again, Steve," she said, being as honest as she could. "It hurt too much the first time."

"It would be different."

"Nothing's different. You're just between challenges, Steve. Once you accept one again, I would get left behind. You're very focused. It's what made you so good at your job."

"No. Not this time." His eyes pleaded with her, as much as Michel cried for relief from his personal misery.

"Yes, it would be the same. I'm the same inside, too," she said, wishing she could relieve both males' unhappiness with a wave of her hand. Her voice cracked with betraying emotion. "I might have a demanding job, but I'm still the same person inside. It won't be different, because *I'm* not different. I'll be waiting for the first time you're late, or you get a promotion, and I'll pounce. I need to start over, Steve. So do you."

"You underestimate yourself."

"I don't think so." Suddenly she felt helpless and restless. The parrot squawked in time to the baby's cries. "Here, give me Michel for a while. You go see if you can settle Max."

Steve came to her. He looked at her, his eyes searching. He leaned over and kissed her. Her lips clung to his, hungry for a taste of him. She wanted nothing more than to take her mother's advice and go to bed with Steve and have sex make everything better. She was vulnerable to him. She always would be.

Between them, Michel cried.

Sara eased away, her lips burning from the kiss. She took Michel from Steve. She walked around the living room and dining room, patting the baby on the back the entire time. Her frustration rose, not so much from the crying in her ear, but from Steve watching her every move as he soothed Max's feathers.

Why couldn't Steve understand? Their broken marriage needed more than a touch of superglue sex to put it back together again. She should have kept her hotel room, no matter what the horrendous cost in the end.

"Five'll get you ten," Max said, then began to cry in unison with Michel.

"Can't you do something with that bird?" she asked, annoyed.

"I could fricassee him, but he'd probably give us indigestion."

She glared at both man and bird.

"I'll put him in my bedroom," Steve said.

"Good."

Max squawked when Steve lifted his standing perch. The bird screeched, "No! No! Max is a good birdie. Max is a good birdie!"

"Right, Max," Steve said. "And if Sara believes that, then you've got a bridge to show her."

"Au secours! Au secours!" Max's French pleas for help grew fainter as Steve took the bird to the other side of the house.

"The noisy bird is all gone," Sara crooned to Michel, who acted as if all hell had just broken loose. "And the big, bad wolf, Steve, went with him."

Michel's crying quieted, although he still fussed a little.

Sara wondered if her mother was right, and envisioned the coming night with a wide-awake, unhappy baby. Tears blurred her eyes at the thought. Some rational instinct, however, grew stronger. The baby couldn't help his unhappiness. He couldn't say exactly what was wrong with him. It could even be simply emotional fright because he wasn't with familiar people. Whatever it was, he couldn't help his crying.

A sense of patience settled over Sara. This was only temporary deprivation of sleep caused by someone who had no clue what he was doing. Eventually, he would stop crying. But knowing Michel was helpless, she could accept the baby fates and handle the situation until then.

Steve came back downstairs. He, unfortunately, was *not* a temporary deprivation. He was permanent. He had to be.

So why was she here? The infant was hardly the only reason.

Not wanting to think about the answer, she pressed her cheek against Michel's curls, inhaling the sweet scent of baby. She was here for him. She had to be.

"Steve," she said, raising her head. "Let's have a truce, please. Let's set our problems aside and devote ourselves to Michel."

"I thought we were already doing that," he replied, frowning.

She smiled wryly. Only a man would see an unsettling discussion as not talking about things. "Let's just say our problems keep creeping in. I think we'd be better off making a conscious effort to avoid them. We need to concentrate on Michel's needs right now."

"We're devoting every second to him as it is." Steve ran a hand through his hair. "What more does the kid need?"

"Our mental attention."

"Fine." He looked at the baby. "Uh-oh. He's asleep again."

Sara lifted Michel away slightly, only to see the closed eyes and hear the little, shuddering breath of slumber disturbed. She set the baby on her shoulder again. Michel snuggled against her. "This is not good. He's already slept all day."

"Maybe everyone is wrong and he'll sleep all night," Steve said, a little too hopefully.

Sara squelched that notion. He wasn't getting away with wearing rose-colored glasses and leaving her out of it. "You know what my mother said. He's slept too much already. It's only seven o'clock now. If he sleeps for four hours, that's what? Over ten hours during the day alone. You sleep ten hours during the day and tell me what happens."

"I can party until four in the morning," Steve said. "I guess we better wake him up."

Sara's brain rebelled, adversely wanting a little more peace and isolation from the baby. Just to refresh herself, she rationalized. But common sense took over. Dammit.

She jiggled Michel. "Wake up, sweetie. You don't want that nasty old sleep now."

Michel's eyelids flashed open at the deliberate waking. He took one look at Sara and bellowed with indignation.

Sara looked at Steve. At least they wouldn't be able to talk about their relationship—and get nowhere fast.

STEVE WISHED FOR a dark and stormy night.

That would have been the capper, he admitted, dragging a weary hand down his face. Unfortunately, he wasn't getting his wish. His watch read three in the morning, and the night was dark but calm outside his living room window. A little cold, but that was it.

Michel had had an hour's nap around ten, then they had wakened him, hoping he'd go down by midnight or one. But no. Michel had preferred being unhappily awake ever since.

"Let's put him down now," Steve suggested, watching Sara as she tiredly bounced the baby. That was another annoyance of the night. She had thus far refused to give up the baby to him.

"He didn't like it last time," she said, looking up with red-rimmed eyes. Her skin was pasty with exhaustion.

"Hell, I didn't like it, either. But if we want to get his days and nights unmixed, then we've got to start him sleeping at night sometime." The notion seemed logical to Steve.

"I don't know. What if it's colic? Or a growth spurt? Trying to get him to sleep will be a waste of all our time."

"Then it doesn't matter if we try it, because this is hardly productive," Steve said. "He's going to be miserable anyway, and our playing with him won't matter. Neither will putting him in the playpen, which would at least give us a little relief. Here. I'll put him down."

"No, no. I will." She got up awkwardly from the sofa while holding the baby.

"Hey, I am competent," he protested, hurt.

She gave him a pointed look.

"As competent as you," he amended.

"I'm a woman."

Steve laughed wryly. "I know that very well. But it's no automatic skill enhancement."

"I want a baby. You don't."

"I want to make one." He raised his hand before she could verbally assault him. "That conversation is off-limits. I understand that. Besides, it's too late to start arguing now. Just put the baby in his playpen.''

"You're finally saying something with some sense to it.''

He got up and fixed the covers for the baby, pushing toys out of the way. Sara laid Michel down very, very gently. Michel cried, as expected. Sara reached for him. Steve pulled her back.

"Let's give him a little time," he said, some instinct prompting him. "He could settle down.''

"Okay.'' She sounded dubious, but she didn't lift the baby out of the makeshift bed.

Michel fussed, cried outright for a minute or two, then seemed to relax. His mouth found his thumb. He sucked. His eyes slowly closed.

"What do you think?'' Sara whispered, raising a hopeful gaze to Steve.

"I think we need to follow his lead and go to bed.'' Steve put his hand to her back, intending to turn her toward the stairs.

Sara resisted. "I'll sleep on the sofa.''

He glared at her. "Don't be ridiculous. I'll use the other bedroom.''

"That's okay. I'll be fine here.''

"No, you won't. You're about to fall over, you're so damn tired. You need a good sleep in a real bed. Take mine.''

"No, thank you. I don't think it's wise.''

"I'm not going to do anything.'' He kept his voice soft, in spite of the anger boiling up inside him. "I'm too damn tired, too.''

"The sofa will be fine.''

"Okay.'' Steve dropped his hand. He'd be damned before he fought with her. He'd be damned before he extended special hospitality again, either. "If you want to be stiff-necked, fine, but I'm going to bed. There's a guest bedroom you're welcome to, if you change your mind. The bed's not the greatest, and you'll have to move stuff off it, but that's your choice."

He left her to her decision, cursing under his breath while he climbed the stairs again. If she didn't want the good bed, then he certainly wouldn't be a gentleman about it.

"Cute butt, babe," Max chirped, when Steve entered the bedroom.

Steve groaned. He'd forgotten he'd put his parrot in here.

"Shut up, Max," Steve said, shucking his jeans.

"Shut up, shut up, shut up!" Max sang back.

Steve stripped off his shirt. To hell with Max, he thought. He was too damn tired for the bird to keep him awake for long.

"She's a lady...whoa, whoa, whoa, she's a lady," Max sang.

Steve flopped on the bed, *his* bed. It felt so good, and he would take advantage of every quiet minute Michel gave them. Sara could be a martyr if she wanted. He wouldn't be. Steve closed his eyes.

"Stayin' alive...staying alive. Whoa-a-a!"

Steve opened his eyes. "Maxie, quiet."

"Polly wants a friggin' cracker!"

Steve cursed. So far Michel was asleep downstairs, which meant Max had only disturbed *him*.

Maybe the baby was crying and Steve couldn't hear him. He got up and opened his bedroom door to check on that theory. Silence reigned downstairs. Maybe Sara, his stubborn, wary, thinking-the-worst-of-him wife, was asleep, too. Now that would really annoy him.

''Macho, macho man...''

Steve shut the door against Max's singing. ''Damn!''

''I thought I saw a putty tat,'' Max announced.

''I wish you had and the cat would eat you, you Tweety bird.''

He lifted Max's perch and moved it to the other side of the room, farthest from the door and downstairs. He stubbed his toe in the process. Max repeated his barnyard curses.

''Any farther away from the baby and you'd be outside,'' Steve said, surveying his handiwork.

''Here, chickie, chickie...''

Steve flopped back in the bed. Max seemed less annoying in the far corner as the bird chattered to himself.

Unfortunately, Steve found himself thinking of his wife downstairs. He was angry that she'd insisted on staying with the baby. He resented her acting like he was some sex ogre.

Okay, so he'd given her that impression. But they had a truce between them now. He was too intent on sleep to break it. Yet he also felt guilty that he was in the nice bed with the parrot while she was on the uncomfortable sofa with the time bomb that could reawaken any moment.

''You ain't nothing but a hound dog,'' Max sang for a lullaby.

Elvis, Steve thought, letting Max's singing roll over him. Max had a jukebox repertoire, thanks to his years living in a bar. Next up would be the twist....

''Steve! Wake up!''

At Sara's frantic voice, Steve bolted upright out of a sound sleep. ''What! What!''

Sara staggered back, startled at his sudden movement. Steve realized the sun was shining through the windows. Last night came back in a rush, even as Sara said, ''Did the baby wake up and I didn't hear him? Did he cry and you took care of him?"

"No." Steve frowned, disoriented and not grasping her worry. "You were downstairs with him—"

"But I wasn't!" Tears swam in her eyes. "I couldn't relax because I heard every movement he made in his sleep. I heard those damn alligators bellowing, too. I finally came upstairs at about four and used the other bedroom. But now it's after eight, and I just woke up. I panicked, then I thought, well, you must have seen to him, and I shouldn't be silly. But then I didn't want to go down and check and wake him if he was up a lot during the night. Oh God, Steve, what if something happened?"

"It's okay." Steve got up and strode downstairs, Sara following. Panic strode with him, terrible panic, although he tried not to show it for her sake. It was too quiet in the house.

Michel lay in his playpen, clearly and contentedly asleep. His chest rose and fell in a nice, healthy rhythm.

Sara burst into tears. "Thank God!"

"See? He's okay," Steve said, letting out his own breath of relief. He put his arm around Sara and chuckled. "Look at us. We want the kid to sleep and then we have alarm bells go off because he is."

"Amateur hour is back," Sara agreed. She put her arm around his waist and rested her forehead on his chest. "I was so scared."

She felt good in his arms. Too good. He was only in his briefs. He stroked her back, half in comfort and half in desire. He wanted her; he could never deny that. Yet he understood her fears. No one could turn around a bad marriage and four years of separation in a few days. He had no right to ask it of her—only he could not let her leave him again, either.

''What should we do now?'' Sara asked, her breath deliciously hot on his chest.

''Exactly what we're doing...and more,'' he said dreamily.

She disentangled herself from him. ''I meant about the baby.''

''Oh.'' He should have known. When had his wife developed such a one-track mind? ''Let him sleep. Anything else would be crazy. Wouldn't it?''

''What about him having his days and nights mixed up?'' she reminded him. ''Shouldn't we be getting him back on a normal schedule? That won't happen if he sleeps until noon.''

''God, that sounds so good.'' Steve looked at Michel. ''But he's so cute right now. And so quiet. The moment we wake him, he'll act like he's possessed by the Evil Baby again.''

''I know.'' Sara smiled ruefully.

Steve sighed. ''Okay, let's get him up.''

Sara brightened. ''There's always morning nap to compensate.''

''I like your thinking. Okay. I'll be the dirty rat.'' Steve bent down and picked Michel up.

Michel blinked a few times, then came fully awake. He frowned at Steve, clearly trying to decide whether he should be awake or not.

''I know how you feel, pal.'' An odor of unwashed baby assailed Steve's nose. ''Woo, boy! You are in need of a bath, my friend.''

Sara leaned over and sniffed. She drew back fast. ''He's one stinky petunia. I suppose he hasn't had a bath since his mother got sick. We've only been sponging the diaper area and cleaning up his face and hands.''

"The trick is," Steve began, "whether we're brave enough to give him a bath."

"The real trick is whether we're *competent* enough," Sara replied. "For his safety, I want to vote no. For his health, we may not have a choice. By the way, we've got to wash his clothes, too. That's the last of the outfits Maisie brought yesterday."

"Okay, you give him his bottle, and I'll go start the water in the tub."

Sara laughed. "Steve, you can't put a baby in a bath-tub."

"But you can throw the baby out with the bathwater. Go figure."

"That's an expression. We'll use the kitchen sink."

"Might as well rename the kitchen Michel's salon. He's the master of that domain."

Sara smiled. Steve bent and kissed her, a short kiss of affection. He should have done more of that before, he thought, when he saw pleasure light her eyes.

"I'll take him," Sara said. She glanced at his briefs, then away. "You get dressed. I'll feed him, then we'll give him a bath, then I'll have one."

"While you feed him, I'll make coffee and take care of the clothes," Steve volunteered. "Hey. We're a team."

"So far."

"Have a little faith, why don't you?"

"I have faith. It's the hope and charity I'm still working on."

He handed over the baby, his hand brushing her breasts. Sweat popped out on his forehead. He wanted nothing more than to cover them with his hands, rub his palm over her nipple and feel it harden. He wanted a lot of things.

Sara flushed after the baby exchange. He wondered if her thoughts had paralleled his.

"Go get dressed," she said.

He nodded.

After dressing, he took the time to move Max back downstairs. He checked Ruby's cage. The crab clung forlornly to the chicken-wire reinforcement. Steve grinned at Ruby before checking the other crabs. The smaller crabs were okay, too; certainly they weren't looking for an escape route.

Michel was chugging down his bottle when Steve walked into the kitchen.

"This isn't bad," Steve announced. "He got a little sleep. We got a little sleep. *Little* being the operative word. In two, three years, we'll have this down to a science."

"I think you run into a whole new set of problems in two or three years. Everyone calls them the terrible twos."

"I didn't say we'd have no problems. I only said we'd have this one solved." Steve put coffee on for them.

Sara sighed happily when the coffeemaker began to run dark liquid into the pot. "I need some of that. *Now.* But not while I'm holding the baby."

"I told you to take the good bed. You would have slept better."

She smiled archly. "I'm sure you would have loved that."

He chuckled. "I won't lie. I would have. Tonight, you take it, though. In fact, if you want a nap during the day, just use it. I'll put Max back in there, so you can be sung to sleep. He does a helluva job."

"No thanks. I heard him. He's a real Bee Gees fan."

"Twenty years in a bar will do that to any parrot."

"Wow. He's twenty?"

"A little older, I think. But he'll go another twenty easy. More. I'll be a doddering old man before he will."

Steve fixed their coffee, then fixed Michel's bath. He took an educated guess that the water temperature should be less than the boiling level he preferred for himself. He put a few inches in the bottom of the sink. He got a bar of soap, some shampoo and a washcloth from the baby bag, as well as a towel and another of his cut-off T-shirts for Michel to wear until his clothes were clean again.

When it was time for the bath, Sara was reluctant to give Michel to him.

"I won't break the child," Steve said in disgust. "You fed him, so I should bathe him. That's sharing the workload. Besides, if anything happens on this new venture, I want it to be on my head rather than yours."

"I don't know if you should," she said dubiously.

"Stand next to me, drink your coffee and watch, just like any other supervisor."

Sara handed the baby over at last. Steve's pride and satisfaction swelled as he bathed the baby with no mishaps. Well, two minor ones, he admitted as he wrapped Michel in the bath towel to dry him. He'd accidentally put too much shampoo on the baby's head, and Michel had christened Sara with a shower of his own when they'd stripped him for his bath. Other than those, Michel had grinned and kicked and splashed the water. Cleanliness was next to godliness, and Michel was obviously headed for angel status again.

"Why don't you go get a shower?" Steve suggested to Sara, eyeing her rumpled, wet-spotted clothes. Michel was in another of his shirts, so she might as well be, too. She looked much better in it.

"I guess I better before I reek to high heavens," she

replied sheepishly. "We did good this morning, didn't we?"

"I told you we make a great team," he said.

She smiled in answer, then tickled Michel under his chin. "And you are positively pleasant now. Why do I expect the other shoe to drop today?"

Michel cooed at her.

"You're telling me something, and it's not good. You're far too happy about it, aren't you?"

"Go take your shower," Steve said, and shooed her from the room. She left, laughing. They all felt good, he thought.

He no sooner had Michel diapered and dressed in his T-shirt when Maisie's car pulled around the back of the house.

Carrying Michel, Steve went out on the back porch to greet her. "Hey, Grandmama!"

Maisie laughed when she saw her grandson's damp curls. "What you try and do? Drown that boy?"

They went inside as Steve replied, "Almost. He needed a bath. Sara declared him a stinky petunia."

"I've smelled that in my time."

"How's your daughter doing?" he asked.

"Much, much better. They're moving her from intensive care this morning, and they expect to release her from the hospital the day after tomorrow. She won't need more surgery after all, so I came to get this stinky petunia. We're all missing him."

Steve's heart lurched. His hands unconsciously tightened around Michel. "Sara and I are doing okay with him. Why don't we keep him until your daughter comes home? That way you can go to the hospital however much you need to, without worrying about the baby."

Maisie grinned. "He got to ya, didn't he? I thought he

might. While I had little choice, that's one of the reasons I *wanted* to leave him with you.''

"I'm just thinking of your needs," Steve said.

"I appreciate that. You've been a real good friend to me in my time of need. And your mojo's way better, I can feel that already. But my baby doesn't need me so much now, and I can handle her baby. Besides, I miss him something awful.''

She held out her arms for her grandson.

Steve handed Michel over, saying, "We got his days and nights mixed up.''

"You did?''

He nodded. "Maybe we should keep him until he's straightened out. That's only fair.''

"He looks straightened out to me.'' Maisie nuzzled Michel, who grinned and made a happy noise.

"We might have given him colic.''

"Nonsense. This baby never had a colicky day in his life.''

"He was fussy. Maybe it's a growth spurt. You don't want to deal with that.''

Maisie glanced up. "Now who's been feeding you that?''

"Well, when he was crying a lot, Sara's mother said that could be his problem.''

"People have a lot of opinions about babies. You just have to feel your way with each one.''

Steve had nothing else to say, his arguments for keeping Michel longer now exhausted. With a heavy heart, he collapsed Michel's playpen and got his car seat, putting both in Maisie's car.

"Behave for your grandmother,'' he told Michel, letting the baby grip his forefinger. "No screaming at three in the morning. No throwing up on her best shirt and no filling your diapers with that toxic-waste stuff. There's a law against it, pal.''

He kissed Michel, then Maisie, goodbye. Maisie thanked him again for his help.

After they left, he went back in the kitchen. A suspicious lump stuck in his throat. Sara came in from the dining room, fluffing her short, damp hair.

"I feel so much better. Did I hear a car? Where's the baby? You didn't put him down for a nap already—"

"Maisie came," he said in a low voice, feeling bad. "Her daughter's doing much better. She's out of intensive care and she'll be home in a couple days, so Maisie's able to take care of Michel."

Sara looked stricken, a clear pain crossing her face. "Michel's gone home? Just like that?"

Steve nodded, frowning from his own emptiness. "Just like that."

"I—I didn't get to say goodbye."

Sara burst into tears.

Chapter Nine

"I shouldn't be crying," Sara cried, wiping at the tears that refused to stop. "I knew he was supposed to go home, but not this fast...."

Steve came to her and pulled her into his comforting embrace. She burst into fresh tears. All her maternal desires had come to the fore with Michel, who had been ripped away in the blink of an eye.

"Did we do something wrong?" she asked. "Did I?"

"No. No." Steve's arms tightened around her. She'd never felt so grateful for his presence in her life. "It was just time for him to go back home, that's all."

"I know that's it. I truly do. So why do I feel like I lost something precious?"

"You got attached." Steve raised her face and wiped her tears. "Hell, honey, so did I. He was a cutie, wasn't he?"

She nodded. Then started crying again.

"You want one of those really bad, don't you?"

"Oh, God, yes. If I wasn't sure before, I am now. Lord knows why. Babies pee on you and throw up on you and scare the hell out of you. I know that now."

Steve laughed and smoothed her hair. "He was great."

"You were," she said. "You took him in and you did

everything for him. Most men would have shoved the job onto someone else, but you...you were a natural at it."

"I don't know about that," he replied.

"I do. Even Michel thought so." She sniffed back the last tears. "You surprised me, Steve."

"You surprised *me*," he said. "There's a lot we don't know about each other anymore."

"No. There isn't."

She gazed up at him, at the sharply defined features that were so familiar and yet so new to her. His body pressed close. It felt so good, reminding her, in contrast, of the many nights she had been alone. Under his shirt, his muscles were lean and hard. His hips intimately met her own. Their legs touched.

She shouldn't want him, she thought. Yet she did.

"Steve," she murmured, needing to be comforted. Something inside her insisted she take back what she'd lost. If she thought about the urge, if she rationalized it, she would lose it and the moment would never come again. She knew she was vulnerable, but it didn't matter. Only need mattered. She needed Steve now as she never had before.

Sara reached up on her toes and kissed him. She blended her mouth to his. Their tongues swirled together and their breathing quickened. She had always loved the feel of his warm breath on her cheek when they kissed.

Steve began to lift his head to break contact, but she pulled him back. Her body ached and yet was satisfied when he kissed her again.

The kiss went on for endless minutes. She became light-headed. Her body throbbed deep within. She took his hand and put it to one breast.

This time Steve did ease fully away. "I shouldn't be

saying this, not with what I want, but be sure about what you're doing, Sara."

"I want you," she whispered. What she didn't want was to hear reason. She didn't want to see reason. She felt broken inside and sensed that Steve would heal her one way or another.

"You're upset. You're—"

"Oh, shut up and kiss me."

This new kiss was fierce, their lips and tongues frantic. His hands covered her breasts, his thumbs rubbing her nipples until they turned diamond hard. Sara clung to him, clutched at him in her desperation to mate. She craved physical intimacy as much as she craved its aftermath. Oddly, she trusted Steve more in this moment than she had ever trusted anyone else.

"Oh, God," she murmured when he placed biting little kisses along her throat and shoulders, "You feel so good."

He kissed her mouth, another devastating kiss that only heightened her body's clamoring for relief from the sensual onslaught.

"Steve," she whispered finally. "Come to bed with me now."

He swept her up in a mind-spinning kiss, then took her hand and led her upstairs.

She thought of all the rational arguments not to, all the resistance she'd had against their making love. But caring for Michel had raised an ache in her that had to be eased. She needed intimacy, a renewal of self, a joy, no matter how temporary. She would deal with reality when it set in.

His unmade bed beckoned, and Sara tumbled onto it, bringing Steve with her. She turned aggressor, kissing his face, his lips, his throat and shoulders. She ran her hands down his back, shivering in delight at the feel of his body, so different and yet so necessary to hers. Their legs tangled together, and he wedged his hips in the cradle hers made.

Even fully clothed, their bodies were incredibly intimate, she thought.

Steve pulled her shirt over her head, then unsnapped her bra. Or tried to. He cursed as he fumbled behind her back.

Sara chuckled. "You never were smooth with that."

"I'll make up for it," he promised, finally undoing the garment.

She knew he would.

"I've never forgotten how soft your skin is," Steve murmured, raising himself on one elbow as he traced the globes of her breasts with his forefinger. "I've never forgotten how sweet you taste."

He replaced his finger with his tongue, laving every inch of her exposed breasts in a decreasing circle. Sara gasped for breath, her hands clasping his head, unconsciously guiding him to a nipple. His lips plucked at it, teasing her and driving her into a frenzy. He finally took the nipple fully into his mouth, his tongue whirling around the sensitive point.

Sara writhed under his ministrations, and when she could stand no more, he moved to her other breast.

Her blood pumped thickly with heat. It pooled low in her belly. She lifted herself into his hips, pleading with her body for him to take her.

Steve knew Sara was vulnerable, all torn up from Michel's abrupt departure. He knew she would have regrets after lovemaking. So would he. But he could no more stop himself than fly to the moon. Sara wanted him, and he wanted her. One thing he would not do was take her. He would make *love* to her with every nuance he remembered, and hope she made love in return. Maybe then they would resolve their marriage limbo.

Sara's hands were like cool fire on his back. Her mouth was like silk and her flesh like satin. Her thighs moved restlessly, and her hips twisted. The combination dissolved all sensible thought.

Steve kissed her flat stomach, unsnapping her jeans with more finesse than he had used when removing her bra. He rose back on his heels and pulled the pants from her legs. Her body had haunted his dreams for years, and he found her as beautiful as ever. Her soft, creamy skin, glowing with health, was enhanced by a dark thatch of hair at the junction of her thighs. Her breasts were still small by general standards, but more responsive than ever. Her rosy nipples distended into sensual points. She half closed her sensuous brown eyes as she watched him watching her.

He sucked in his breath, marveling at the perfection once more in his bed.

Sara reached up and pushed his shirt up over his waist and chest, her palms deliciously tickling his skin. He took it the rest of the way over his head, then leaned down and kissed her in the most intimate of places.

Sara moaned.

Steve tasted her womanly sweetness, her unique scent flooding his senses. Her body tensed at his ministrations, clearly throbbing with her growing pleasure.

He might have continued until her release, but Sara reached between them, stroking him boldly. Steve gasped in his own pleasure.

She unzipped his shorts, pushing them down his hips. All his common sense dissolved with the brazen move.

Steve shoved the last of his clothes off, surrendering to his own needs and hers.

Sara pressed her hips against his. He lost any thought of sending her over the brink time and again before seeking his own satisfaction. He was helpless to stop her when she urged him closer. He eased himself into her, her moistness capturing him fully. So many times they had been one, he thought, and yet each time was so unique. The way he and Sara made love had always been unique, different from anything else he had experienced.

They moved together in rhythms as ancient as the earth, yet sweetly remembered and as new as the first time. Sara's legs came around his waist, opening her fully to his thrusts. Her trust and her vulnerability wrapped around his heart, and he met her hips again and again, trying to tell her with his body how he felt. He fought the primal need to spill himself within her, waiting for her satisfaction. At last Sara's fingers dug into his shoulders and she called out his name, her body stiffening in the way he remembered so well and had always craved so much. He gave himself up to velvet depths, his own satisfaction roaring through every inch of him, draining him of all that he was until he was totally blended with her.

As they had been meant to be.

SARA SLOWLY OPENED her eyes after the most incredible lovemaking she had ever experienced. Steve's body was heavy on hers. She closed her eyes again to savor the moment and push reality away for a few minutes longer. All the emptiness that had provoked their joining had been replaced with total contentment.

But reality crept back all too soon. She had allowed a moment of vulnerability to get to her—and had made herself more vulnerable in the process. Wanting to test her heart's emotion, yet not daring to, she admitted only to confusion.

Steve kissed her cheek. "I'm too heavy for you."

"No." She tightened her arms around his shoulders. As much as she was confused and didn't want to think, she also didn't want to lose the warmth and the closeness she had with him. Her body and mind had hungered for this for far too long not to keep it as long as she could.

Steve relaxed on top of her again, his weight, as it always had, deliciously pressing her into the mattress.

She wondered if they had made a little Michel. She wondered what she would do if they had. A baby would be the culmination of her quest, yet she would have achieved it without the essentials she felt were needed. To top it off, she would have made a baby with the man she'd least expected to. Could she truly trust him again for the long haul of a marriage?

Sara groaned as reality finally dug in a little deeper. What did she want?

"We're still under a truce," Steve whispered.

"What?" Sara gaped as he raised his head.

"We're still under a truce. This doesn't count."

She swallowed. Maybe their lovemaking hadn't been as soul satisfying for him as it had been for her. Maybe he had regrets of his own. "Okay."

His gaze searched hers for a long moment, then he lowered his mouth to hers. The kiss was as tender as the earlier ones had been fierce. Sara gave herself up to it.

After the kiss and all the unsaid things it betrayed, Steve rolled to his side, taking her with him.

Sara closed her eyes and let him hold her. She refused to think.

Eventually she fell asleep.

STEVE COULDN'T TELL what Sara was thinking.

Or feeling.

He wished he could. His life hinged on what her reaction would be to their lovemaking. He had insisted on
keeping the truce only because he hadn't been ready to
hear her ask for him to sign the divorce papers.

Sara lay nestled against him, like she had when they'd
lived together. He knew she was sleeping, her breath even
and regular. Skin on skin. *Mated,* he thought.

He remembered her nonsense about another man named
Mike. She had been prophetic; she had fallen for a Mike.
Little Michel had stolen his heart as well—and maybe
changed things between him and Sara.

The late afternoon sun filtered through the west windows' broken shutter slats. Steve felt no inclination to get
up. He grinned. He and Sara would have their days and
nights mixed up next.

Downstairs, the telephone rang. Steve raised his head
to listen to his answering machine, his only concession to
the disturbance.

The owner of the cleaning company was on the other
line.

"Where the hell are you and what the hell's going on?
I'm getting calls from clients that their places aren't being
cleaned. Ya'll want to get fired? Call me."

Steve cursed, wishing he didn't keep his machine's volume control on the highest notch. Maisie's emergency had
so occupied him that he'd forgotten work altogether.

Sara shifted onto her back, the call having wakened her.
"I think you're in trouble."

"Wouldn't be the first time." He smiled at her. "Feeling better?"

"Confused," she admitted.

"I'll take it." Confused was better than adamantly determined to have a divorce.

She rubbed her eyes. "What time is it?"

"After five."

Her eyes widened. "Wow. We've slept the afternoon away. Michel really wore us out."

"I like to think we helped wear ourselves out."

She glanced away, then back. "Steve—"

He kissed her, to stop what she would say. She firmed her lips for a moment, but he prevailed, and she eventually responded.

"Why do you have to be so good at that?" she asked, when the kiss ended.

"It's nice to know you think so," he said, chuckling.

She covered her face with her hands. "This was an aberration, you know."

"A *great* aberration." He couldn't let her get away with dismissing the ramifications of their lovemaking. "This changes everything."

She lowered her hands. "No. It doesn't. I was feeling sorry for myself and needed the closeness of another human being."

He bristled. "Are you saying I could have been Charles Manson and you would have made love to me?"

"Don't be ludicrous, silly and ridiculous," she snapped. "You aren't just a warm body, and you know it."

"I sure sound that way."

"I was vulnerable and I…we're comfortable sexually."

"More than comfortable. Very in tune. And that's not the only reason we wound up in bed."

A blush stained her cheeks. "I guess what I'm saying is that I responded to a moment. I'm sorry."

Steve's anger rose several more notches into the dangerous zone. He recognized, however, that how he responded could break any bond now between them. "Then why did you say you were confused before? That's not the automatic response for an 'aberration' or a momentary need fulfilled by a temporary body."

"You make it sound tawdry—"

"Me? You're the one calling it an aberration." He realized he was losing his temper again and reined it back in. "If it's just sex, then it shouldn't matter if it's tawdry. You want it to be more, but you're not willing to really accept that it is."

Her lip trembled slightly with emotion. "I am confused, aren't I?"

Steve felt as though he'd made some progress. "I don't think that's a bad thing. I'm starved. Let's go eat something and be confused together."

"All right," she conceded, in a very progressive move. "You should call your boss back, too."

"To hell with him." His job was the least of his worries.

They took separate showers, to Steve's disappointment. But he didn't want to push. Maisie was right about his mojo. His luck was changing. His *wanga* wasn't doing badly, either.

Halfway through his shower, it occurred to him that Sara could be packing her bags and running out on him once more. He raced through the rest of it, emerged almost rinsed and still half-damp from his cursory toweling.

"Sara!" he shouted the moment he opened the bathroom door.

"What?" she called back innocently and reassuringly from downstairs.

Steve sighed in relief. "Put on the coffee, will you please?"

"Already done."

"God love her," he murmured. "I do."

Maybe he hadn't told her yet, but he did love her. She was more than good-luck charms and making babies. He loved her, plain and simple. And Sara loved him still. He was banking on it.

He joined her in the kitchen. She sat at the table, a filled mug in front of her.

"Don't worry," she said. "I disinfected the table five times."

"I appreciate that, believe me." He got a mug from the cabinet and filled it with the coffee she'd made. "Seems too quiet without a screaming baby."

Max squalled from the living room.

"Thank you, Max," Steve said, grinning.

Sara grinned, too, when he sat at the table opposite her. "Spoke too soon."

"I forget we have Mr. Impression in the living room."

Max squawked a stream of obscenities.

"That's his Eddie Murphy," Steve added.

"He's diverse," Sara said, laughing.

Her amusement faded, but Steve saw its appearance as a good sign. At least she wasn't determined and confused. He took a sip of coffee.

"I think I should leave," Sara said.

Steve nearly spit out the coffee. "No, Sara."

"It figures that I would give up my hotel room too soon," she added.

"They were gouging you."

"Steve, how can I stay here? I was only staying because of Michel. It made sense for the situation and now the situation's changed."

"Yes, and that's why you should stay," he said.

"You're confused. What better way to get unconfused than to stay and work things through?"

She shook her head. "That's too dangerous."

"Dammit, I knew I should never have allowed you out of my bed."

She chuckled ruefully. "I knew I never should have gotten in it."

"But you did." He reached across the table and took her hand. "Leaving won't solve anything."

"I don't know that staying will." She sighed. "It's me. I'm too afraid to start over again. I told you, I just don't think I can go through a relationship with you, only to find we can't be together without destroying each other. I—I care too much."

"So you're going to give another man your leavings," he countered. "How fair is that to *him?* It's crappy, Sara."

She opened her mouth, then shut it. Her expression showed the dawning realization of the truth of what he'd said.

"There's another factor now," he said. "What if you're pregnant? We didn't use anything. We didn't even think about it. If you are, then it changes everything."

Again she didn't answer. Her eyes widened, however. Surely she'd known the possibility existed.

"You could be," he repeated. "And I would be the happiest man in the world, if you are."

"Thank you," she whispered, a catch of emotion in her voice.

"So stay here and we'll work it out, okay?" He smiled at her. "If you're pregnant, I'm not signing the papers. You can't expect me to give up my wife *and* my child. I've had a taste of life with baby. It wasn't bad."

"Oh, God." She began to laugh and cry at the same time. "I've really messed myself up."

He squeezed her fingers as she wiped away her tears with her free hand. "I think of it as serendipitous planning. Hell, I do it all the time now. So, will you stay with me and get to know your husband better before you dump him for the great unknown?"

"I shouldn't," she said slowly. "But I've made stupid choices so far when I've tried not to. Maybe I ought to deliberately make the biggest mistake of my life, and things might come out all right."

"That's the spirit," he said, undaunted, and kissed her hand.

"But I stay in the guest room. No more sex."

He gripped her hand. "How are we gonna learn anything if we're not reexperiencing *every* aspect of married life?"

"I think I need to make a rational decision, not an emotional one."

"Hell, woman, that's what marriage is. Emotional decisions on a daily basis." He saw her expression harden into stubborn lines. If he didn't back down, she'd be out the door. "Okay. But I'll use the guest room, not you. And no argument about that."

Her face became only a little less mulish. "All right."

"And I get to court you," he said. "I've been meaning to do that."

"Oh, Lord. What have I done?"

"Made the biggest mistake of your life," he said expansively. "What the hell, Sara. You married me to begin with, now let's eat. I'm starved."

He barbecued a couple of steaks he found buried in his freezer. They talked as they ate, the conversation mostly about Michel and how resilient he had been under their naive care. That kept the mood lighthearted for the rest of the evening.

Steve taught her how to polish shells, the patience involved amazing her. He had trouble keeping his libido under control. Every time he gazed at Sara, he wanted her. Occasionally, a look or a touch would heighten the underlying sensuality between them. But Steve ignored it, determined to do the right thing. Sara, if she knew his internal struggles, would say it was about time he stopped acting like Macho Man. A little sensitivity shouldn't kill him. He hoped.

About midnight, they climbed the stairs together to go to their separate beds. With every step, Steve reminded himself he was "courting" only.

At the top of the stairs, he said, "If you get too warm, just open a window. Don't worry about the shutters, they'll let in plenty of air."

"Okay," she said. "Good night."

This stinks, he thought, his baser nature getting the better of him for the moment. But he gathered his control, gave her a chaste kiss on the forehead and said a cheerful, "Good night."

When he turned away, she took his hand. He turned back.

"Thanks for being so understanding," she said.

He nodded, afraid he'd croak like a frog if he spoke.

She tugged on his hand, urging him down for her kiss. He reminded himself that it had to be a chaste one. Again. Her lips were soft and sweet, drugging him with the depth of the kiss.

When he eased away, she pulled him back, clearly intent on making another big mistake.

He wrapped her in his arms and happily let her.

Chapter Ten

Late morning light flooded Sara's senses. So did the naked male body against her equally naked back. Cool air coming through an open window fanned her skin as she lay next to Steve.

She opened her eyes, then closed them again. Dammit, she hadn't even lasted ten hours on her No Sex rule.

What if she was pregnant?

Sara's heart beat faster for a moment, before confusion stepped in. For someone who wanted a husband and marriage and a rose-covered cottage with her babies, she was way off course.

A voice inside reminded her that she already had a husband, and a marriage as well. And a cottage of sorts. Two. His moss-covered one here in Louisiana, and her condo back in Philadelphia. But that wasn't what she had planned for her future. Yet at one time her future had very much included babies with Steve.

He had asked her to work things out with him. Only she didn't know if they were workable. She doubted that they were, but she had to try. If she didn't, all her life she would wonder if she and Steve could have made marriage work the second time. He had been right, too, that she would be giving less to another man. She wouldn't be fair, something she hadn't thought possible until she came here to get her divorce papers signed. Steve had always been a good negotiator, making critical points at the right moment. She had grown enough to recognize the critical points he'd made with her.

As if he sensed her thoughts, Steve snuggled closer in his sleep, his arm tightening around her waist, his breath hot on her back.

Sara put her hand on his forearm, her fingers exploring the corded muscles. He was the same in many ways, yet different in others. She wished she could trust him completely again.... Maybe she asked too much of him to even try.

A door opened downstairs. Sara tensed. She shook Steve's arm. "Wake up. Someone's here."

"Wha...?" Steve raised his head sleepily.

Sara turned to face him. "Someone just opened a door—the back one, I think."

He frowned and listened. They both heard a door close.

"Hello!" Steve called out.

Sara was about to lecture him on the stupidity of calling out to murderers when Maisie called back, "Hello!"

Sara relaxed. Steve grinned at her, then called downstairs, "What are you doing here? I thought you'd be home with Michel, waiting for your daughter. How's she doing?"

"She's coming home tomorrow, for sure. Meantime, I figured this place needed some cleaning up. As soon as I get the baby settled, I'll get to it."

Sara and Steve bolted upright. "The baby!"

"Morning, Sara. I hear you up there. Yes, I brought the baby. What'd you think? I'm bringin' a frog?"

Sara whipped the covers off her even as Steve scrambled out of bed. They raced around the bedroom, gathering clothes.

"Those are my jeans!" she yelped, grabbing them from Steve.

"How the hell can you tell?" he asked.

"Are you wearing Lady Branded?" She showed him the patch on the back pocket.

"Only on my good days," he replied. He looked around the bedroom. "Dammit! If those are yours, then where did mine go?"

"I tossed them by the headboard, I think."

He laughed. "You were some wild woman."

She grinned, although she felt heat on her cheeks.

They were still doing the last of their buttoning and snapping while they tried to beat each other down the staircase. They skidded to a halt in front of Maisie.

"I thought I had a herd of elephants on a rampage coming at me," the housekeeper said when she spotted them. She held Michel, the object of their haste.

"She pushed me into the banister," Steve immediately complained.

"Did not, you big baby," Sara countered, and took Michel from his grandmother. His slight weight was satisfyingly sweet. She kissed his cheek. "I didn't get a chance to say goodbye to you yesterday, so I'm saying hello first."

Michel grinned, recognizing her. Sara was thrilled.

"Not fair," Steve said. "I'm the man. I should get him first."

Sara stuck out her tongue and blasted a juicy raspberry at her estranged and yet not estranged husband.

"You'll kill poor Michel with your morning breath," Steve said.

"Oh. Like you brushed."

"I'm sweeter any way you cut it." Steve reached for Michel and Sara gave the baby over. Steve kissed him on the other cheek. "Hey, big guy. How they hanging?"

"Steve!" Sara scolded, as Maisie howled with laughter.

"I have to correct all the mushy slobbering you just did," Steve said in his defense.

Sara giggled.

"Well, well," Maisie interrupted, eyeing them. "If you all don't make a pretty picture with my grandbaby. I won't ask what you're doing here, Sara, at ten in the morning. Your hair's lookin' like spikes and your shirt's buttoned wrong."

"Oh!" Sara blushed and ran her hands through her hair to settle it down. "The curse of morning short hair."

"Steve looks like he stuck his finger in a light socket."

"The blessing of making love to your wife all night long," Steve said, as Michel grabbed an unbound hank.

Sara flushed again. She had played with Steve's hair half the night, not to mention nearly yanking it out during certain climatic moments. Feeling guilty, she disentangled Michel's fingers from Steve's hair and smoothed it down in the back.

"Looks like my Love Chicken worked," Maisie said with satisfaction.

"It's not what it seems," Sara began.

Maisie raised her hand to stop her. "Don't spin anything on me, child. I know what my skills are."

"I'm not arguing with her," Steve said. "She might not let us play with the baby."

Sara made a zipping motion across her mouth.

"That's better," Maisie said. "Steve, you get the playpen out of my car, and Sara, you go clean up first."

"Yes, ma'am."

They handed the baby back to Maisie and did as she ordered.

Michel was as pleasant a baby as he could be when they were cleaned up and fed and finally allowed to play with him. He really was an angel, Sara thought in amusement, remembering Steve's "Evil Baby" comment.

She watched Steve challenge the baby to a peekaboo game. Michel gurgled and kicked his legs in delight. Steve would make a wonderful father, she admitted. Provided he didn't revert to the power-driven man he'd been.

Leopards couldn't change their spots and old dogs were incapable of learning new tricks. Did the old sayings have any validity? Could a man's nature change?

The questions ate at her.

Maisie called them over to Ruby's cage. "What's all this?"

Steve grinned. "I didn't want Ruby escaping while Michel was here. We just didn't know where he'd wind up, so we didn't take a chance he wouldn't do one of his escapes. I'll take it down now. He needs fresh water, anyway."

Maisie left him to it, returning to the kitchen.

Steve gave Michel to Sara. She sat down on the easy chair to watch Steve at work. She liked watching him do things. She always had.

Steve cursed as he unraveled the chicken wire. He never had been great with tools. His hands excelled with other things. Sara smiled, feeling extremely content. Michel leaned back against her.

Max, on his perch, sang his favorite song. "When the moon comes over Miami, I'll be a fool for you...."

Steve finally got the wire off the cage. He opened the door and turned the shells over, checking for the hermit crab.

"Uh-oh," he said, turning to Sara. "He got out."

She sat up straighter. "How could he? That thing is wrapped tighter than Fort Knox."

Steve looked helplessly at her. "I don't know."

Sara just started laughing. She couldn't help herself. "To think you used to run an entire division of over a hundred employees and now you can't keep one little hermit crab in its place. How the mighty have fallen, Michel."

Steve smiled. "I keep telling you that."

"Here chickie, chickie, chickie," Max called.

"No, Max. It's 'Here Ruby, Ruby, Ruby,'" Sara corrected.

"Polly wants a friggin' cracker," Max said, changing his tune, although not for the better.

"Lord knows where he's going with that one." Sara stood. "Come on, Michel. Let's go look for Ruby."

She carried the baby over to the shelves of shells. Remembering all too well her introduction to Ruby, she began turning them up cautiously with her free hand. Michel tried to grab the shells but she kept them just out of reach.

"Any luck?" Steve asked, joining her.

"Nope."

"Damn!" He started turning shells, too.

"I think you two better get in here," Maisie called from the kitchen.

Steve looked at Sara. Sara looked at Steve. He shrugged. They went into the kitchen.

Maisie had a small glass jar on the counter. In it was the missing hermit crab.

"What's Ruby doing in there?" Sara asked, while pointing the crab out to Michel. Not that the baby knew what he was looking at, but it was fun.

"I found him in the recycling basket," Maisie said. "I think he picked another pretty shell."

"An empty sweet-pickle jar?" Sara replied. She and Steve had finished the jar off at last night's dinner.

"I'd like to know how he got past the chicken-wire reinforcements in the first place," Steve said.

His telephone rang.

"I'll get it," Maisie said.

Sara studied the crab, which was all scrunched up and "hiding" inside. "Now I can see the back part of him. That's all soft, isn't it? But the rest of his body is a shell. How odd."

"The soft part's his lungs. Crabs use shells to protect that vulnerable portion," Steve explained.

Sara felt like Ruby, but with her vulnerable heart now exposed.

"It's for you," Maisie said to Steve.

As he took the call, Sara watched Ruby slowly emerge to investigate his surroundings. He walked with his front claws while dragging the jar behind him. It bumped along the counter.

"I'd hate to think what would happen if that jar broke," Sara said, not liking the fragile new shell for the crab's sake.

"But you can't get the silly thing out of it without pulling him apart, honey," Maisie said, putting him in the porcelain sink, where he couldn't get a purchase with his claws to climb out.

"Let's put him back in the cage then," Sara said. "He hates it there, so he'll escape again and leave the jar behind. Then we can throw it away or put the recycling bin someplace where he can't get another jar."

Maisie chuckled. "You've got a good brain on your shoulders."

Steve's voice rose, catching their attention. His face was flushed and he suddenly banged the receiver down hard on the wall phone.

He turned to face them, his jaw tight as if he was trying to control anger, then announced, "Well, ladies, you are looking at an unemployed man."

Sara and Maisie gasped together.

"He fired me and I quit. So much for good mojo."

"Now, don't you be blaming mojo," Maisie said.

"Steve!" Sara exclaimed, shocked.

"I never called him back from yesterday. I told him about Chloe's operation and having to help her. That I couldn't leave the baby, but he doesn't give a damn. His customers didn't get their rooms cleaned on time. That's all he cares about."

Sara stared at him, surprised by his outraged pronouncement. Never would she have expected to hear condemnation from him about a company's needs as opposed to an individual employee's.

"You shouldn't be fired for that," she said. "What about the other employees? You're management, aren't you? Shouldn't they have been cleaning the customers' places? Don't they have schedules to follow?"

"I have two people out sick," he said. "Or rather, I had. I was picking up their work until they came back."

Sara would have loved to have seen him with a vacuum and dust rag. When they'd been married, he, in typical male fashion, had thought the house magically cleaned itself.

"I'm sorry," Maisie said, her eyes tearing.

"Don't be ludicrous," Steve said, borrowing Sara's famous words. He put his arm around the older woman. "I would have lost a thousand jobs to help you. You helped me when I first came down here."

"I'll put a hex on that boss of yours," Maisie vowed. "I'll send his mojo straight into the gutter until he's begging you to come back."

Steve chuckled and hugged her. "Forget it. A junkyard dog would turn his nose up at that job. You wouldn't be doing me any favors to get it back. I hope you don't mind not getting paid for a while."

Maisie chuckled. "Honey, you never paid enough anyway."

"I know it."

The turn of events appalled Sara, yet she knew Steve's boss had every right under the law to fire him. Maisie's emergency wasn't a family hardship for Steve.

"What will you do now?" she asked.

He shrugged. "Who knows? But I'm not going to worry about it now."

His attitude was alien to her. Never had her Steve Johanson been laissez-faire about work and career.

Never.

STEVE WHISTLED as he packed the playpen back in Maisie's car for the evening.

"Sure you don't want to leave half this stuff for the next time you bring Michel?" he asked, when his now way-underpaid housekeeper came out with the baby and Sara.

"No, we'll need everything at Chloe's tomorrow," Maisie said.

"Damn, that's right. We won't see you two for a few days, will we?" he asked, but grinned.

Michel's own mother took precedence over him and Sara. Not that he was complaining—just missing the baby. However, the lack of interruption would give him and

Sara plenty of time to make one of their own. That was great compensation for not seeing Michel.

"Don't worry, I'll bring this muffin back," Maisie promised, settling Michel in the car seat. "I've made a dinner for you two. You have to go to the store, boy, you got nothing now. And I've left a few things in certain places in the house. Don't disturb them."

Maisie looked at him pointedly.

"What things?" Sara asked.

"I think the priestess is back at work," Steve said.

"Never you mind," Maisie told him sternly. "Don't forget to feed Max—"

"Like he lets me forget. Polly always wants a friggin' cracker."

"And keep an eye on that crazy crab!"

After her parting words, Maisie kissed him and Sara goodbye. They in turn kissed Michel, who gurgled happily at them. As Maisie's car pulled down the long drive, this time the baby left behind happy hearts at his departure.

"That dinner she made is Love Chicken," Steve said, having smelled it cooking earlier. "Let's go eat and get turned on."

"You're in a cheerful mood," Sara said.

"I'm not upset like before about Michel's going back home," he said, putting his arm around her waist and walking with her into the house. "I guess I knew all day that this was coming. After all, it is the kid's mom—"

"Steve, I didn't mean the baby. I meant you're very cheerful for someone who just lost his job."

"That was no job, believe me."

"Maybe not, but no one loses a job like that without anger or repercussions. What will you do? How will you live? Do you have a lot of money saved that you don't have to worry about working?"

"I'm flat broke and I don't know what I'll do, but I'll get by," he replied, shrugging. "Somehow. I've lost it all before."

When they were inside, he shut the door behind him and kissed her thoroughly. "Who needs Love Chicken when you've got the Love Man?"

"Oh, good Lord," Sara groaned, laughing. "That was awful."

"Not as smooth as I used to be, am I?"

"Not even close. First we'll eat and then we'll talk," she said.

"Can we have sex first, then eat, then talk?" Steve asked hopefully.

She smiled, raising his hopes higher. She started raising something else, too, until she said, "No."

He felt deflated on both counts. "You're no fun."

"So you've been telling me since I got here."

They put dinner on the table together, although Steve was still unhappy with the scheduled order of events. He preferred to handle the important business right away, namely getting Sara naked in his bed.

Damn, he thought, sitting across from her. He just loved knowing that was happening again for them. He had a chance now; he would not neglect it this time.

"I think you should talk to your boss," Sara said finally, after they were down to the picking and nibbling stage of dinner.

"That's the last thing I want to do."

She leaned forward. "Look, you have to try and work it out with him. Explain the emergency so he *will* understand. Persuasion is your best skill."

"In some cases." He grinned at her before sobering. "He won't understand. I should have arranged for everything to be covered, and I didn't. He's got a point on that.

On the other hand, he was a jerk about it, too. Ultimately, Sara, it's not a job worth fighting for.''

"Maybe not, but you've got to get a decent recommendation out of him, which you won't get if you don't smooth things over.''

"I could have been national employee of the year and this guy wouldn't give a good recommendation. At my level, it won't hurt me. You get down this low and nothing really does.''

"Steve, you're not going to build yourself back up *unless* you get a decent word from an old employer to a new one. You better think on that.''

Steve thought. "Valid point. I just don't care.''

Sara grimaced in exasperation. "This isn't like you, to be unambitious and uncaring.''

"I care," he said. "But I've learned what's important. Killing myself for a job isn't one of them.''

"Living on the streets isn't another?" she countered.

"It won't come to that." He reached out and took her hand. "Thank you.''

"For what?"

He rubbed her thumb gently. "Just for caring.''

She smiled a little. "I do care.''

"I know. Don't worry about me, Sara. I'm fine." He grinned. "In fact, I feel damn good at the moment. It must be the Love Chicken kicking in.''

He lifted her hand and kissed her fingers.

"Steve, we really need to talk—''

"We've talked already. And we've eaten. Now it's time for sex.''

"No, really. You have to make a plan for yourself.''

"I just made a plan for us. That's better than any plan for me." He rose and pulled her up into his embrace, kissing her thoroughly.

"Steve," she murmured after the kiss was over. Her tone was half pleasure and half frustration.

Steve kissed her again and again until her tone was all pleading and her body hungering for him, as his was for hers.

Now that, he thought, was exactly the help he needed.

THE NEXT MORNING, Steve filled the coffeemaker. He felt as if the strength had been poured out of his body just as the heated, brown liquid poured out of the coffee filter into the pot.

What a great feeling, he acknowledged with a tired grin.

"Good thing I'm not working," he said when Sara came down from her shower. "I don't have the strength for it. Thanks, honey."

He kissed her.

Sara blushed, but only held up a glass jar. "Ruby made a great escape again. I knew he'd let go of the jar if we put him back in the cage. I checked the shells on display but he's not in them."

"He probably found that new box of shells that came in yesterday. I'll look for him after breakfast." Steve brightened. "Hey! I'm not a total bum. I polish shells. Feel better now?"

She chuckled. "Oh, sure."

He put his mouth to her ear. "I'll be okay, Sara, as long as you're with me."

"I've been thinking about that," she said.

He sucked in his breath. "And...?"

"I'm going to help you get a new job."

Steve gaped at her. "What?"

Sara's gaze never wavered. Her brown eyes held all the trust in the world. "I said, I will help you get a new job.

First I'll talk to your boss. Then I'll talk to some people I know and come up with something good for you—''

"Hell, no!" he snapped, angry. "I'll do my own job hunting when I'm damn good and ready."

"And you have enough savings to do that?" she asked archly.

He had no resources between him and disaster, and he knew it. But he'd been living on the edge for a long time. He'd survive this further push toward the cliff. His ego couldn't handle Sara pulling him back from the brink. Truth to tell, he didn't know how far back he wanted to be pulled. His ambitions lay elsewhere than with a career.

"Sara, I'm okay," he said.

"No, you're not. Anyone who knows you can see that." She poured herself some coffee. "I am going to help you get back on your feet, Steve. Isn't that what you told me when I first got here? That you wanted our marriage back because I was some kind of good-luck charm that made you successful? Clearly, we're going to have to make some luck for you, to do it again."

Steve groaned. "You're more than that to me."

"And you're more than bad luck waiting for my cure."

She didn't budge from her position during breakfast or afterward.

"This is no way to rebuild a marriage," he said finally, accepting the stalemate.

"Neither is your being down-and-out in New Orleans," she replied.

"I live in Saint Sebastian," he corrected.

"I was close enough. Steve, you need your self-respect back, not to mention a means to eat."

"That batch of Love Chicken must have had a bone stuck in the wrong place," he grumbled.

Eventually, he gave her the number for his boss, figuring a chat with that clown would make her see how futile getting a "good" recommendation from the man would be.

"What a cretin," she said when she hung up.

Steve smiled in satisfaction. "I told you."

"But he did agree that circumstances were an emergency. He won't crucify you with a prospective employer."

"Wanna bet?" Steve muttered.

"We'll find out." She picked up the phone again.

He cursed under his breath and left her to her calls. If his mojo was better, then he was chief executive officer of General Motors, RJ Reynolds and Microsoft combined.

"She works hard for the money...." Max sang in the living room.

"Unfortunately, she does," Steve muttered in agreement. He looked for Ruby inside the new shells waiting to be polished and found him there. He had been escaping more than usual since Sara arrived. Ruby's wanderlust meant something; Steve just didn't know what. After settling Ruby back in the cage, he took Max from his perch and carried him outside. After setting the parrot on the outside perch, Steve sat down on the wicker chair. He put his feet up and closed his eyes.

The sounds of the distant highway reached him faintly, the cars and trucks roaring by from a half mile off. Closer, birds called to each other. A warm breeze rustled the Spanish moss on the trees. The scent of honeysuckle played with his senses. Everything was easy. Peaceful.

The pace of his life was more leisurely now. He appreciated things to which he had once paid no attention. He liked putting his feet up and listening to nature. He liked not worrying about clients and million-dollar deals. He liked worrying about babies. And Sara. He wanted time for things with her, time he wouldn't have if she "helped" him.

Sara came out onto the porch. "There you are."

"Boy, what a pair!" Max announced, giving a wolf whistle.

"What kind of bar was this degenerate in?" Sara asked. "A strip joint?"

"I think so," Steve said, opening his eyes.

"It figures. I have good news," she said, smiling with pleasure.

Steve felt his stomach drop.

"I talked with my company. Our personnel director knows a recruiter down here. She's calling her for me. And pulling a few favors. Isn't that great?"

"No. Sara, I don't want a headhunter," he said, using the business slang for recruiter. He straightened in his chair. "I don't need help finding a job."

"But I want to help you," she said, looking somber.

"I appreciate it. I truly do, but I'll be okay."

"Steve, how can you ask me to work out our marriage when you're not working at all? You need help I can give. I wouldn't feel right if I didn't. Not after we…not after we're trying to see if we can have a real marriage again."

Steve sighed. "Sara, I can take care of myself. And I can take care of you."

Even as he said the words, he knew the odds against him were growing on both counts. Renewing his marriage was nearly as precious as his unemployment. He wanted both for different reasons. And he was mired in the question of what he could offer her in the future. Right now, all he had was a mouthy parrot, four hermit crabs, one with a major roaming problem, and himself. In other words, nothing of material value.

But he didn't want to go back to his old life. Maybe

he was suffering from the worst case of career burnout in the entire annals of Western civilization, but he would not go back again to the corporate world. He'd lose her once more if he did.

"Steve, you will be taking care of yourself and me by getting your life back on track," Sara said. "I know it."

He knew, too. He knew she was wrong.

Chapter Eleven

"Thank God you still have a suit," Sara said, looking in Steve's closet.

"I should have thrown the damn thing out years ago," Steve said from the bed.

Sara turned. Her husband was lying naked on the mattress. Why did he have to look so damn sexy? She could easily have a job for him as her sex slave. No doubt he'd adapt to it like a duck to water.

"Steve, you've got an interview this afternoon," she said. "You've got to get dressed."

"Why?" He looked up and ran his forefinger along the curved molding of the headboard. "I've got time."

She sighed. "You're not helping. Okay, so this is for a middle-management, sales-rep job with a petroleum company. But it's a good start with a good salary." She frowned. "I think you should get a haircut."

"Oh, no. Hell, no!" he replied, sitting up. His hair fanned out around his shoulders. "They'll look past my hair or to hell with them."

Sara firmed her lips. If she didn't know better, she'd think he didn't want a job. But she did know better, and she knew he *needed* a job. Not just to survive but to thrive. And he needed a good one. No more of this marking time in a dead end. Steve must have a proper job again.

And she had to see if he really had changed. Only by him returning to his former corporate circumstances would she know if he truly was a different man. She had accepted every lure he'd held out to her, despite her misgivings. But she refused to be fooled into accepting their marriage again without really seeing him as he was. The same Steve or a different one.

She had to know.

"Sara, come back to bed," he said. He smiled and raised an eyebrow. "I'll do that thing with my tongue that you like so much."

Sara moaned.

"See? Even thinking about it makes you horny."

"Ah-h-h!"

"And screaming. Just imagine how you'll scream with delight when I actually *do* it."

She reached in his underwear drawer, got a pair of briefs and flung them at his head. "You're not that good. Now get dressed."

"Hey, so I need some practice—"

She rounded on him in exasperation, keeping her gaze on his face. "Steve, I went to a lot of trouble for you. Please don't do this."

She walked out of the room and downstairs. She did take a peek at his body before she left. She might be frustrated but she wasn't dead.

"Ugh, I'm turning into my mom," she muttered.

In the living room, Max squawked and rustled his feathers. "Take it off, baby! Take it off!"

"You're as dirty as the male upstairs," she said.

"Woo-wee, baby!"

She looked heavenward. But Steve was her main concern. She would have thought he'd jump at the chance to get into the corporate life again. Maybe he was nervous, she thought. Maybe he was afraid he'd be rejected. Maybe that was behind his reluctance to go to the interview. He'd been through some bad times, fallen way down the success ladder, if not right off the thing. She supposed it was harder to climb out of the hole than to fall into it in the first place.

"Sara? I'll get dressed and go to the interview," he called from upstairs.

"Good!" she shouted back, then smiled.

He was just nervous.

"When the moon comes over Miami, I'll be a fool for you," Max sang. It was his one sensible piece of advice.

"You just love that song, don't you?" she asked, stroking the parrot's back.

He reached his claw out and she allowed him to climb up to her shoulder. His feathers tickled her neck as he cuddled under her ear.

"Come on, baby, now. Twist and shout!" he sang.

Sara chuckled. Another horny male she had to contend with.

She looked at Ruby, now back in his cage. No doubt his containment was temporary.

"What a house," she said out loud, watching the crab cling, seemingly content, to the wire side.

She still marveled at Steve's living quarters. Eclectic was an understatement. Her place seemed so sterile next to it. Even the old house they'd had together lacked the liveliness here. She missed Michel, however. The baby added that special noise. Okay, at the top of his lungs. But his coos and oohs overshadowed the wails and yowls.

"*Brack!* Dinner!" Max announced, then started playing with her hair.

"Tell me I should be on the cover of *GQ*."

Sara rose slowly from looking at Ruby and turned to face Steve. She gave a wolf whistle. On her shoulder, Max did, too.

Steve did look great in the light brown suit and pale cream shirt, the last of his Armani wardrobe. He had matched a subdued, maroon brocade tie to his clothes. With his hair slicked back in a neat ponytail, he looked very much the corporate raider.

Sara wondered if his image was over the top. The job wasn't very high level.

Steve made a face at her. "I'm not saying a thing."

"That'll be a change," she murmured.

As she coaxed Max off her shoulder and back onto his perch, she wondered what she was doing with Steve. Why was she living with him now? Why was she trying to get him a job? Why hadn't she stuck to her original purpose in coming here?

The answer was easy. Too easy. She refused to examine it, nowhere near ready to do so. *Let it be,* she thought. Max hadn't sang that old Beatles tune yet, but it was apt for her and Steve.

"Okay," she said. "I'm ready to go."

Steve stared at her. "Why are you going?"

"For your moral support," she said, smiling. "If you're a good boy, I'll take you out to lunch afterward."

"Hot dog. There's a thrill."

"Stop moaning and come on. Your appointment's in less than an hour and you don't want to be late."

The heat, back after the cool front of the other day, whacked them both in the face as soon as they went outside. The air seemed motionless, hanging, dripping like the moss beards on the trees. All she needed was an alligator bellowing in the distance to cap off the soupy atmosphere.

"I'll melt before I get there," Steve said.

At least he was worried about his appearance, Sara acknowledged. That was a good sign. "Let's take my car. It's better than the truck."

"Forget it. Like the ponytail, the truck stays."

Sara smothered a groan. He intended to make one helluva mixed impression.

The oil company offices were attached to the refinery plant. They were stopped at the main gate by company security. Steve gave his name and his purpose for visiting.

"Who's she?" the guard asked, looking across Steve at Sara.

"My wife."

"Not on the list," the guard said, tapping his clipboard. "You can't go in, *chère*."

"The hell she can't," Steve snapped. "She doesn't go in, I don't go in."

"Oh, no," Sara said, opening the truck door and getting out. She knew he'd make a terrible impression if they had to call to get permission for Steve to bring the "wife" in on his interview. "You're going in. I'll wait here with the nice guard. Pick me up on the way out."

Steve glared at her when she walked around to his side of the truck. The guard chuckled and handed over an elastic cap that looked exactly like one for the shower.

"Long hair has to be covered 'cause it can pick up the oil in the air and catch on fire near a spark. You got to wear this as you travel through the plant to the offices."

"The hell I will!" Steve yelped, outraged. "Get back in the truck, Sara."

She leaned into his window. "Steve Johanson, you *will* go to that interview. You *will* wear the cap and you *will* cooperate on every level. I went to a lot of trouble for you, and you *will not* blow it.''

"Man, she's hard," the guard said, laughing.

"And *you*," Sara added to him, "will pass my husband through without further comment. I have had enough of this macho male nonsense."

"Good luck, pal. You're stuck with her now," Steve said, snapping the cap over the very top of his head. His ponytail hung out of the bottom in splendor as he drove off.

Sara leaned against the shady side of the guard hut, her back absorbing the heat of the wood walls.

"I think I'll go back to work," the guard mumbled, entering the hut. "You want a soda, *chère?*"

"That would be lovely," Sara replied. "Thank you."

The soda didn't help. As the minutes turned into an hour, then more, Sara felt as if she was roasting in an oven. Her head planned to explode at any moment, despite the two aspirins she eventually swallowed. The guard couldn't let her in the air-conditioned hut—regulations, he said; revenge, she surmised—but in a courtly gesture, he left the door open so the cool air could reach her. Unfortunately, not much did.

People stared at her as they entered and exited the plant. Sara felt like a two-bit hooker looking for business in desperate places. Moral support her backside, she admitted. She'd come to make sure Steve kept the interview, and this was her punishment. She hoped things were going great inside because it was going bad out here.

Steve finally pulled up at the gate. He wore the shower cap just on the ponytail itself. Sara shook her head in disgust. When had he turned into a comedian? Steve pulled off the cap and held it out to the guard.

"You keep it, *mon ami*. Our gift to you."

"What a company," Steve said, as Sara got in the truck. He floored the vehicle and sped away from the plant.

"So how did it go?" she asked, blessing the cool cab interior and ignoring the truck's rapidly rising speed.

"All right. Hell, it was an interview." He made a face. "I haven't been on one in years, and it was as humiliating as always. I hate them."

"Everyone does," Sara said. "Don't worry about that. Did they have any comment about you?"

"Only that they were doing a favor to Debbie to see me."

"That's not good." Debbie was the recruiter who was the friend of Sara's friend at work.

"Oh, that wasn't the bad part," Steve added. "They complained that I was overqualified and too long out of their kind of work and that I hadn't brought a résumé with me."

"Oh." She'd assumed he had one from before. She'd assumed he would bring it. Everyone in corporate America had a résumé, one's lifeline to the next job. "We'll make one up for you."

He grinned. "Hell, honey, I'm thrilled they were not thrilled. That place wasn't for me. I knew it as soon as I had to put on a shower cap just to go to a damn interview. You look wiped."

"I'm getting better," she said, her body reviving slightly in the car's air-conditioning. She waggled her clothes to get air under them.

"You're nuts," he said. "You know that?"

"Me?" Sara chuckled. "You're the nut. Well, not to worry. I have a few more interviews lined up for you. But not today."

"Sara—"

"I'm not feeling so good again," she said, forestalling any argument.

She leaned her head back and closed her eyes.

She'd whip him into shape yet.

STEVE TOOK THE PHONE CALL late that afternoon.

"Steve Johanson?"

"Yes?" he replied cautiously, wondering if it was a creditor. Not that he owed much and not that he'd missed any payments yet, but those guys were sharks sometimes.

"This is Debbie, the recruiter. George Budreau, the sales manager at Ship Oil, called me. He liked what he saw of you today, and so the job's yours. He thinks you'll move up quickly."

Steve gaped at the receiver. He couldn't believe he'd heard right. He'd had a better interview for his paperboy job, twenty-five years ago.

"I appreciate that," he finally said.

Panic shot through him at the thought of the job. The whole place had scraped his insides raw, starting with the stupid cap and having to leave Sara at the gate. He'd hated the confining office walls, the negative tone of the personnel director, and George Budreau hadn't been any better. Steve had shown his dislike, too. He knew he had. Why he'd been offered the job was beyond him.

But taking it, going back into the life again...

He couldn't.

He glanced around the corner of the kitchen. Sara was napping on the couch. She had been since they'd returned from lunch, and he hoped she still was.

"I'm sorry, but I've got to decline the job," Steve said, trying to keep his voice normal for the recruiter, but too low for Sara's ears. "I would be moving in another direction as soon as an opportunity came up, and that wouldn't be fair to them.''

"Oh," she said, annoyance clear in her voice. "I'll tell George."

She hung up without saying goodbye.

"And that's why I wouldn't work for any of you people," Steve murmured, hanging up the phone.

He felt good, though, at doing the right thing for himself. No matter how one sliced it, that job was *not* for him. Sara, however, would have something else to say. If she knew.

He strolled out to the living room, hoping he looked as nonchalant as he prayed he did. Sara lay on the sofa, her eyes closed.

"Who was on the phone?" she asked, not moving.

"Solicitor." Not a lie. He had been solicited to take a job. Steve knelt down and stroked her forehead. "Still have a headache?"

"Not really. Just lying here listening to Max ruffle his feathers and Ruby claw at his cage. Did he get loose again? I didn't feel like getting up to look."

"No. He's still hanging."

"I think the baby crabs are up. I heard something clunk in the dining room."

"One of them probably fell off the log. You're not opening your eyes." He kissed her nose. "Why not?"

"I have no clue."

"What are you thinking about?"

"Why I'm here."

"Any conclusions?" he asked softly.

"No. Yes." She smiled slightly. "I'm in it for the sex."

Steve laughed. He ran his hand over her breast.

Sara opened one eye. "You will go on the other interviews, won't you?"

Steve paused. Had she heard him turn down the oil company job? "Is sex contingent on my going?"

Sara opened the other eye. "I've never bargained like that."

"I know. Yes, I'll go." But he wouldn't like it. He ran his hand over her other breast. "Now, where were we?"

"YOU DON'T HAVE a résumé?"

"Nah," Steve replied to the personnel manager's question.

Frowning, the woman eyed him critically. Banks liked prim and proper employees. Steve knew he had been too cooperative in the last interview. Maybe that was why he'd been offered the job.

With that in mind, he deliberately slouched in the chair. He stared insolently at the manager and poked a finger in his ear. He reamed his appendage for good measure. Having finished his ablutions, he smiled at the woman.

She blinked, clearly astonished at her interviewee's lack of manners. Lack of written history bothered her, too, for she said, "I would have thought you'd have a résumé with your background. Or was I told wrong about that?"

He hadn't gotten around to doing a résumé yet, so he recited, "Summa cum laude from the Wharton School for Business Management…sales manager for the northeast region of ABM Computers when I was twenty-four…third executive vice president of RMX Peripherals at thirty." Steve paused. "Yeah, that's it."

He loosened his tie, scratched his head until some hair pulled out from its band, and cleared his throat loudly, as if he were about to expectorate onto the mauve carpet. If

Sara saw him now, she'd kill him. Steve grinned at the irony. He was only doing this for her, after all.

"This opening is for a regional coordinations officer," the manager said. "Banks have to sell themselves now, too. Your duties would include traveling the southeastern United States—"

"I hate travel," Steve said. "It cuts into my free time."

"You'd also oversee the sales staff and advertising—"

"I think advertising a total waste of time."

"And you would oversee marketing our services to their utmost potential."

"A bank is a bank is a bank," Steve commented. "Hell, advertising won't make a damn difference. People just use the one closest to their house."

The woman gaped at him, frozen, as if he'd turned into a male gorgon. Deciding to help the thought along, he took the black band holding back the ponytail and shook his hair free.

"Damn thing was annoying the hell out of me."

The woman stood and put out her hand. "Thank you for coming, Mr. Johanson. We'll let you know."

"Yeah, sure," he said, and gave her hand a single shake. He grinned wryly at her. "Thanks."

Outside, he whistled happily. That interview had gone down the tubes faster than a nuclear torpedo.

He only hoped the details didn't get back to Sara. How could they?

He wished he hadn't had to go through the farce at all. He'd tried to reason with her last night that this was no longer his way, but she had been adamant. She was corporate now, and she didn't understand that he couldn't handle it. While he was touched by her caring, he was frustrated by her insistence. Finally, he'd decided that the best way to handle her "help" was to go like a lamb to the interview, then sabotage it. Maybe it wasn't honest, but it was efficient. He'd find the right thing for himself eventually. He wanted to support marriage and family, but not at his own expense. He had done that once. Never again.

He remembered how, when Sara had arrived in Louisiana, he'd thought she was his good-luck charm, his return to success. He knew now he measured success differently than he had before. Success now was making Sara happy. Going on the interviews made her happy. Sabotaging them satisfied him. It was a nice compromise.

"How did it go?" Sara asked him when he got home.

"Very well," he said honestly. From his point of view it had.

"Good." She smiled.

"But I don't think I'll get the job," he told her.

Her expression fell. "You don't?"

"Too long out of that kind of work, for one thing. They weren't happy about that." He got a beer from the refrigerator and opened it. The first sip of the yeasty nectar soothed his dry throat.

Sara sighed. "I was really hoping that wouldn't be too much of a problem. Everyone's been downsized like mad, so big gaps in employment aren't unusual nowadays. My friend at home says that's playing less of a role, with jobs opening up the way they are."

"Well, it did in this one," he said, guilt riding him a little. He shouldn't lie to her. "Sara, you know I've told you this is not what I want."

She firmed her lips. "It's only a temporary solution if you want something else. I never meant it to be more, okay? But you were happy before when you were at RMX. Don't say you weren't."

"I was a fool before. And you hated it. How can you ask me to go back into that life?"

"Because I think you don't know what you want, and this will help you define it."

"I want you. I want to make babies with you." He grinned. "I'd be a helluva kept man."

Sara laughed. "You wouldn't last a week."

"Hey, I was doing good with Michel. There you go! You have the babies, and I'll take care of them. If male seahorses can do it, why can't I? Now there's a job for life."

"We couldn't even do it together with Michel!"

"We were new at it, that's all. I bet by the third or fourth kid, I'd have it down to a science." He liked the idea.

Sara just chuckled. "You would be bored out of your skull in ten minutes."

"Try me."

"Steve…"

"Okay, I'm rushing things again." He'd pushed enough, and he was only half teasing as it was. Yet the idea had a special lure to it. He'd love to be focused on Sara and children. He'd be flying in the face of convention. The world wasn't nearly as progressive as it thought it was.

"Steve, we need to talk about something else," she said, taking his hand and urging him to sit down at the kitchen table.

"I don't like this," he said, before swallowing a bracing gulp of beer.

"I don't, either." She gazed at him. "My vacation time is almost up. I have to go home."

"No," he said, his stomach lurching. "Stay with me."

"I can't—"

"I thought we were trying to rebuild a marriage. I thought we were doing great the last few days. Are you telling me that's already over?"

"No." She squeezed his fingers. "I'm not explaining this right. It's got nothing to do with our relationship. It's just…logistics. My job's in Philadelphia. So are my parents and my family. I have to have a job, Steve. How far would we get in a marriage if we're both unemployed? I still want to try. If we're strong and committed to each other, the separations won't matter."

"Can't you get a transfer down here?" he asked.

"We don't have offices down here. Besides, I'm a Northern girl. This heat's making me wilt already."

"Then if your future is North, why am I looking for a job in New Orleans?" he asked in frustration.

"I won't feel right asking you to leave your life here."

He laughed. "What life?"

She grinned wryly. "You've got a point."

The only thing was Steve wasn't sure how much he wanted to go back. Maybe the old surroundings would draw him into his old life again.

Yet letting Sara go home scared the bejesus out of him. If she got home and changed her mind… He refused to think about it.

"I can't let you go home," he said. "We haven't had nearly enough time together."

"Steve, I have to go. I have my job."

"You sound just like I used to."

She laughed ruefully and shook her head. "Steve, you wouldn't have even come looking for me like I did you. The job would have meant more."

She had a point. Suddenly, he knew what would make him feel better about her having to leave. And her feel better about it, too. "Tear up the divorce papers."

Sara sat back, his demand taking her by surprise. "What?"

"We'll tear up the divorce papers," he repeated. "At least let's make it clear to each other that we *are* committed to fixing our marriage."

"I see your point," she said slowly.

"You sound like you're going in for oral surgery," he said, disappointed with her attitude. "I love you, and I want to stay married to you. Don't you feel the same?"

"You hadn't said the words yet," she whispered, tears filling her eyes.

Steve frowned. "Of course I did."

"No. I know. I was never sure if I was just a reconquest of a failure for you, so I've been waiting to see if you would say you love me. I've needed to hear it."

He tried to think back on their time together. He had to have told her he loved her. It seemed so obvious to him. "Hell. How could you not know when I'm talking about our marriage all the time? Or when I'm making love to you? I guess I'm a stupid man."

"And I'm a not-so-bright woman."

"Do you love me?" he asked, wondering just how stupid he might be.

Sara drew in a deep breath. "Yes."

He smiled and relaxed. "Boy, I was hoping you did."

She grinned at him, then grew serious. "Steve, we have a long way to go."

"I know that. But what if you get home and decide you want out again?"

"What if you do?"

"I won't. This all hinges on you, Sara." He grimaced. "Burn the papers. At least I'll feel like we're starting things right."

She nodded.

"Go get them."

Sara went to retrieve the divorce papers, while Steve took matches from a kitchen drawer. When she came back, he put the papers he hated so much in the sink.

He lit a match, and when the flame was bright and glowing, he dropped it on the papers that had threatened to dissolve his marriage. He drew Sara close to him, and they watched together as the papers caught flame and burned to ashes. He turned on the water and rinsed the residue away until the sink was clear again.

"Here's to a second chance at our marriage, and having a family and an old age together," he said. "I love you, Sara."

She looked up at him. "I love you, Steve."

They sealed their vow with a kiss.

Chapter Twelve

"Damn, I'll never get through this."

Sara cursed again as the long line of passengers snaked across the airline terminal check-in area.

"No problem," Steve said. "Just stay."

Sara half laughed and half cried, wishing she could. She wasn't wealthy and he certainly wasn't, so they could hardly chuck life and make love all day.

Though it did sound wonderful.

"You're driving me nuts," she said.

"I know, but I'm hopeful." He gazed around. "Hell, everyone must be leaving New Orleans at the same time. Wait here."

He left her with her bags and talked to a skycap.

Sara shivered, although the day was hot. She was frightened to leave Steve. Despite her brave words, how could their relationship survive even a short separation? It was so fragile even when they were together.

What if he took one of the jobs down here? What if he wanted to stay in the South? She loved her job and didn't want to leave it. Would they be right back where they'd started? What if she had helped him too well? The questions had haunted her ever since she'd realized she was out of vacation time and had to leave.

When Steve returned, he said, "You've got your ticket, so you can check in with the security outside. He says this is for people who need changes in their tickets. A flight got canceled and that's why it's so bad."

"I hope it's not my flight," she said. She should have called about the flight's departure time before they left his house.

"I checked." He chuckled. "It's not." He looked at her somberly. "Sure you want to go?"

"No," she said. "But I have to. Steve, if we're meant to be together, then this won't matter."

He nodded and rubbed her back. "I've been casting a lot of things to the winds in the last few years, but you're not one of them. I'll make sure this won't matter. Be prepared to be courted long-distance."

"If I know you, I'll be bombarded long-distance," she replied.

"I'm no fool. I'll run with whatever works," he said. Then added, "We'll be okay."

"We will be." She knew she sounded as scared as he.

"I'll drive up in a few weeks," he said.

"I hope the truck makes it."

"It will, even if I have to push it to Philly."

"I'll come down and help."

He glanced at his watch. "You've only got an hour before the flight leaves."

"Oh, Lord." She hated this. Earlier, she had said good-bye to Maisie and Michel. Maisie had given her a gift and mumbled some things—a blessing, she'd called it. Sara didn't want to know. Michel had just gurgled.

"Don't go," Steve murmured.

She pressed her face into his shirt and whispered, "I have to."

He rubbed her arms. "I know."

When she regained control of her emotions, they walked to the security gate. Sara set off the metal-detector alarm.

Steve laughed. "We know who's got the money in the family now."

"Great," she muttered, taking off her earrings, necklace and bracelet. Wanting to look her best, she had worn a lot of silver jewelry with the blue, sleeveless vest and flowing skirt. She'd never given detectors a thought. Now that was dumb, she admitted.

The woman guard ran the detector wand over Sara's form. The alarm didn't go off, but the woman touched the small leather pouch nestled between Sara's breasts.

"Someone made you a powerful charm," she said.

"Oh." Sara touched the pouch, remembering Maisie's admonition when she'd given it to her as they said goodbye, insisting that Sara wear it. "I'm not a great flyer and a friend said this would help."

The guard laughed. "Did she?"

Sara turned to Steve, who had just come through the detector without a peep from man or machine. She frowned. "That is what Maisie said. That it was for flying, right?"

"Hell, I never ask what she's doing. I only do what she says."

"You're a smart man," the guard said. "Someone powerful made that. I can feel it."

"It is for flying, right?" Sara asked the guard, wondering what the heck Maisie had hung around her neck.

"Flying and more."

The guard moved to the next passenger coming through the detector.

"What do you suppose she meant?" Sara asked, as

Steve handed over her purse and picked up her carry-on from the baggage scanner.

Steve shrugged. "Who knows?"

"Maybe I should take it off."

She moved to lift the fetish from around her neck, but he stopped her.

"Leave it," he said. "I trust Maisie, and I feel better knowing you've got it on."

"All right." He did have a point. Maisie would only ask her to wear something she felt was useful, not harmful.

They got her checked in at her gate, then sat together and waited. The area was full, indicating a booked flight. Steve didn't say much. Neither did Sara. His thumb caressed her fingers as they held hands. A lump of unshed tears clogged her throat.

"You'll go on that last interview tomorrow," Sara said finally.

Steve glanced at her. "Hell, no."

"Yes, you will." She bristled. At least her unhappiness faded, although frustration wasn't much better. "My friend went to a lot of trouble to arrange this for you. Steve, you have to have a job. How can you not?"

"Easy." He grinned at her.

"This isn't like you," she said.

"That's the point I've been trying to make."

"You've just been down on your luck so long you're afraid to try and come out of it."

"But why should I get a job in the South when you're going North?"

"Because you need to restart your career. If this works out, you can come up North then."

"If it works out down here, then why am I coming up North?" he asked. "Your logic is skewed, girl."

"You'll *transfer* or move on after a year or so, but you'll have a career foundation upon which to build. Geez, Steve, you should understand that more than most people."

"Passengers with tickets in rows thirty-six through twenty, please board now for Flight 874 to Philadelphia."

Steve cursed.

Sara smothered a whimper of pain. She was in row twenty-two. "I have to go."

"I know."

He walked with her to the jetway, as far as he was allowed. They waited until all the passengers went down the ramp at the last call. Steve faced her, then kissed her so thoroughly they held up the closing of the gate door for a full five minutes. Sara clung to Steve, feeling as though she would board the plane and this lovely dream would be over.

"Please," a steward said, tapping them each on the shoulder. "You've got to board the flight now."

Sara nodded. Steve let her go. He gazed deeply into her eyes, then kissed her ring finger, still missing her wedding band.

"I'll be up in a few weeks," he said.

She nodded.

Somehow she got on the plane and found her row. Her whole body hurt as she stowed her purse and carry-on. She sat down. Her seatmates, two women, smiled at her. She tried smiling back. It was useless.

Every bone in her body screamed for her to get off the plane, to go back to Steve. Yet she knew this separation was like a test they both had to pass. They had to be sure of each other. *She* needed to be sure. Was that too much to ask?

The plane rolled back from the gate and toward the runway.

When it lifted into the air, Sara burst into tears.

"Damn," she murmured, horrified by her display.

A pack of tissues was pressed into her hands. Sara looked up to find the woman next to her smiling sympathetically.

"My book couldn't have been that bad," the woman said.

Belatedly, Sara realized it was one of the romance writers from the hotel, the one who had given her a book that night Steve had escorted her back and handed her his ultimatum. "I'm sorry."

"It was that bad?" Her seatmate's expression was crestfallen.

"Oh, no." Sara chuckled despite herself. "I haven't read it yet. I was apologizing for blubbering all over you. Here." She held out the rest of the tissues, after taking one from the pack.

"Keep it," the woman said. "It's a relief to know *Doctor Valentine* still has a chance, although that hunk you were with at the gate would give all my Holiday cousins a run for their money."

"Oh, that was my husband."

"Lucky girl. I'd cry, too, if I had to leave a guy like him."

"That's the problem."

Somehow, Sara found herself telling the writer about her situation. The woman listened to it all, giving only an encouraging comment or two.

"I'm sorry," Sara apologized again. "I've dumped on you and that wasn't fair."

"Hey, I'll do anything to make a sale," the woman

said, grinning. "Actually, writers are good listeners. We never know where our ideas will come from."

"Oh, wonderful. Now I'll be in a book."

The woman laughed. "And me risk being sued? I don't think so."

It occurred to Sara that this woman might know a lot more about love than most people. After all, she wrote about the emotion every day.

"Am I being dumb?" Sara asked.

"About your husband?" The woman shrugged. "It's hard to say. I write about people following their hearts. Maybe that's what you need to do. Maybe you're already doing that."

Sara didn't know if she was or not, but she wondered if the writer was right. But wouldn't her heart make her go back to Steve, rather than return home?

To HER SURPRISE, her mother met her at the arrival gate in Philadelphia.

"Hi," Sara said, kissing her cheek. "Where'd you come from?"

"Just hanging out. Your dad sends his love. He's got an early appointment tomorrow or he'd be here, too." Her mother hugged her. "Did you have a good flight?"

"Other than crying on some poor woman's shoulder, yes."

"You didn't."

Sara grimaced. "I did, and it wasn't because I was afraid of flying. What are you doing here?"

"Giving you a lift home." Her mother grinned. "Steve called and told me when you would be in."

"I would have gotten the shuttle."

"Yes, but this is so much nicer of me."

"Why do I feel like I'm about to be pumped for every guilty detail?"

"Because you are. If you can tell a perfect stranger, you can tell me. I'm your mother."

"Telling perfect strangers is easier. They're nonjudgmental."

"I promise to judge only a little bit."

"I'm sure Custer said that to Sitting Bull right before the Little Big Horn."

"Sitting Bull won, dear. You never did manage more than a *C* in history. Come on, let's get your bags."

Sara was whisked along by her mother. Despite knowing where her parent would side on the matter of Steve, she felt better in her presence. As they walked, Sara talked. Her mother listened nearly as well as the romance writer on the plane.

"I think you did right to come home," Marj said.

"You do?" Sara gaped. "I would have thought you'd want me to stay with Steve."

"I do, ultimately. But you've gotten back together with him, to try again. That's all I ever truly wanted. The separation will not crumble a good foundation."

"Damn, but I wish I had a tape recorder," Sara said. "I don't believe the total reversal by my mother."

"I'm not reversing myself," Marj said, sniffing at the notion. "I've always felt you two didn't give the marriage a chance the first time. Now you are, and I think it's good that you recognize what I've always seen."

"That's a real nifty way of saying I told you so," Sara said.

"I'm glad you appreciate it. Now tell me how you did with the baby. Was it so bad you've sworn off giving me grandchildren?"

"No." Sara laughed.

She felt much, much better by the time her mother dropped her on her doorstep. Sara propped the feather mask Steve had bought her on her mantel, once she settled into her condo. She called Steve. The moment she heard his voice, however, she wanted to get on the next plane back to New Orleans.

"I miss you," he said.

"I miss you." She swallowed around a lump of emotion. Pulling herself together, no easy feat, she asked, "How's Maisie and her daughter? How's Michel?"

"Fine, so far as I know." He chuckled. "I think Max misses you, too. He doesn't want a 'friggin' cracker.' And he won't sing."

Sara grinned. "I bet you're hopping mad about that."

"I'm crying in my beer." He paused. "Actually, I am. Why are you there and I'm here?"

"Because we're being sensible about this and going slowly," she replied. "I hate sensible and slow."

"Not as much as me."

Sara sighed. Maybe this was all wrong. Maybe she ought to chuck everything and go back right now.

Unfortunately, sensible and slow, the *S* and *S* twins, prevailed.

Sara trudged into her office the next morning, not off some plane in New Orleans. The gray Philadelphia day didn't add to her mood. Neither did the mountain of paperwork on her desk.

She cursed as she glanced through it. Correspondence, computer printouts, buyer memos and other items demanded her attention. Only her attention was more than a thousand miles away.

She had come home in the same condition she'd left—married...without children. But with hopeful prospects.

Hopeful in an entirely different way, she admitted. She drew in a deep breath. Steve and she *would* work out. They would put their past behind them and move on to the future. Together. She had to believe that.

Her "hopeful" attitude allowed her to tackle work with a good heart. About midafternoon, she ran into Barbara, her company's personnel director, who had arranged for her recruiter friend to work with Steve on prospective jobs.

"Thanks again for helping out my husband," Sara said, wanting to thank her in person. She'd already done so over the phone from New Orleans.

"Why?" Barbara asked, her tone tinged with sarcasm and her expression far from pleased. "My headhunter friend told me this morning that your husband turned down one of the jobs. He acted like a pig and a jerk in another interview and he didn't show up for the one he had today. She's ticked and won't do me any more favors. And I'm ticked, too, for having my time wasted. What the hell were you doing down there, Sara? Trying to get *my* job?"

Sara gaped at the woman, shocked by her words. "No! My God, but it's impossible. Steve couldn't have done that."

"I'm hardly a liar, Sara." Barbara snorted in disgust and walked away.

Sara caught up to the woman. "Barbara, I'm sorry, but I have no idea what you're talking about. Steve went on two interviews while I was there. I even went with him for one. He wasn't offered any job, believe me. And he told me last night on the phone that he was going to to-day's. He couldn't have canceled it. Your friend must have gotten it wrong."

"I doubt that," Barbara said. "She went to a lot of

trouble to arrange those interviews and talk him up. She said she really had to compensate with the companies, because of his recent work record. She got complaints from all three personnel people about him. I don't know what went on down there, Sara, but my friend—my *former* friend—and I got zapped."

Barbara went into her office. Sara just stood in the hallway, stunned and confused. Some kind of wild mix-up must have happened down there.

She went back to her office and called Steve. His answering machine picked up, but he never did. She rummaged around in her purse until she found the business card from Barbara's recruiter friend. She called and talked to the woman. When she hung up, she had a much clearer picture of things.

There had been no mistake.

"I'll kill him," Sara exclaimed, furious with the headhunter's detailed information. Steve had made them all look foolish.

She called and called him, but only got the damnable machine. She wanted to take a bat to the thing. Steve's message, "Hi! I assume you know how to use this, so leave a message at the beep!" now bordered on insolent.

What the hell was he doing down there? Why had he made a mockery out of what she'd done for him? Especially after she'd gone to bed with him!

She had fallen in love with him all over again, and he had given her the figurative slap in the face once more.

Steve never did answer his phone. She tried getting Maisie's number from information. New Orleans, Saint Sebastian and surrounding parishes had about eighty million Tippedeaux listed but none with the additional first name of Maisie.

By the time Sara crawled into bed that night, a numbed

anger had taken hold of her insides. Steve had humiliated her with her co-workers. He had treated her help with disdain. Worse, he had trampled over all that was important to her. Once again.

He hadn't changed. He had probably felt embarrassed in that macho male way that she had gotten him interviews he could no longer acquire himself. But that was no excuse. She should never have trusted him again. Never.

But she had. Now it hurt worse than the day she'd walked out of her marriage. She never should have walked back in again. The moment she'd seen him, she should have twisted those divorce papers around his neck until he had signed the damn things.

Her doorbell rang. Sara glanced at her clock. It was after eleven. When the bell rang again, she got out of bed, her treacherous husband temporarily forgotten. Probably it was some nut, but on the off chance it wasn't...

Using caution, she peeked through the door's security peephole. Throwing caution to Hades and back, she flung it wide open.

Steve stood there, in the flesh. He held a small cage containing Max in one hand and a smaller mesh cage containing the hermit crabs in the other. He had a big grin on his face.

"Hi, honey, I'm home," he announced.

"You bastard!" she snapped, and slammed the door in his face.

STEVE STARED at Sara's front door, feeling like a man who had just met his wife's hitherto unknown evil twin.

"Hey!" he shouted through the vinyl-covered, made-to-look-like-oak, steel portal. "I drove all night and day to get here."

"Drive the hell back right now."

Something was definitely wrong with his wife, evil twins notwithstanding. This was not the same Sara he had put on the airplane yesterday. That Sara had been clinging and declaring her love for him.

What a difference a day made.

"Sara, what's wrong?" Steve shivered in the night air, far cooler than Louisiana's gulf breezes. He wasn't used to the northern version of spring, and a cold spring it was, too.

"You're a bastard. That's what's wrong." Her voice was faint, but clear.

"What did I do?"

"You lied and humiliated me and made me into the world's biggest fool."

"Uh-oh," Steve muttered, wondering how she had found out that he'd canceled that interview scheduled for today. "Honey, I'm sorry about today's interview, but I couldn't stand being away from you. Let me in and let's talk. Max is cold, not to mention the crabs."

"Turn the heat on in the truck on your way home to Saint Sebastian. And I know about that job you turned down, and how you sabotaged another. You haven't changed, Steve. You're as arrogant as you ever were."

He muttered a barnyard curse. Someone must have talked a lot.

"I can explain, Sara."

"Go away before I call the cops!"

"Sara…Sara!"

Max squawked and ruffled his feathers, puffing them up to keep warm. Steve called out a few more times, but Sara didn't answer. He considered his options.

He could keep calling until the cops did come. Then she would have to open the door and maybe he could elude the police, get inside and straighten this out with her.

Or, since his hands were occupied with pet carriers, he could kick the door down. Again, he would probably have to elude cops, but he would have the advantage of talking to her uninterrupted first.

Or he could walk away tonight, allow her a little time for cooling off and then straighten things out.

The last option seemed the most sensible.

He chose number two anyway.

Steve kicked the door with all his might, the sole of his foot squarely hitting the overlaid steel right above the latch.

He yelped in agony as horrible pain shot straight up his leg and into his brain. The door, on the other hand, never budged.

"Au secours! Au secours!" Max screeched loudly, startled by the attempted door breaking. The crabs rustled in the mesh cage.

"Sara! Open the damn door!" Steve shouted.

No answer.

Lights flicked on at nearby condos. Steve knew that in a matter of minutes he'd be caught up in a "domestic dispute" with the law. There would be no going back after that.

He now chose discretion, option number three, over stupidity, option number two, and returned to his truck. Better late than never.

A string of curses, all his own, accompanied his starting the vehicle and driving out of the condominium's parking lot. Max gleefully matched him curse for curse.

Anger and bewilderment seethed inside Steve. After their emotional farewell, he had gone home and realized he had no home without Sara. After their phone talk last night, he couldn't stand being away from her. No marriage could survive separation for long, and he wasn't about to lose what he had regained. So he'd driven over a thousand miles in less than twenty-four hours to be with her again. Instead of the hero's welcome he'd been expecting, he'd gotten the emotional pie in the face.

Okay, so she had found out about the interviews and the job. He'd tried to tell her more than once that his former life was no longer for him. She hadn't listened. If she had, none of this would have happened, but what else could he have done? She wasn't listening now, either.

Steve drove around a bit, not sure what to do. He had about twenty bucks in his pocket and nowhere to go. The area eventually looked familiar, and Steve realized he was near Sara's parents' house. He drove there and knocked on the door.

The house didn't look any different, Steve thought. The rhododendrons and azaleas still competed for space in the front garden. Steve hoped the reception would still be the same.

Sara's father answered, the man's mouth forming an O of astonishment at finding his estranged son-in-law on his doorstep at midnight.

"Hi, Bob," Steve said. "Got a spare room I can borrow for a while?"

"Hell, Steve." Bob Carter started laughing, then wrapped Steve in a bear hug. "Where'd you come from? Marj! It's Steve!"

Sara's mother wrapped Steve in another hug. "Steve. My God! What are you doing here?"

"It's a long story. And a long drive," he said. "Can I come in?"

"Of course, of course."

Steve started across the threshold, then turned around. "I forgot a few friends."

He retrieved Max and the hermit crabs from the truck.

"Hello, baby!" Max shouted, then made kissing noises as they passed Sara's mother.

"He's cute," Marj said, eyeing the bird, who eyed her back through the bars of his temporary cage. Steve set it on the coffee table and opened the cage door.

"Don't worry," he said. "Max's wings are clipped so he can't fly. But he's been cooped up in there since we left Saint Sebastian."

"Shake it up, baby! Twist and shout!"

"I see his point," Sara's father said. He glanced at the other cage with the hermit crabs. "I hope they don't need to be let out."

"Just Ruby, but he can keep for a little longer. He's not hurting the babies."

"Your female crab is a he?" Marj asked.

"That's a long story, too." Steve sighed and sat down on the sofa. "I think I made a mess of things with Sara. Again."

"Probably," her mother agreed. "Men usually do with their women. Why don't you tell us? From the beginning, when Sara went down to your place with the divorce papers. We need a clear picture to understand the problem. Besides, I'm dying to hear your version of it."

Steve smiled, glad that he had come to Sara's parents. They had received him warmly and were willing to listen. He doubted his own parents would have reacted this sympathetically. Since his marriage, he had found his in-laws always more willing to hear his hopes and dreams. In fact, he had probably expressed them better to Sara's parents than to her, another mistake he had made in his marriage.

He told Bob and Marj what had happened between him

and Sara from the moment she had walked back into his life. He explained how he had tried to tell her how he felt about a heavy corporate career again, and her insistence that he try anyway. "But when she came back here, I couldn't stand it. The house was so damned empty. I was coming up in a few weeks, but after she called to let me know she got in safe, I realized nothing held me back from coming up now. So I packed Max and the crabs in the truck and drove through the night, only to have her refuse to open the door because she found out about those interviews and the job."

"If that wasn't the direction you wanted to go in, son, you had to make her see that," Bob said.

"I know you're right," Steve replied. "I told her more than once, but she paid no attention."

"Not surprising. I practically have to hit her mother over the head with a two-by-four to get her to listen to me."

"Nonsense," Marj said. "You never say anything important. When you finally do, then I'll listen. Now, Steve, I think Sara wasn't listening because she's still afraid."

"Of what?" Steve asked. Sara hadn't sounded full of fear when she'd called him a bastard. She'd sounded all too positive.

"She's afraid that things won't work out, and she'll be hurt again. That's why she's not listening. It seems to me that she's pushing you to be the old Steve so she can point the finger and say, 'See? I knew it. Goodbye.'"

"I can't fight that," he said.

"No, no," Sara's father countered. "I think Sara wants to have the old Steve back, to prove she can handle the situation better this time around."

"She said I can't be happy unless I'm successful," Steve said.

"In other words, we have no clue what Sara's doing," Marj added, summing up.

"Let's rock and roll!" Max squawked.

"To what?" Steve asked Max.

"Let's rock and roll to bed." Sara's mother rose. "We'll think better in the morning. One point is clear. Approaching Sara anytime soon is useless for you. Stay here. You know you're welcome."

"Thanks," Steve said gratefully as she left to fix up the guest room for him.

"Sara's right about one thing," Bob said, turning to him. "You do need some direction in your life again."

Steve groaned. "Now I know where Sara gets her stubbornness from."

"Damn straight. But you need to decide what you want to do with your life and then pursue it. What makes you happy?"

"Sara." Steve's answer was prompt, and he was proud of it.

Bob grinned. "Other than Sara. What makes you feel complete inside? Satisfied with life in general? We are more than who we love. And who loves us."

"I thought I knew once what made me complete," Steve admitted. "Now I'm not so sure."

"Find that again, and you'll show Sara a man she can stay in love with."

"Damn," Steve said in awe. "I hope I'm as smart as you when I'm a father."

Bob leaned forward. "You can't let it show too much or the family will stop paying attention. Pick and choose when to reveal your common sense. That'll make it count. But never tell the wife that's what you're doing. Let her think she's the problem solver in the family. Makes life a helluva lot easier for you."

Steve chuckled. It was good to be back home.

Chapter Thirteen

"Come over for dinner, dear. I'm making Chicken Caesar Salad. Your favorite."

Sara poked a pencil at the papers on her desk as she considered her mother's invitation. She loved the spicy grilled chicken, glistening with dressing over a bed of croutons and romaine lettuce. Her mother had a special touch of laying purple onion slices across the chicken. The dish always looked so good—and smelled as if it had been made in heaven. It was good healthwise, now that her mother had a low-fat version.

"I don't know, Mom," Sara began, hesitating. Chicken Caesar Salad also entailed a grilling of her. She wasn't dumb to her mother's motives. Marjorie Carter had brought out the big guns for a meal. Sara wasn't sure she was ready for it.

She hadn't called or seen her parents since her mother had taken her home from the airport. She hadn't seen anything except work. She hadn't seen Steve. No doubt he had driven back to Saint Sebastian. Half of her was glad...and half of her had died a little more each day.

Having a pretty good notion of the dinner conversation topic, Sara said, "I'll come if you promise not to steer the conversation to my marriage. Or Steve."

"I'll make tapioca pudding."

"Mom."

"From scratch."

Oh boy, her mother was pulling out the nuclear bomb of favorite food, Sara thought. She had been teased since she was a kid about loving a turn-of-the-century dessert like tapioca pudding. Her mother had only to add her special sauce of fresh-sliced strawberries to detonate the meal to torture level.

"And with that strawberry sauce you like," her mother added.

"No deal," Sara said, holding on to her willpower by a pinkie finger. "Come on, Mom. You know it's unhealthy to bribe your kids with food. It should be a form of simple nourishment, not a tool of power for mothers."

"Boy, you are getting very good with the guilt," her mother said. "All right. I promise not to say a word about Steve and your marriage."

"I'll hold you to it," Sara said.

"I solemnly swear, although I want you to remember this was your idea."

Sara ignored the last bit. "And Dad doesn't talk about it, either."

"Fine, fine. Will you come to dinner? You are our daughter and we love you."

"Now that I can't resist," Sara said, smiling.

As she hung up the phone, she wondered where the subject of the now-off-limits dinner conversation was. She still couldn't believe he had blown off an important interview to drive up here, no doubt as a surprise. Well, surprise, surprise. Steve was still Steve, not the least concerned with anything beyond his own self-gratification.

How could he have done that to her? After making her believe they had a growing love and trust again, he had jeopardized her own job. Barbara had complained to a senior vice president, and a memo had gone out about asking for "outside favors" from co-workers. Sara was sure she had a black mark on her name with her superiors, not a healthy thing to have careerwise.

Steve had protested her job search on his behalf, then had made it clear it meant nothing. No, he had not wanted "little wallflower" Sara's help and had made sure she would know it.

As she arrived at her mother's after work that evening, she admitted she ought to tell her parents about this latest fiasco with Steve—she supposed they should be informed. But she'd do so on her own terms, she decided. She'd like to enjoy her meal first.

"Hello, honey," her mother said, kissing her on the cheek when she walked in the door. "How was work?"

"Exhausting, but all right," Sara said. She glanced around the living room. "Where's Dad?"

"Oh, he'll be home soon. Don't worry. Come in the kitchen. You can watch me shred romaine. If you're a good girl, I'll let you eat some."

"Wow. What a mom."

"Just remember that."

Her mother settled her into a chair at the kitchen table and gave her an iced tea. Sara heard a noise from above them on the second floor. It sounded like someone talking.

"Your father must have left on the TV again," her mother commented, shredding lettuce into a colander.

"Want me to go up and turn it off?" Sara volunteered.

"No, no." Her mother glanced at her. "Umm...leave it on. He's always forgetting about things like that, and when I tell him I've had to turn off something he's left on again, he claims I'm making it up just to annoy him. This time I have proof."

"What a marriage," Sara commented, with a grin.

"It works for us."

Marriage talk was the perfect opening for her mother to bring up Sara's, but the older woman was true to her promise and never mentioned it.

The television upstairs sounded noisy at times, silent at others, like someone was playing with the volume control.

"I think you need a new TV up there," Sara said, before taking a sip of her iced tea. The cold liquid poured down her throat like chilled honey, relaxing her.

"A new television would be a nice anniversary gift. Hint, hint," her mother said, chuckling.

"I think I've got it."

Sara heard the front door open.

"Hi! Hi, Sara!" her father called out.

"Hi!" her mother chirped.

"Hello!" Sara added, then found herself in a footrace with her parent. Her mom hustled past her, out the doorway and into the living room. Sara came through second...and skidded to an abrupt halt.

Steve stood next to her father.

His jeans hugged his lean thighs and hips, his sex bulging visibly under the heavy cloth. His buttoned shirt emphasized his shoulders and chest. Sara wished she didn't notice his body first, before shock and anger shot to the fore.

She rounded on her mother. "How dare you?"

"What's wrong?" Marj asked, arching her brows. "You haven't told me anything is wrong between you and Steve."

"That is *not* the point."

"I wanted to tell you Steve was staying with us," her mother added.

"Staying with you?" Sara staggered back at this piece of news.

"Yes, he had nowhere else to go."

"He could go back home to Louisiana."

"No, he couldn't," her father said. "His truck needed work. That's where we were just now, getting a new head gasket put on."

"What's there for him in Louisiana anyway?" her mother asked. "His family's here. I would have told you Steve was with us, but you made me promise not to discuss him or your marriage. So I couldn't tell you...by your rules, which I respected."

"That is ludicrous!" Sara exclaimed. She headed for her purse, which sat next to her mother's on the foyer table. Then she was heading for the door, she thought murderously.

Steve blocked her path. "Don't go. These are your parents. I'll go. All I ask is that you listen first."

"More conditions and negotiations," Sara said sarcastically. "Don't you ever stop?" She turned back to her parents. "And I can't believe you two would take him in like this. Do you even know what he did?"

"Yes," her mother said. "He told us how stupid he was. Very stupid. We told him that. But we weren't about to turn him out on the street. Or his pets. He is our son-in-law."

"Not for long."

Sara sped around Steve and out the door.

"Sara, honey, calm down!" her father called after her.

"Not on your life," she muttered, furious with all three of them.

How could they all have done that to her? Never had she felt so humiliated. And angry. Her own parents cared more for her husband than they did for her. He was *living* with them!

She got into her car without interference and drove off, tires spinning. She went through town on an unseeing tear, too mad to be bothered with scenery. She barely bothered noticing the traffic.

Why her? Anyone else would have received tea and sympathy from parents. Anyone else's parents wouldn't have insulted their daughter by taking in a rotten husband. And his pets. No doubt the "TV" left on was Max talking to himself upstairs.

Anyone else's parents would have *understood*. She hoped Max burned her mother's ears right off with his less-than-stellar language.

She finally pulled up to her parking slot, only slightly cooled down since she'd left her parents' house.

A shadow moved just as she reached her door. Sara jumped and screamed.

"Easy, honey. It's only me."

Steve grinned wryly as he came fully into the parking lot's light.

Sara gritted her teeth together, her blood pressure shooting up again. "Dammit, do you have some evil, stalking twin?"

"I thought you had one, with the way you changed since you got home here."

"Me!" Sara felt ready to explode. She realized that if she began a defense, she would argue with him all night, not a smart move. "Excuse me. I need to go in my house now. I missed dinner."

"Oh, yeah." He held out something in his hand—a bag. "Your mother sent it over."

"You mean my *traitor* mother sent it over."

"I think your parents wanted to give me a chance to

make it up to you and that's why they let me stay with them. Besides, Max was freezing his feathers off. Spring in the northeast is *not* spring in Louisiana."

"Take the food back and tell my mother I can't be bribed with a lousy chicken dish and mealy tapioca dessert."

"Okay. Sara, I was wrong. What can I do to make it right?"

Sara closed her eyes to his earnest face and shut her ears to his earnest tone. When she was under control, she opened her eyes and said, "Steve, it's not a question of making it right. It was a question of trust and honesty. I trusted you and you weren't honest with me. You didn't like my getting you those interviews, ones you could no longer get yourself. You threw it back in my face."

"Is that what you think?" His gaze hardened. "Did you listen to me at all, Sara, when I told you I didn't want any of that?"

"You don't have to play this game," she said. "We both know that's who you are."

"That's who I *was*. I told you more than once, but you ignored me. That, too, was a matter of trust and respect. You threw those back in my face."

"Then it's obvious we're not meant to have a marriage," Sara said. "We never were."

"Now there I think you're very wrong. But I'm tired of trying to prove it to you."

Steve shoved the unwanted dinner into her hands and walked away.

STEVE LAY on his in-laws spare-room bed and stared at the ceiling. Early morning light streamed through the lace curtains.

Although the Carters were annoyed with their daughter's reaction to his presence in their house, Steve knew he couldn't impose on them much longer. If he did, he would cause a rift between her and them.

He should pack up and go home to Saint Sebastian today. Knowing Maisie, she would have really cleaned the house the way she always threatened, and he wouldn't be able to find a thing for six months. That should keep his mind off Sara.

"When the moon comes over Miami…" Max began.

"I'll be a fool for you," Steve finished with the bird. "I know. Hell, do I know."

"Sara, Sara… Here, chickie chickie… *Au secours!* Help, I've fallen and I can't get up…waa-waa… Why don't you come with me, little girl, on a magic carpet ride…. Hey, baby, nice butt!"

"That's right, bird. Make my whole life flash before my eyes."

"Polly wants a friggin' cracker."

"Take that cracker and—"

"Be nice, Max," Max squawked.

Steve sighed. The bird would drive him nuts. Right now Sara had that privilege.

Unfortunately, when he added up the who-did-what-to-whom, he had done the most "whats." Sara's father was right. He, Steve, should have made it much more clear to Sara that he had long since moved to a different career style. Certainly, he shouldn't have lied about being offered a job, or acted like an animal in an interview or skipped the third. He could have handled that situation so much better.

No matter what Sara's mother's theories were regarding Sara's motives, he should have gotten through to her. At the moment when both of them were most vulnerable, he had blown it.

Unforgivable. Which was Sara's point.

"Hell," he muttered.

"Hell," Max repeated.

Steve's logic urged him to recognize a disaster, pack it in and go back to his bare-bones life. His heart urged him to continue the fight. Both alternatives seemed hopeless.

But he had to do something.

It occurred to him that he owed an apology to the woman at Sara's office who had arranged for the recruiter to get him those interviews. Maybe he ought to go and apologize. Not only would it salve his conscience and maybe make amends for any blame to Sara, but it would put him in Sara's office building. A chance meeting, another opportunity to talk...

No, he thought. It was a great idea, but for the wrong reasons. He had to apologize, and that was his sole reason for going. It would not be used as an opportunity to see Sara. That was her workplace, and he would not interfere. In fact, he would go out of his way to avoid her there.

But he was going.

Steve rose from the bed. Max gave a wolf whistle at the human nakedness.

"Must be the hair," Steve muttered, smoothing his hand down his long tresses. He liked it long, liked the individuality it gave him, its departure from his old self. But maybe it was time for a change.

He slipped on a pair of jeans and went in search of scissors. He found a pair in the bathroom. Staring in the mirror and taking a deep breath, he lifted a hank of his hair. He boldly cut it off.

Later that morning, he stood in front of Sara's office building. He pressed down the short, almost bristly hairs at the back of his neck. Sara's mother had gaped at his hack job when she'd seen it. His hair had stood up everywhere after his amateur cut, despite being shampooed and conditioned. Sara's father had rushed him to a barber, who'd fixed the mess. Steve felt naked without the hair, a little the way Samson must have felt. He looked too much like his old self, not an image to which he wanted to return.

Give it a few months, he thought, and his hair would be long again.

Bob had also fixed him up with a decent shirt and an old, yet serviceable, hopsack jacket. Bob was as tall as he, but paunchier. Steve stuck with his jeans, knowing Bob's pants would practically slide off him.

He walked inside and asked the receptionist for the personnel director. He couldn't remember the woman's name and wasn't sure if Sara had ever mentioned it, but he did remember the title.

"And your name?" the girl asked, her tone half curious, half snooty.

"Steve Johanson."

"Johanson..." The receptionist smiled. "We have a Sara Johanson here. Any relation?"

"My wife."

The receptionist's jaw dropped, then she pulled herself together. "Do you want to speak with her?"

Tempting, he thought. "No, your personnel director, please."

"And the nature of your visit?"

Steve was tempted to tell her to stuff it, but knew the receptionist was trained to weed out the unwanted. "I owe her an apology."

The girl's eyebrows shot up in surprise, but she finally called. When she hung up, she said, "You can go in. Down the right-hand corridor and turn right at the second hall. It's the third door on your left."

"Thanks."

He followed the directions, his gaze spearing people in case he saw Sara. He was here for one reason alone. And she wasn't it.

The personnel director waited at her open door. She was a pretty woman about fifteen years older than himself.

"I probably shouldn't see you, but I couldn't resist," she said. "I'm Barbara Martin."

She didn't offer her hand.

Steve didn't, either, as he said, "Steve Johanson. Thanks for seeing me."

She waved him into his office. He sat in the chair opposite her desk.

"I want to apologize for what happened over those job interviews your friend arranged," he said. "It wasn't fair of me to agree to them in the first place when I knew I wouldn't be taking any of the jobs offered to me."

"Then why did you agree to interviews?" Barbara asked.

Steve paused for a moment. "That's hard to explain."

"Try."

"I had lost my job down South while Sara was there, and she tried to help me with those interviews. She and I were just getting back together. Hell, not even that close, but I was desperate to solidify our renewed relationship any way I could." He shifted in the chair, uncomfortable with talking about his private life. "I didn't want to upset things, so I thought I'd handle the interviews quietly and Sara would never know. It was stupid, childish. But I know working seventy- and eighty-hour weeks are no longer for me. I lost Sara the first time because I put that kind of job ahead of her. I wasn't about to be trapped by the same lifestyle again."

"I see."

"This wasn't Sara's fault at all. It's mine."

"Why didn't you just tell Sara thanks but no thanks before she called me?"

Steve coughed. "I did, but not loud enough, I think. Sara and I have been apart for four years. It's difficult for people to see change. Sara thought I still hankered for the corporate world, and I wasn't as clear as I should have been that I didn't."

Barbara straightened in her chair. "With your résumé, I can understand why she'd put you back into corporate. It's what you're qualified for."

"I'm too qualified." He chuckled wryly. "Or I was. I've got to say that even then I envisioned only working at that pace for a few years or so, making big money, then retiring when I was forty."

Barbara laughed. "I've seen that pipe dream. I have to say I admire you for coming today. You had no idea what kind of reception you would get, but you braved it."

"You've been far more polite than I have a right to expect," Steve said. "If there's anything I can do for you, I'd be happy to help."

"Actually, since you offered…" Barbara paused. "I've got a sales-manager position open—"

"Uh…not that much help, please," Steve corrected.

"I understand that, I assure you. Besides, you're overqualified for the job."

As he had told her, he'd heard that plenty when he'd been looking for a corporate job, Steve thought.

"Unfortunately, the group manager had to have surgery and she'll be out for several weeks with follow-up therapy. We have no one who's proven they can organize the department while I'm trying to fill the job."

"The assistant sales manager can't move up into the job?" Steve asked. That would be the logical step.

"Unfortunately again, I believe the sales manager hired him for his square jaw and cute behind as opposed to any experience or talent for the job. None of the other people have the talent, the experience nor the inclination to take on the position. I'm sure you can guess what's happened to the department. It's a mess. I don't know how long you'll be up here, but would you be willing to look at things and advise us, maybe give some direction so work can get done? Even if it's for a day or two, that would be great. With Mary out sick, I don't even know what she's really looking for in a sales manager, which makes my interviewing all the more difficult."

Steve hesitated, wondering just how much help he would be to Barbara. Still, he needed money to live on here, or to get home, and he owed Sara's parents a few bucks. He also owed Barbara a big favor. "Okay. I'll come in tomorrow and look things over. But if I can't help, I'll be up-front about it. I won't waste your time again."

"Good enough." Barbara rose and held out her hand. Steve stood and shook it. "Thanks, Steve. Want to go tell Sara the good news?"

Oh, boy. Out loud, Steve said, "I'll tell her later."

Barbara frowned, clearly wondering about his hesitation, then she smiled. "She'll be surprised."

"I don't doubt it," Steve admitted.

But what she'd do afterward was another matter entirely.

Chapter Fourteen

"Wow, Sara. Your husband's hot, and I didn't even know you were married."

On her way out for the day, Sara whirled back to the receptionist's desk. "How do you know I have a husband? And how do you know he's hot?"

Corinne's smile faltered. "He was here earlier...to see Barbara."

"Barbara Martin?" Sara exclaimed. "Why was he seeing Barbara?"

"I don't know. He said something about apologizing." Corinne looked away.

"Apologizing! Is Barbara still here?"

"She left for the day. I'm sorry I said he was hot."

"Me, too." Sara headed for the exit, and when she got in her car, she headed for her parents' house.

Steve's truck was in the driveway. Sara blocked it in. It was all she could do not to run right over it. She had no idea why he'd gone to her company and apologized, but it couldn't be good for her.

"I knew you would cool off," her father said, as she entered the house.

"Steve!" she shouted at the top of her lungs.

"Or maybe not," her dad added, and focused his attention on the crab cage sitting on the coffee table. "These guys are cute."

"Don't bet on it," she said, annoyed. "Ruby escapes whenever he can."

"Oh."

Steve came down the steps two at a time, Max on his shoulder, wings flapping in protest at his speed.

Sara stared at him, shocked. "You cut your hair!"

"Yeah." He touched his bare nape. "It feels weird."

"Well, I'll leave you two alone," her father said, lifting the crab cage. "And I'll keep your mother out of here."

He disappeared into the kitchen, cage in hand.

"Why did you cut your hair?" she asked, all her concerns flying out the window at his dramatically changed appearance.

"I don't know. Yes, I do. I had to go do something important, and I felt I needed to make a very good impression."

"Barbara," she guessed. "You went to see her and apologize."

"Did she tell you?"

"No. Corinne did."

He frowned, puzzled. "Who's Corinne?"

"The receptionist. She told me you were...hot." She spat the word out. It angered her more than anything.

He grinned. "Then I guess it's a good thing I cut my hair."

"Why did you apologize to Barbara?"

"Because I owed her one, after she arranged for the recruiter on my behalf. I'll catch the recruiter when I get back to Saint Sebastian."

"You didn't apologize to me," Sara said.

Steve's grin vanished. "Yes, I did. The night I arrived and you slammed the door in my face. I apologized. I've been apologizing all over the place ever since. You just haven't been accepting."

No, she thought, she hadn't. She didn't know what to make of this revelation, either. "What did you say to Barbara?"

"That I was sorry I wasted her time."

"What did you say about the memo?"

"What memo?" he asked.

Sara waved a hand, half wishing she'd never brought it up. But she had. "She had one of the VPs write a memo warning everyone against asking outside favors of co-workers."

"She never said a word about that." Steve grimaced. "If I'd known I wouldn't have apologized so nicely. I wouldn't have taken the job she offered me."

Sara staggered toward the ottoman, feeling like she'd been hit by a grenade. She sat down on the large footrest, her legs no longer able to hold her up. "A job!"

"It's consulting work. Evidently, the sales department needs guidance while the group manager's out sick, and she's trying to replace the sales manager. I'm told the boy toy isn't ready."

"James will never be ready, which is why Christine got fired from the sales manager's job. She put together a staff of idiots." Sara paused. "I don't believe this! I arrange for you to get job interviews, and you hate them so much you act like an ass about them. And now you take a job out of the blue. With *my* company!"

"It's only for a day or two," he said. "A week at the most."

Sara's head spun. She felt like the world had some conspiracy going. First her parents, now her company worked against her.

"Take it off, baby!" Max shouted.

That was all she had left to do, Sara thought. Just strip and say, "Take me."

"Be nice, Max," Steve admonished in a gentlemanly tone.

"Polly wants a friggin' cracker."

"Dinner!" Sara's mother called, poking her head in from the kitchen. "Sara, dear, how nice. You're staying, of course."

"Not." Sara rose, her legs still wobbly. "I'm on a diet."

Steve sighed loudly, his exasperation clear as Sara walked to the door. She heard her father say, "Well, at least she didn't yell."

The next morning, at work, Sara admitted she should have yelled. And yelled loud.

"Hey, Sara," yet another co-worker said. "Is that your husband in sales today?"

"You make number fourteen," Sara told the man, by way of reply. "Yes, he is and yes, he's hot."

"Actually, I haven't seen him yet, but thanks for the tip."

"Great," Sara said, belatedly remembering the guy was gay.

As she walked along the corridor, numbers fifteen, sixteen and seventeen stopped her before she reached her office. They each asked the same question and made the same observation about Steve. Fuming, she detoured to sales.

Steve was in the sales manager's office, sitting behind the desk, using the computer's mouse to guide him through software programs.

Sara stopped on the threshold, finding it disconcerting to see the old Steve again. This was the man she remembered. Focused. Intense. Oblivious to all that surrounded him. To her surprise, she realized she liked the new Steve, who nurtured cranky babies and odd pets, and who cared about his friends more than his job. That Steve had been more relaxed and easygoing, more willing to share himself with her.

He glanced up, then smiled. "Hi. You look great."

"I do?" She glanced down at her vest and above-the-knee black skirt.

"Absolutely." The computer beeped rudely. "Damn!" He fiddled with the mouse until the beeping stopped. "To think I had heavy computer use in the old job. I'm just about finding my way around this new system."

"That looks like the tie I gave my father last year for his birthday," she commented, the black-and-white music-note pattern looking very familiar.

"Could be. I borrowed it from him. And I borrowed the shirt from him, too, just in case you got it for him for Christmas or something." He held up a paper bag. "Chocolate chip cookies. I feel like I'm at my first day in kindergarten."

Sara shook her head. "My mother would feed Ivan the Terrible."

He chuckled. "Want a cookie from Ivan?"

"Sure. She makes a great cookie." Sara walked into the office. She took a cookie from the bag and bit into it. The rich chocolate blended magnificently with the soft, crumbly dough. "These are from scratch."

"Your mom always could cook."

Sara shut the office door, sat down in the visitor's chair and got to the point of her visit. "Steve, this is an impossible situation. Everyone's talking about you."

He shrugged, unconcerned. "I suppose I would be the new, hot gossip. Sara's long-lost husband come back to pull the sales department together. I'll be gone in a few days, and it will all die down. Don't worry."

"This isn't right," she began.

"What's wrong about it?" he asked. "I have a job, which is what you wanted for me. It's consulting, so I'll only be here a little while, which suits me. And I need the money to get home."

"I'll give you money—"

"I wouldn't take it, and you know it."

Sara sat for a moment. "Anything I say, I'll look like a witch, won't I?"

He grinned. "That's an interesting point. I promise I'll behave."

"I don't believe this. First my parents take you in, then my company takes you in. Is this a conspiracy against me?"

"Maybe I'm not as bad as you think I am." He held up a hand when she would have spoken. "I admit more than half of what's happened is my fault, okay? I should have been better at telling you that those jobs were useless for me, but maybe you should have been better at listening. You owe me that much, Sara, even if you won't admit it. I don't know what scares you about our marriage, but I'd do whatever it takes to make it better."

"I don't know if it can be made better," she said. "That's the problem. Will we go through life doing this to each other again and again?"

"What the hell are you talking about?" he asked, frowning.

"This. Us. Not talking, not making things clear. Not listening to each other. We're still doing it." She rose and walked to the door.

"Sara."

She turned. He stood and came to her.

"We're not perfect people," he said, gazing at her intensely. "We never will be perfect people. But we owe ourselves the chance we didn't have before."

He kissed her. She wanted to pull away, but his mouth had that wonderful gentle fire she had always craved. His lips quested over hers, searching, promising. Even in the fiercest of kisses, he always conveyed that hesitancy, waiting for her approval. Maybe that was why they were so attuned physically.

She wrapped her arms around his neck, her fingers digging into his shoulders. His hands coursed down her back, strong and sure. His palms kneaded her derriere, pulling her intimately against his hips. Her mouth opened to his, their tongues exploring, teasing. Sara's blood flowed thickly through her veins, warming her, making her feel faint.

"I'm sorry," he whispered in her ear, when the kiss eased. "Let's try again."

Sara slipped out of the embrace. "I have to go."

"Sara."

This time she got herself through the door before he could stop her. She hurried down the corridors, barely acknowledging people as she passed them. Heat seared her cheeks, whether from sensuality or embarrassment, she didn't know. She didn't want to know. If she analyzed her actions just now, she'd have an answer she was unprepared to handle.

STEVE DRAGGED HIMSELF to his truck at seven in the evening. Four days it had been like this, he thought, exhausted. Sometimes brain work took more out of a person than physical work. He was wiped.

Worse, he was at it again. The sales department really needed a major overhaul, not the patchwork magic he was trying to make. He had told Barbara he could do a few things to help, but she really needed to get a strong manager in there to do what was required. Part of his problem was that several people knew he was only a temporary department head, and they were taking advantage of it.

Others, however, paid attention, and so he focused his energies with those employees. One person would eventually make an excellent manager. She had the educational background and the skills; she only needed a little more experience with the job. He had already recommended her to Barbara. One thing he knew was that, while he could resurrect his own skills for a short time, this world was no longer for him. Besides the sales department's state of flux, half the people specialized in backbiting and get-ahead games. Things he used to do himself. He might be there only a few days, but people gossiped even to him. The sooner he was out of it all, the better.

"Hi, Steve!"

"Hi." Steve waved to a group of marketing people leaving for the day. They must have had a late meeting, he decided. People at the company were very nice—and curious. Sara's concern did have a point. He was asked all kinds of questions about his marriage. Or lack of it. He said as little as possible, feeling discretion worked better in his favor with Sara.

He wondered what she still thought about his being there. She hadn't visited his office again to complain. In fact, he'd barely seen her at all. That talk they'd had, calm and direct, had been extremely promising...he hoped. That kiss had promised even more. Maybe it was good she hadn't returned. If she did, he knew he'd be tempted to shut the door and clear the desk.

One question burned in him. He wanted with all his heart to ask it, but was afraid to. Was she pregnant? They hadn't used anything when she had been at his house. Several weeks had passed. Surely she must have an idea by now.

She wanted a baby so badly, and he wanted to be the one to give her one. But would it solve anything between them?

When he arrived at her parents' house, he was surprised to see her car parked in front. He parked the truck and went into the house, his heart beating faster with hope and his stomach churning with anxiety at the same time.

No one was in the living room.

No one was in the kitchen, either.

Bewildered, Steve shouted, "Hey! Anyone here?"

"Up here." Sara's father's voice boomed from above.

Steve took the stairs two at a time. Sara poked her head out from the bathroom.

"Ruby made the great escape again," she said. "My mother called me in a panic."

"Damn! Why didn't she call me?" Steve asked, going into the bathroom.

"She didn't want to bother you because you were working," Sara replied, then bent over to look behind the sink.

Every fiber of Steve's being froze at the beautiful view. Heat roared through him, and his body stiffened in reaction. "Sara. Get up."

"What?" She straightened. It didn't matter; his body was feeding on memories. As soon as she looked at him, she knew what he'd been thinking. Her eyes widened with the clear knowledge and her face flushed.

"You're killing me," he said in a low voice.

"I don't mean to."

"I know. That makes me want you even more."

He reached for her. She stepped toward him.

"Hey! Did you find him?"

Bob Carter's voice broke through the sensual spell.

Steve blinked, then let out his breath. He dropped his arm away from Sara. She stepped back just as her father walked to the bathroom door.

He took one look at their faces, which no doubt revealed their state of mind, then said, "I'll, uh, leave you two to look."

"We haven't found him, Dad," Sara said.

Sara's father didn't quite meet her eyes, Steve noted. Neither did he quite meet Steve's. "Okay, we'll keep looking. Your mom's having a fit."

"I'm sorry about this," Steve said. "I thought he was pretty secure in the mesh cage."

"He found a loose edge, so far as I can tell." Bob smiled slightly. "The other three are still in there. I fixed it for them."

"You two should have called me, not Sara," Steve said. "Hell, it's my crab."

"I didn't mind," Sara said, fully recovered. "I'm used to Ruby. Besides, it was fun to see my mother in a panic. She's at the neighbor's."

"She says she's not coming back until we find him," her father added.

Sara grinned. "Let's not look too hard, okay?"

"Did he leave his shell behind again?" Steve asked.

"No. He managed to get that out, too."

Steve frowned. "That's unusual. He's always looking for a new place to live."

Sara shrugged. "Maybe he just had enough room to take it this time."

"Let's keep looking," her father said, and put action to words.

When they were alone again, Steve took Sara's arm to

stop her search. He set the lid down on the commode and sat on it. He urged her to sit on the tub edge. When she did, he said, "Are you pregnant?"

Sara gaped, surprised by his bluntness. "I…no."

"Are you sure?"

"Yes. I have been since yesterday."

"Dammit," he muttered under his breath. "I was hoping."

She shrugged. "I will be when I'm supposed to be. Not before."

He stared at her, astonished by her philosophical attitude. "But I thought you were desperate for a baby."

"I want one, yes. And wish for one. But I learned I wanted a lot of other things to go with it, things I was maybe forcing. That's not good."

"What do you mean?"

"Well, you were right about not picking just any man to be husband and father. I've got a lot of baggage about you that I have to get rid of first."

"Maybe you don't need to get rid of it," he said.

"No." She smiled tremulously. "I need to, one way or the other. I'm angry and I'm confused. I have to stop being both."

"What does that mean for me?" he asked. "For us?"

"I don't know."

That wasn't the answer he wanted, but it was a better answer than he'd been getting lately from her. "Okay. You better know some things about me, too. I'll be done with this job in two days, and I'll be glad of it. I know, really know, it's not what I want to do with my life."

"But Barbara is very happy," Sara said. "She even told me she's planning to offer you the job permanently."

"She did offer me the job. I said no. That damn thing sucks you in like crazy, and I won't give eighty-hour weeks again unless it's to my family. Your father suggested once that I find my direction, rather than waffling around like I have been. No wonder you're confused about me.''

Sara stared at him, shocked.

''You—you didn't take the job?'' she asked. He'd looked so happy in that sales manager's office.

He shook his head. ''Nope. Too many hours, too much opportunity to climb to a CEO spot, too much time and work with too little self-satisfaction. I want a Michel of my own to take care of. And a couple of Michelles, with the extra *l* and *e* on their names. Girls. What do you think?''

Oh God, she thought. She didn't know what to think. He was so different, reacting in ways that were the antithesis of the old Steve. And yet at times she saw the old Steve.

''Leopards don't change their spots and dogs don't learn new tricks. Men don't transform,'' she said, repeating the old sayings that had haunted her.

He stood. ''You know, Sara, you've turned into me.''

''What?'' she gasped.

He nodded. ''You don't listen, you don't really look and you think everyone's got to do it your way. Granted, I gave you good reason to be cautious, but now you're way over on the punishment end of the meter. Let me know when you're objective again. In the meantime, I'll look for my crab.''

They eventually found Ruby in the living room, buried in the dirt of the ficus tree's pot. Sara was glad. Her brain still pondered the discussion she and Steve had had in the bathroom. She didn't know what to think. She hadn't listened to him about those interviews, positive she'd known what he really wanted. And she'd been furious when she'd found out what he'd done. But was she now punishing him for the past, rather than just being careful with her heart?

It seemed far too late for that, she admitted. She'd wept when she woke up to her period yesterday, crying because there would be no baby from Steve. She had avoided him at the office ever since that kiss, too. She would find it very easy to fall into his arms again and make love. Somehow, she trusted him to father her child, yet didn't trust him with her heart again.

Never had she been so confused.

"I think he's molting," Steve said, studying the top of the shell just peeking out from the soil. It looked like a striped mushroom.

"Molting?" Sara frowned. "What's that?"

Steve smiled. "You've forgotten your first hermit-crab lesson. They shed their entire body shell every so often. Remember? It's how they grow. Ruby hasn't hidden in soil like this for about a year. I think that's what he's doing."

"That's right."

Steve sighed. "I better get him a tank to molt in. He can't go into the mesh cage with the others. Because it's temporary, I don't have any sand or gravel in it for him to burrow into. And even the little guys could kill him when he's soft and vulnerable."

"They're like Lazarus," her father said. "It's like they become reborn."

"That's about it." Steve smiled. "I should have named him Lazarus."

"I like Ruby better," Sara said.

Buried and reborn. She wondered if humans could do the same.

Steve and her father went out and bought a small tank

with a handle for Ruby to molt in. They carefully dug him up from the ficus pot, disturbing him as little as possible. Steve even put a few new shells in the tank, for Ruby's shell-changing pleasure after he molted. Sara's mother came home finally, but she wasn't thrilled with the wandering hermit crab, in semistasis or not.

"I'll take him home with me," Sara volunteered. "Much as I would like to see Ruby make you nuts, Mom, I'm used to his escapes."

"You always were a wonderful daughter, Sara," her mother said.

Sara smiled evilly. "I'm tempted to leave him just for that alone."

Her mother's eyes widened. "Please, no. I wouldn't be able to sleep."

Her father clamped his hand on her mother's mouth. "Quit giving her ammunition, Marj."

Sara laughed.

"You sure?" Steve asked.

She sobered. "Yes. I'm kind of liking Ruby now."

"Okay. I'll come back up and get him when he's done."

"You'll—you'll come back up?" she repeated numbly.

He nodded. "It could be a couple of weeks. With his size it's hard to tell. When I'm done with my job for your company, there's no reason to stay any longer."

Sara stared at him.

"Sara," her father prompted.

Sara's mother clamped a hand over his mouth. "Common sense is setting in with me. Let's go into the kitchen."

Her parents left. Once she was alone with Steve, Sara swallowed, then said, "I—I don't know what to say."

"Me, neither. I'm tired of fighting you, Sara. If you

can't see the truth, then you can't. But my truck is fixed, I can pay back your parents, get myself back to Saint Sebastian and have enough left over to live on for a little while. Maybe you ought to go find a real guy named Mike. Maybe I'm not listening one more time and that's what you really need. You've tried to say it just about every way possible."

"I'm afraid," she said.

"You're the one who's got to get past that. I can't get past it for you." He handed over the cage with Ruby now ensconced inside. "Spray the tank daily with water. Keep some food and a filled water dish in there all the time. Call me when he's ready."

Steve went up to his room.

Sara stood in the living room for a long time, not thinking at all. Eventually, she went out to her car and drove home. Her heart was frozen. She didn't understand herself and she didn't want to try.

Two days later, she knew Steve had left for his house in Louisiana. She didn't have to be told; she felt a sudden loss right down to her bones. Her mother had no recriminations. As Marj Carter put it, "He had his second chance, and you still felt the same. No one could ask for more."

Sara pondered that last little bit in the days that followed. Did she feel the same? She watched the crab tank in the evenings. Ruby burrowed even deeper in the dirt and gravel. Sara couldn't even find him one day. She poked around until she felt the hard shell under the gravel. Assured he was still in the container, she didn't disturb him otherwise.

She read the romance novel. To her surprise, the story was about people in emotional conflict. She felt an affinity for their struggle. And when the two people found each other in the end, Sara could see they were changed. But it wasn't real life, she admitted. People didn't regain trust. Yet she wondered what it would be like to try.

She thought about Steve all the time. She missed him terribly. She loved him. More and more she wondered if what she had wanted was a perfect marriage to a perfect man. More and more she wondered if an imperfect marriage to an imperfect man she loved with all her heart was a happier recipe for life. Oddly, her urge for children diminished. She couldn't envision anyone other than Steve as their father. Even more oddly, her dreams were continually sexual in content. Her psyche, unleashed from conscious restraint, relived every moment of pleasure Steve had given her. She woke each morning drained and exhausted and confused even more about her husband. She knew one thing, though. The romance writer had that part right on the money.

One morning, about two weeks after Steve left, she found Ruby above the gravel surface. No seashell home that he'd carried on his back, just Ruby's body.

"Oh, no," she whispered, horrified that the crab had died in her care.

Reverently, she lifted the body with a paper towel, intending to dispose of it. Ruby looked strange in death. Looked empty....

She raised it to eye level, examining it suspiciously. It *was* empty. She could see a split down the back of the hard little body. She ran her finger in the gravel and dirt until she found resistance. She dug out the shell. Turning it over, she peeked inside.

Sure enough, Ruby was there. But he was so pink he looked sunburned. Sara remembered that he would be in his soft state and very vulnerable.

Ruby was alive. Reborn.

The old Ruby was a new Ruby. The old Steve was a new Steve.

Her husband had buried himself in Saint Sebastian, and when she'd found him, he was different. His philosophy of life was new, more in tune with her own. He cared about things he never would have looked twice at before. He refused to do things he would have jumped at before because they would take away from the simpler pleasures in life. She had looked far too long for the old Steve, afraid of the new.

Maybe she had been afraid too long and now it was too late.

TWO DAYS LATER, she crawled out of her car, exhausted and terrified. Holding Ruby's tank by its handle in one hand, she climbed the old veranda steps, the Louisiana heat back in force. Max sat on his perch. He began to bob up and down, flapping his clipped wings.

"*Au secours, au secours!* Hot stuff! Hey, baby! Woo-wee! Shake it up, shake it up! Here, chickie, chickie, chickie," the bird squawked.

"Hi, Maxie," Sara said, grinning at the parrot. Pleased that he remembered her, she held out her free hand to him. Max stepped onto it and climbed up to her shoulder.

He cuddled under her ear, murmuring, "Take it off, baby, take it off."

"You randy old thing," she murmured back, shifting the cage to her other hand so she could stroke the parrot's feathers.

Max muttered a few more endearments from his strip-club days. The front door opened. Sara turned, expecting to see Steve. Instead, Maisie grinned at her.

"I thought he was fussing about something," the older woman said. "What took you so long to get here?"

"Ruby just finished molting." Maisie made it sound like she had been expecting her days ago.

"Of course, I did," Maisie said, her grin widening. "I put a strong gris-gris in that leather pouch that would pull you back to your heart. Damn crab would hold up the works."

I'm not asking, Sara thought. Maisie's abilities amazed her yet again. "Where's Steve?"

"Right here." His voice came from behind her.

She turned around. He stood on the bottom step, looking up at her. Once again, he wore only cut-off jeans. His chest and shoulders looked thinner, as if he'd lost a little weight. His hair was already shaggy on the nape of his neck. But his features were expressionless, giving away nothing of his emotions at seeing her.

"I brought Ruby back," she said, holding out the cage. "He's new and improved, yet still the same. He's already been in every new shell you put in the tank."

"I would have come up for him."

"No. I needed to come down. I need to apologize for not listening and not trusting you. Some things take a while to get worked out of the heart. Sometimes people need to give a new chance more time. I needed to."

Steve came up the steps slowly. "What are you saying?"

Sara swallowed. "That I love you, that I haven't stopped. That I let fear override trust. That I should have listened with my heart instead of my head. That I can see you are a new Steve, one who finds personal success in small things now. It took a hermit crab to make me see that people can change, that you aren't the same man. And I'm not the same woman I was, either."

"I don't have a damn thing to offer you," he said in a low voice.

She grinned. "You have yourself and that's all I want."

He kissed her gently, both of them conscious of the parrot on her shoulder.

"Voulez-vous coucher avec moi, ce soir?" Max asked. They broke apart, laughing.

"That's my line, pal," Steve said.

"Steve is a dirty bird," Max announced.

"Boy, I hope so," Sara said.

"Here. Let me take him." Maisie offered the parrot her hand. Max climbed on and up to the housekeeper's shoulder. Maisie relieved Sara of Ruby's cage. "I'll just take these two bad boys into the house. Ya'll keep doing what you're doing."

After she disappeared, Steve kissed Sara very thoroughly. "I thought I'd lost you again."

"No chance," she murmured, nuzzling his mouth. "I was down for the count the moment I met Max."

"Thank God."

Steve rested his forehead on hers. "I love you, Sara."

"I love you."

"We'll work everything out this time."

She smiled. "I *know* we will."

He kissed her again. "No more Mikes?"

She laughed. "Plenty more Mikes. That's *your* middle name, ding-a-ling."

Steve grinned. "I never made the connection."

"I did, eventually." She kissed his bare chest. "My heart was thinking right all along, while the rest of me was acting crazy."

"Welcome home, Sara."

"You are my home. You're where my heart is."

Epilogue

"Hi, honey! I'm home!"

To Sara's dismay, her usual evening greeting went un-
answered as she came through the front door. "Hey, guys!
I'm home!"

"Blow it out your—"

"Now, Max, be good." Sara talked over the parrot's
last word. "There are children in the house. Somewhere.
Hello? Anyone home?"

On his perch in the living room, Max fluffed his feathers but was otherwise silent. Sara checked on the hermit
crabs. The smaller ones were fine. Ruby, as usual, was
missing. Oh, well, she thought ruefully. They'd find him
later.

She walked through the old farmhouse she and Steve
had bought in New Jersey after they had renewed their
marriage vows. Steve had insisted on that sentimental
touch.

What a man, she thought happily, never once regretting
her decision. Unfortunately, he had hidden himself and
their three kids away somewhere. "Hey! Where are you
guys?"

The scent of spaghetti sauce wafted through the
kitchen, although no one was there, either. The pot was

hot to her touch, and the burner was on low. Her wayward husband had to be around.

She took a water bottle from the refrigerator. After making sure she was alone, she took a healthy swig from the bottle in memory of her first reunion with Steve. Afterward she put the bottle in the sink to be washed, maternal standards winning the germ war.

The sounds of numerous barking dogs reached her ears. She glanced out the back window above the sink, then grinned at the activity at the kennels.

She walked into the backyard, about two acres of land in all, toward the group of people in front of the low buildings. "Hey! That was one heck of a greeting for the corporate parent in this family. Where were you all?"

"Mommy's home!" her youngest, Brian, shouted. The three-year-old ran over and wrapped his arms around her legs. "Daddy's got some more dogs to take care of. Willie and Jenny and a guinea pig named Brownie. Can I keep Brownie in my room?"

"Brownie's a client, sweetie. You know it has to stay out here," Sara replied to her son's usual request. Brian always wanted the kennel guests in the house. The kid wasn't satisfied with a parrot, four hermit crabs and their own dog, Bummer. Bummer, a mixed breed of undetermined heritage, followed Brian to her and wagged his tail when she patted his head. Steve had named the animal after his new occupation, as he liked to say.

"Hi, honey!" Steve said. He had one arm each around Mike and Michelle, their older children. "You're home early. I was just settling in the Stowkowskis' dogs and guinea pig."

"Only you would board a guinea pig for vacationing clients. I hope that small-animal room is soundproof. Those dogs are barking enough to wake me up."

"I keep telling you, I soundproofed everything, including our bedroom. Trust me." Steve kissed her hello.

So did Mike and Michelle, the five-year-old twins. That had been a surprising first birth. Sara had been secretly glad to go back to work while Steve stayed home with them. He handled all their children while she worked full-time.

A few years back, he had begun taking care of the pets of her neighbors and co-workers when they went on vacation. Out of that had come his home business, Animals On Board. He would board anything from small hamsters—even snakes and a tarantula once—to the normal dogs and cats. Steve was the ultimate nurturer, and he did it to the tune of a hundred grand a year.

He had never been happier. Anyone could see it. Neither had Sara been happier. Her life wasn't perfect—and that was good.

"Tell Mom," Steve said to the twins.

"Uh-oh," Sara murmured. "Is someone flunking kindergarten?"

The twins giggled, looked at each other, then said together in that disconcerting way they had, "Maisie and Michel are coming to visit."

Sara grinned. "Honest? When?"

"Friday. I'm picking them up from the airport. I'm sure she'll have a few words of wisdom about my mojo."

"I'm in charge of that," Sara said.

"My mojo is extremely happy. My *wanga*, too." Steve laughed and put his arm around her. "I missed you today. I miss you every day."

"I missed you, too." She kissed him again. "I'm glad to be home."

"Me, too." He smiled. "I'm happier than I have a right
to be."

Sara chuckled. "I was just thinking the same thing."

They went into the house, their brood following behind.

He's every woman's fantasy, but only one woman's dream come true.

For the first time Harlequin American Romance brings you THE ULTIMATE...in romance, pursuit and seduction—our most sumptuous series ever. Because wealth, looks and a bod are nothing without that one special woman.

THE ULTIMATE...

Pursuit

They're
#711 ~~SHE'S~~ THE ONE! by Mindy Neff
January 1998

Stud

#715 HOUSE HUSBAND by Linda Cajio
February 1998

Seduction

#723 HER PRINCE CHARMING by Nikki Rivers
April 1998

Catch

#729 MASQUERADE by Mary Anne Wilson
June 1998

Take 4 bestselling love stories FREE

Plus get a FREE surprise gift!

Special Limited-time Offer

Mail to Harlequin Reader Service®

3010 Walden Avenue
P.O. Box 1867
Buffalo, N.Y. 14240-1867

YES! Please send me 4 free Harlequin American Romance® novels and my free surprise gift. Then send me 4 brand-new novels every month, which I will receive months before they appear in bookstores. Bill me at the low price of $3.34 each plus 25¢ delivery and applicable sales tax, if any.* That's the complete price and a savings of over 10% off the cover prices—quite a bargain! I understand that accepting the books and gift places me under no obligation ever to buy any books. I can always return a shipment and cancel at any time. Even if I never buy another book from Harlequin, the 4 free books and the surprise gift are mine to keep forever.

154 HEN CE7C

Name	(PLEASE PRINT)	
Address		Apt. No.
City	State	Zip

This offer is limited to one order per household and not valid to present Harlequin American Romance® subscribers. *Terms and prices are subject to change without notice. Sales tax applicable in N.Y.

UAM-696

©1990 Harlequin Enterprises Limited

BESTSELLING AUTHORS
IN THE SPOTLIGHT

WE'RE SHINING THE SPOTLIGHT ON SIX OF OUR STARS!

Harlequin and Silhouette have selected stories from several of their bestselling authors to give you six sensational reads. These star-powered romances are bound to please!

THERE'S A PRICE TO PAY FOR STARDOM... AND IT'S LOW

$1.99 U.S.
$2.50 CAN.
Special Offer

As a special offer, these six outstanding books are available from Harlequin and Silhouette for only $1.99 in the U.S. and $2.50 in Canada. Watch for these titles:

At the Midnight Hour—**Alicia Scott**
Joshua and the Cowgirl—**Sherryl Woods**
Another Whirlwind Courtship—**Barbara Boswell**
Madeleine's Cowboy—**Kristine Rolofson**
Her Sister's Baby—**Janice Kay Johnson**
One and One Makes Three—**Muriel Jensen**

Available in March 1998
at your favorite retail outlet.

PBAIS

DEBBIE MACOMBER

invites you to the

HEART OF TEXAS

Join Debbie Macomber as she brings you the lives and loves of the folks in the ranching community of Promise, Texas.

If you loved Midnight Sons—don't miss Heart of Texas! A brand-new six-book series from Debbie Macomber.

Available in February 1998 at your favorite retail store.

Heart of Texas by Debbie Macomber

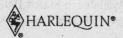
HARLEQUIN®

HPHRT1

Don't miss these Harlequin favorites by some of our top-selling authors!

HT#25733	THE GETAWAY BRIDE	$3.50 U.S.	☐
	by Gina Wilkins	$3.99 CAN.	☐
HP#11849	A KISS TO REMEMBER	$3.50 U.S.	☐
	by Miranda Lee	$3.99 CAN.	☐
HR#03431	BRINGING UP BABIES	$3.25 U.S.	☐
	by Emma Goldrick	$3.75 CAN.	☐
HS#70723	SIDE EFFECTS	$3.99 U.S.	☐
	by Bobby Hutchinson	$4.50 CAN.	☐
HI#22377	CISCO'S WOMAN	$3.75 U.S.	☐
	by Aimée Thurlo	$4.25 CAN.	☐
HAR#16666	ELISE & THE HOTSHOT LAWYER	$3.75 U.S.	☐
	by Emily Dalton	$4.25 CAN.	☐
HH#28949	RAVEN'S VOW	$4.99 U.S.	☐
	by Gayle Wilson	$5.99 CAN.	☐

(limited quantities available on certain titles)

AMOUNT	$ _____
POSTAGE & HANDLING	$ _____
($1.00 for one book, 50¢ for each additional)	
APPLICABLE TAXES*	$ _____
TOTAL PAYABLE	$ _____

(check or money order—please do not send cash)

To order, complete this form and send it, along with a check or money order for the total above, payable to Harlequin Books, to: **In the U.S.:** 3010 Walden Avenue, P.O. Box 9047, Buffalo, NY 14269-9047; **In Canada:** P.O. Box 613, Fort Erie, Ontario, L2A 5X3.

Name: _____

Address: _____ City: _____

State/Prov.: _____ Zip/Postal Code: _____

Account Number (if applicable): _____

*New York residents remit applicable sales taxes.
  Canadian residents remit applicable GST and provincial taxes.

Look us up on-line at: http://www.romance.net

075-CSAS

HBLJM98

**Make a Valentine's date
for the premiere of**

HARLEQUIN® Movies

starting February 14, 1998 with

Debbie Macomber's

This Matter of Marriage

on the movie channel tmc

Just tune in to **The Movie Channel** the **second Saturday night** of every month at 9:00 p.m. EST to join us, and be swept away by the sheer thrill of romance brought to life. Watch for details of upcoming movies—in books, in your television viewing guide and in stores.

If you are not currently a subscriber to The Movie Channel, simply call your local cable or satellite provider for more details. Call today, and don't miss out on the romance!

the movie channel tmc
*100% pure movies.
100% pure fun.*

HARLEQUIN®
Makes any time special.™

An Alliance Production

HMBPA298

Cupid's going undercover
this Valentine's Day in

The Cupid Connection

Cupid has his work
cut out for him this
Valentine's Day with these
three stories about three
couples who are just too *busy*
to fall in love...well, not for long!

ONE MORE VALENTINE
by Anne Stuart
BE MINE, VALENTINE
by Vicki Lewis Thompson
BABY ON THE DOORSTEP
by Kathy Gillen Thacker

Make the Cupid Connection this February 1998!

Available wherever Harlequin and Silhouette books are sold.

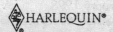 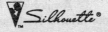

Look us up on-line at: http://www.romance.net   HREQ298